Teaching wasn't supposed to be dangerous...

Clara was pleased to see the walls of her office had been repainted and Vivian's nameplate had been removed.

Ron from facilities dropped by to see if everything was all right, and she thanked him for his efficient help. "Is there anything else I can do for you?" he asked.

"In fact, yes, if you don't mind. I'd like to have my furniture rearranged a little. The desk is too heavy for me to move without your help."

"No problem. How do you want it?"

She explained she wanted it set so her back would be to one wall and thus she could see the window to the outside in one direction and the door to the hall in the other direction. Ron had no trouble moving it by himself, and in minutes it was exactly the way she wanted it.

"Thanks so much, Ron. You're a prince."

He grinned as he answered the vibrating phone in his pocket and took off for his next task. She settled in and was absorbed in her computer research when she was startled by a strident voice at her door.

"Who are you?" the voice said. It came from a thin, wild-eyed woman who was unkempt and had bad teeth. She looked anxious and without taking a breath repeated, "Who are you? Who are you?"

"I beg your pardon," Clara said.

"I said who are you? You're not Hall for sure. What happened to her name on the door?"

"Professor Hall is no longer with us. May I help you with anything?"

"I know damn well she's no longer with us. Goodbye and good riddance to her. God won't forgive her no more than I will. And I never will. It's all her effin' fault. She ruined my life."

San Francisco attorney Clara Quillen is contacted by SFPD Detective Roy Travis again, this time because Vivian Hall, a beautiful young professor who went to the same law school as Clara, has been murdered. The body was found in the same place where Kim Novak jumped into San Francisco Bay in the movie *Vertigo*, and Clara considers some of the film's other locations for possible links to the murderer. She also takes a part-time teaching job at the law school where Vivian was a professor. As Clara digs for the truth, various suspects gradually emerge: students, professors, and others related to the work Vivian did on be behalf of abused and neglected children. Meanwhile, in the course of the investigation, Clara finds herself becoming romantically involved with an attractive judge—who she suspects may not have been completely honest about his relationship with Vivian…

KUDOS for *Second in Her Class*

In *Second in Her Class* by J. E. Gentry, Clara Quillen is a San Francisco attorney with a knack for solving murders. She gets a call from her friend, SFPD Homicide Detective Roy Travis, who is investigating another murder. The victim went to the same law school as Clara, and Travis thinks she might be the best one to interview the people, at the law school where she taught, for possible involvement. Clara goes one better and gets a part time job at the law school, taking over the victim's classes, in hopes that she can get information without making the murderer suspicious. Clara also finds that she needs to step in and take the victim's place in the work she was doing for neglected and abused children and quickly discovers that this is not the safest or most peaceful occupation. Angry parents and ex-lovers quickly move to the top of Clara's suspect list, but how to narrow them down? Well written, fast paced, charming, and interspersed with flashes of humor, the story will catch and hold your interest from the first page to the last—a mystery you won't figure out until the end. ~ *Taylor Jones, The Review Team of Taylor Jones & Regan Murphy*

Second in Her Class by J. E. Gentry is the story of Clara Quillen, an attorney in San Francisco, California, who is also a mystery buff. When a woman who went to the same law school as Clara is murdered, Detective Travis calls Clara for information on possible suspects whom she may know from her law school days. Delighted to help Travis with another case, Clara quickly agrees and even offers to teach the murdered woman's classes at the law school where the victim, Vivian Hall, was a professor. But taking over Vivian's duties also includes taking on her cases in family court where she was a children's attorney for abused and neglected children, working with the foster-care system to protect the rights of children who needed to be removed from a bad home situation. But parents don't often take kindly to losing their children, sometimes taking their anger out on the attorney for the child. As Clara deals with these cases, she can't help but wonder if Vivian's work in family court was the reason for her murder, and if Clara, herself, is going to become the next victim. *Second in Her Class* is an intriguing mystery that gives us a glimpse at how difficult working in the family court system can be. Clever, charming, and educational, it will keep you guessing right to the end. ~ *Regan Murphy, The Review Team of Taylor Jones & Regan Murphy*

ACKNOWLEDGEMENTS

Members of my local Mystery Book Club deserve special thanks for the lively discussions we have every month. I have benefited from their astute observations about mysteries and mystery writers.

My thanks also go out to my "Faithful" editors at Black Opal Books, whose helpful efforts are much appreciated.

Second
in Her
Class

J. E. GENTRY

A Black Opal Books Publication

GENRE: MYSTERY/DETECTIVE/WOMEN SLEUTHS

This is a work of fiction. Names, places, characters and incidents are either the product of the author's imagination or are used fictitiously, and any resemblance to any actual persons, living or dead, businesses, organizations, events or locales is entirely coincidental. All trademarks, service marks, registered trademarks, and registered service marks are the property of their respective owners and are used herein for identification purposes only. The publisher does not have any control over or assume any responsibility for author or third-party websites or their contents.

*To Laura, whose excellence as a daughter is equaled only
by her excellence as a mother;*

and

*To Keil, whose excellence as a son is equaled only
by his excellence as an officer and a gentleman.*

Prologue

I *can't leave her here. Somebody might figure out what happened, how it happened, and then trace it back to me somehow.*

But what can I do with her? How can I get her out of here anyway? She's not very big, but I still have to move her so I can drive her somewhere—away from here.

I have to clean up. It doesn't look too bad. Not much to do, just wipe fingerprints and a little blood. There's not too much blood. I'll take her phone with me, get rid of it somewhere. It might give away something. Then I have to get her out of here.

How can such a small woman be so heavy? Dead weight—I had only a block to carry her, but I wasn't sure I'd make it. With the light from the moon, somebody could've seen me at any time. Almost gave up and left her. I have to take her somewhere—but where?

༄༅༄

I've been driving for hours. Not really. Only seems like hours.

What's all that wooded area up ahead? There's the sign—the Presidio. I've been here before, but not for a long time. There must be a good place to leave her somewhere around here. The Presidio has secluded spots all over the place.

Maybe I need more than just a secluded spot. I need someplace to cover up how she died. The rocks, it could seem like she fell on the rocks. I remember now—Fort Point. Rocks all along there, surf pounding. It's pounding like my heart.

If I put her there, they'll think that's where she died. Maybe she slipped, maybe she jumped, like Kim Novak in Vertigo. Can I find it, even with the moonlight?

I thought I'd never find the turn off. I've been driving in circles. But then I saw the sign to Fort Point, down this little road. Not another car in sight. Not likely to be seen here.

I have to do it fast. Take her body and toss it onto the rocks with one big shove.

ℯ↷ℯ↶

Now I can go home. Not be tormented any more. She can't haunt me anymore. Back up the hill and out of the Presidio. I can breathe easy again.

I almost forgot. Have to stop for a minute and toss the phone into the bay. Did I forget anything else?

Chapter 1

Battered Body

The battered and mangled body of a young woman, marred by bloody bruises, with seaweed matted in her blonde hair—this was not the usual image for Clara to start her day.

It was a mundane Monday, the first week of August. Clara automatically thought school should be starting within a month. She'd gone to school so many years, taught school after that, and then gone to law school. Last year, she'd started a new job at a law firm in September, making a significant break from her pattern of starting school in September.

This year, she had no particular plans. That was all about to change.

Her day had started as it typically did, with a cup of coffee and the *San Francisco Chronicle.* While she may have gotten most of the latest news online now, she still liked the feel of a newspaper in her hands.

This morning she was intrigued by a small story below the fold on the front page of the Bay Area section about a suspicious death the day before. The story described the victim as Vivian Hall, age twenty-six, who had graduated second in her class the year before Clara graduated third in her own class from UC Berkeley School of Law, also known as Boalt Hall. Clara thought she recalled the name, although she didn't know her.

The body had been found on the craggy rocks in the bay, near Fort Point, in the shadow of the Golden Gate Bridge. The story reported that the exact cause of death was unknown but was under investigation. Something about the tone of the article implied it might have been a suicide, but Clara wondered if it could have been an accident or even homicide. She couldn't imagine how anyone with as much going for her as Vivian Hall would have any reason to kill herself.

She was interrupted by the telephone and was glad to hear the familiar voice of SFPD Detective Travis on the other end of the line. But she could hardly believe what he said.

"Clara, how would you like to do some snooping around some people connected to your old law school? I'll stop by and fill you in on my way back from Fort Point."

"You can't be serious, Travis. Are you investigating that suspicious death by the bridge?"

"I must be. I've barely gotten a wink of sleep since I got the call about the body early yesterday morning. It was a crummy way to start a Sunday. I'm just getting back from taking a look at the scene a second time, without all the crime scene guys milling around, and thought I'd stop by and check in with you for a minute before I go back to the office. Okay to come by?"

"Sure, but don't think you're going to hook me into this one. I learned my lesson last time."

Roy Travis was the San Francisco homicide detective who had lured Clara Quillen into helping him investigate the murder of her former boss a few months before.

She had been instrumental in solving the murder, but she had come close to losing her own life in the process. She wasn't about to let Travis talk her into getting involved in police work again.

"I thought I might get a little perspective from you. I'm actually in front of your door now. Want to buzz me in?"

"Travis, you're shameless. Okay, come on up."

ℰↃℰↃ

He looked about the same as usual, except more tired. The bags under his eyes reminded her of an old cartoon character, a loveable hound dog named Droopy. The detective's gray sport coat and black slacks were more disheveled than usual, and he'd shed his tie, meaning he was off duty, at least for the moment. He gave her a slightly awkward affectionate hug, mindful that with his big, beefy frame it would be all too easy to crush her.

"So tell me about it. How did she die?" Clara asked.

"The first question, of course, is whether it was an accident, suicide, or homicide. I'm banking on homicide, but we'll know more this afternoon when we have the full autopsy report."

"What makes you think homicide?"

"First, an accident makes no sense, because we didn't find a vehicle that would have brought her to the spot where we found her. She lived more than five miles from there, so it's not very likely she'd have been out for a stroll and somehow slipped on the rocks."

"What about suicide?"

"In all my years of doing this, I've never known of anybody throwing herself off of anything to kill herself unless it was from a pretty high point. These rocks are only a little below the Fort Point parking lot. By the way, the spot is just about where Kim Novak jumped into the drink in *Vertigo,* before she was fished out by Jimmy Stewart. But that was Hollywood."

"Maybe she was a Hitchcock fan. She might've been a Novak groupie who wanted to copy her. Sorry, Travis, I couldn't resist. I really shouldn't be making light of what must be a genuine tragedy. Are there any specific indications of homicide?"

"A few things make it look that way. There were no overt signs of drowning, and the heaviest mark on the body is a distinct blow to the back of the head. Of course, that could've been her head striking a rock, but somehow it looks more like a deliberate blow to me. Most of the other marks are abrasions from scraping against the rocks."

"Do you think she died where you found her?"

"Unlikely. My guess is she was knocked out somewhere else and dumped on the rocks in the dark sometime during the night when the moon was almost full. She was discovered by a jogger about an hour after daybreak."

"How did you identify her?"

"She didn't have a handbag or a wallet, not even a cell phone. She was wearing black jeans and a yellow cotton sweater, black sneakers, with one missing, and black socks. There was a key ring in a pocket of her jeans with a laminated picture ID card attached. It was for the faculty of Bay Area School of Law. There were two keys, and later I found out one key was to her apartment and the other was to her office."

"So she was teaching there?"

"Yeah, I managed to reach the dean at home as soon as I left the scene. The dean is Britt Penner, and she came to the morgue to ID the body. Vivian hadn't been missed because the faculty doesn't have to be back till new student orientation the last week of August. And it was a weekend anyway."

"Was there anything else in her pockets?"

"Her other pocket held a BART card, a ten-dollar bill, three ones, and two quarters. The bills and the card were all soggy, of course."

"Do you have anything to go on?"

"Not much, but we're only getting started. Dean Penner told me Vivian was highly regarded by both faculty and students after her first year of teaching. She said since the law school is a small one in San Francisco, they thought they were lucky to get her. She had been on law review, and she graduated second in her class at UC Berkeley law school. Did you ever meet her when you were there?"

"No, but I remember hearing her name. She was on law review before I was, and I think she may have been one of the two graduation speakers the year before I graduated. But I don't recall ever having seen her. What did she look like?"

"Basically, you'd say she was a real looker—pretty with a good figure. She had blonde hair and blue eyes with fair skin. I learned something funny about that. She had mentioned to Dean Penner that, when she started law school, she was a natural blonde, but a lot of people made jokes about her being *Legally Blonde,* you know like in the movie. She actually dyed her hair brown for a while. First time I ever heard of a woman deliberately going from blonde to mousy brown. Dean Penner said she went back to blonde again after she finished law school."

"I can't say it surprises me. It's hard enough for a woman to be taken seriously in law school without being glamorous on top of it."

"Guess that makes a certain amount of sense. I've known of good-looking women on the police force who had similar problems. I've seen uniforms that were a little baggy on women who had great figures." Travis nodded and yawned.

"Do you want a cup of coffee? You look as if you're about to drop."

"What I need is to go back to the office and take a nap. I can't do much till I get the autopsy report anyway. They should be finished pretty soon. She'll still be dead when I wake up."

"That sounds pretty callous, Travis. You usually show a little more feeling for the victim."

"Sorry, I'm just tired. I really do need that nap. They'll call me as soon as the autopsy is done."

"Will you call me when you know more? I'm really curious about this one."

"You're always curious, Clara, but I knew you'd want to know about this case. I'll give you a call this afternoon."

෨෨෨

As soon as Travis left, Clara went to her computer and did some searches on Vivian Hall. On the state bar website, she entered an attorney search and discovered Hall had received her undergrad degree from Amherst before earning her Juris Doctor degree at Boalt Hall and had been admitted to the California bar the December after she graduated. Now she was listed as being at Bay Area School of Law. A search of that website indicated it's a relatively small accredited law school in the Glen Park area of San Francisco, a little to the southeast of Diamond Heights.

She was amused by the BASL acronym on the law school website, which immediately made her think of a culinary herb. The faculty listing with a photo of Vivian in a neat gray blazer showed a pretty young woman who had blonde hair that looked natural with her blue eyes and fair skin. It was a little disconcerting when she noticed Vivian's hairstyle in the photo was a sort of French twist, similar to the one Kim Novak wore in *Vertigo.*

She learned that Vivian had taught Torts and Juvenile Law, and she was active on various faculty committees. The class schedule showed her Torts class for two semesters, and Juvenile Law was divided by Juvenile Dependency Law in the fall and Juvenile Delinquency Law in the spring. Some of her time was devoted to working with the staff of the law school's children's rights center on various legal issues that affect minors.

She read the bios of the fourteen full time faculty members, whose credentials indicated the usual highly rated law schools—Harvard, Yale, Columbia, Stanford, UCLA. She skimmed the list of adjunct faculty members who supplemented the full-time faculty. She saw a few names that were vaguely familiar, a couple of judges and one she remembered as having been a past president of the local bar association. They all seemed well credentialed.

Interestingly, the dean's alma mater was not a top-tier law school. Dean Britt Penner had received her JD degree from Southwestern University School of Law in Los Angeles. Clara couldn't help wondering how difficult it would be for the dean to replace Vivian Hall's teaching position with only about a month to go before classes started in September.

At first, Clara couldn't place why Dean Penner's name rang a bell, but then she recalled and confirmed it by checking her file on a meeting she had attended through the San Francisco Bar Association. The dean had been one of the presenters at a continuing education meeting focused on juvenile law, an area of the law Clara

had been considering. It was a special interest of the
dean, and she had established a children's rights center at
BASL.

Clara remembered chatting with Dean Penner after
the meeting and getting more information about California's juvenile dependency system. She was impressed by
a comment the dean made: "This can be very rewarding
work if you can withstand the grim facts of the cases.
Some of these kids have had the most appalling things
you can imagine inflicted on them by their parents, everything from general neglect to extreme abuse."

As a result of what Clara had heard at the meeting,
she took a two-day seminar on juvenile dependency law.
Then she had applied and been appointed to a panel of
appellate attorneys who represent abused and neglected
children in California courts of appeal. In the juvenile
dependency system, children become dependents of the
court because of parental abuse or neglect. In the most
serious cases, parental rights are terminated, and if the
parents appeal that decision, the children cannot be
adopted by new parents until they are freed for adoption
after the appellate process is complete.

Clara had done a lot of research since then and become familiar with the relevant sections of the California
Welfare and Institutions Code, starting with section three
hundred. When she applied to be on the dependency panel, a significant part of her qualifications included already
having had experience as an appellate attorney. So she
had been appointed to her first case and was waiting for
the appellate record in the mail any day now. And she
wondered how she would handle the anticipated sad facts
of the case.

She looked again at the faculty bios on the BASL
website, and she was impressed with the ethnic diversity.
There were three African-Americans, one of whom was a

woman. Two faculty members were Asian, three were Hispanic, and one had a name that sounded Indian or Pakistani. Of the two white legal writing professors, one was male, which from her own experience she knew to be unusual. The two other white males were John Knox MacArthur and one with flowing white hair and a matching beard. At first, she could picture him as a holiday Santa, even to the twinkle in his eye, but the name Greenburg didn't seem to fit that. The remaining faculty member was Vivian Hall.

ℰ⊃ℰ⊃

Clara couldn't stop thinking about Vivian Hall's murder, but the meager facts Travis had told her hadn't given her much to think about it. Impatient to hear from him, she did what she usually did when she had nervous energy to burn—she cleaned her house.

Not that it actually needed much cleaning—after all, Clara was a neatnik. But she was always amazed at how much dust could accumulate in only a few days. Even she didn't clean every day.

It wasn't that she couldn't afford to have someone else do the cleaning for her, of course. She lived in a penthouse in Pacific Heights, overlooking San Francisco Bay, and at thirty-eight, she already had more money than she could spend in a lifetime. Her dear second husband had left her well fixed, and she was eternally grateful for the freedom and independence that benefit provided in her life.

With her built-in vacuum cleaner, Clara took care of the floors and dust in record time. She considered reorganizing her closets, but she knew they were already pretty well organized. There was barely enough laundry in the hamper to make a small load, and the dishwasher was only half full. Considering the drought, she'd never think of running them without full loads. Showering didn't take long because she forced herself to keep it under five minutes and always hated having to turn it off so soon. Would it ever rain again so using water wouldn't have to be a guilt trip?

She slipped into jeans and a fresh T-shirt, and still, it wasn't even lunchtime. She was well aware she should start giving serious thought to pursuing some kind of meaningful work. She knew that even her court appointment to the child abuse cases wouldn't be enough to fill her time.

She picked up the latest mystery novel she had started the night before and began to read. But her mind kept wandering, and she found herself reading the same paragraph over and over again. She wondered if age was beginning to catch up with her, but she was a long way from being over the hill. At least she hoped so.

Damn Travis, she thought. She had to admit, though, since he and his wife had become her closest friends, she had pumped him for information about his cases. She had been fascinated by police work as long as she could remember, and she felt very lucky to have access to Travis's inside information. After years of reading mystery novels, she loved being able to learn about the real thing.

Okay, it was almost noon. She took as long as she could to make herself a salad and a grilled tuna sandwich and ate them slowly. She went down to check her mail, but it hadn't arrived yet. She took a vigorous walk across the way in Lafayette Park, checking to make sure her cell phone was on. She climbed to the summit at the three hundred seventy-eight-foot elevation and surveyed the view of the city and the bay, even grander than the view from her own penthouse.

From this vantage point, she could see more of the nearby white limestone Spreckels mansion, now occupied by superstar romance novelist Danielle Steel. The impressive structure always reminded her of the Grand Trianon palace at Versailles, or at least it might if it were not hidden behind a massive hedge that obscured more than half of the façade. She supposed she could understand the writer's desire for privacy, but if so, why would she choose to live in such a conspicuous mansion?

When she got back home, she decided she didn't need to walk up the four flights of stairs as she often did, but instead took the elevator. Finally, a little after two the phone rang.

"Yep, the coroner thinks it's a homicide," Travis said.

"Why is that? What was the condition of the body?"

"First, the coroner confirmed almost no water in the lungs. Actually, the water's pretty shallow where we found her, so that doesn't really tell us much. But most of the wounds on her hands and face are abrasions and bruises from the rocks, consistent with the similar kind of damage to the jeans and sweater she was wearing. There were a few hairline fractures in the bones of her face and hands, but none of them would've been life threatening. Her left shoe was missing, but she still had a sock on that foot."

"So, what killed her?"

"I was right about the blow to the back of her head. It was a single blow, very solid, and it cracked her skull. From the size and shape of the wound, the coroner's best guess on the weapon was a good-sized hammer."

"What about time of death?"

"It was between eleven p.m. and one a.m. So the body was apparently dumped between that time and sometime before dawn."

"Any sign of a weapon?"

"No, we've combed the scene, and if it was a hammer, it would hardly have floated away. She may have been killed somewhere else and dumped on the rocks where we found her. It doesn't look like she floated, but we already thought that because she was wedged pretty firmly in the rocks when we found her."

"How about other crime scene evidence?"

"There were fibers from her clothes along the edge where she went onto the rocks, and we found her missing shoe in the Fort Point parking lot. We couldn't get anything definitive on tire marks. The pavement is solid, and lots of cars go in and out of the parking lot every day. Nothing significant on footprints either."

"Any other evidence from the body?"

"No defensive wounds, nothing under the fingernails. She had a nice manicure. The only bloodstains tested out probably to be her own. We're not sure yet about any other DNA, but I'll be surprised if we find anything. No evidence of sexual assault. No drugs and only a trace amount of alcohol. So basically, nothing that points to any particular theory at this point."

"Have you notified relatives?"

"Yeah, Dean Penner gave me the emergency contact information, and I called her parents in Massachusetts. They're due to arrive this afternoon on a five o'clock flight. I've arranged for a police pickup to take them to a hotel. Understandably, they had no desire to go to Vivian's apartment, at least not yet."

"They must be devastated."

"No doubt. They haven't seen her since she went home for Christmas. Her mother started telling me how awful it was to have her so far away. She said she'd never get over her daughter going to California for law school when there are so many good schools in New England."

"Maybe that was the point—getting away from home."

"That sounds like the voice of experience talking."

"Yeah, maybe. So what's the next step?"

"This afternoon I'll go back to interview her room-mate, a woman named Marilyn Aiello who is on the editorial staff at the California Supreme Court. They shared a place in the civic center area. When I talked to her yesterday, she was such a basket case I decided not to press. Sometimes you learn more by waiting—establish a little rapport first."

"That sounds a little cold and calculated, Travis."

"Not really, merely good procedure."

"Sometimes I can't tell the difference."

"You're still a rookie, Quillen."

"Speaking of which, I suspect your calling me about this case was more than merely a little idle chitchat. You could've told me about the case just as well a month from now."

"You're getting to be very suspicious, Clara. But now that you mention it…"

"Okay, out with it. What do you want from me?"

"I thought you might be willing to go over to Berkeley and see if you can pick up anything at the law school. I got a copy of the vic's transcript from the dean at BASL, and you could check and see if you had some of the same professors."

"I might consider it, with one basic condition."

"What's that?"

"Don't call her a vic. Her name was Vivian, or Ms. Hall if you want to be formal."

"Sorry, Clara, force of habit. You know how police jargon is. We tend to depersonalize stuff. It's easier to deal with that way. Anyway, Vivian it is."

"Fine. If you scan the transcript and email it to me, I'll see what I can do."

After all, how difficult could it be to ask a few questions? she thought. Besides, she hadn't been back to campus since she had graduated the previous year. It might be nice to see if things were the same.

ഗരുന

Five minutes later, she was going over the transcript in Travis's email. She saw that she'd had several professors in common with Vivian, but the best bet to start with was their Constitutional Law professor, David Murdoch. She had been his research assistant, and she saw Vivian had made the top grade in his class when she took Con Law.

She immediately dialed Professor Murdoch and was pleased to hear his voice, even though it sounded somewhat listless at first. Then he seemed to perk up.

"Ms. Quillen, how lovely to hear from you. What can I do for you?"

"I'd like to drop by to chat with you for a few minutes, if you can spare the time."

"Of course, my dear, I always have time for you. I am getting ready to retire, and truth be told, I have more time on my hands than any respectable person should have."

"Would it be convenient for you to see me this afternoon? I could make it any time that's a good time for you."

"Yes, that would be fine. I'll be here until about six o'clock. I am in the same office, but it is getting to look a trifle bare. Most of my books are packed up or already gone."

"I'm not sure I'll recognize you if you're not surrounded by books, but I'll see you soon."

Chapter 2

Back to Law School

Professor Murdoch's door was partially open when she arrived. He welcomed her with open arms—literally. It was the first time he had ever embraced her. Maybe he was mellowing in his old age.

He still looked the same: neatly trimmed beard, natty bow tie with a crisp blue oxford shirt and tweed jacket. He was as neat as his desk was cluttered, almost a cliché law professor. The only thing missing was an ashtray with a pipe.

In the same spot on the credenza behind him, Clara recognized the eight-by-ten framed photo of a youthful Murdoch with his stunning wife, well matched as the perfect attractive couple. They had still been an attractive older couple a little more than a year before when Clara and a few chosen students had been invited to their home for his annual get together.

"It is a delight to see you, Ms. Quillen. You look well, and I am eager to hear what you have been doing since you left these hallowed halls. Would you care for some tea?" He always seemed to have tea available at a moment's notice. He poured without waiting for her answer.

He still spoke in the precise, slightly formal manner that he typically used with students, and she found herself tending to respond the same way.

"As I recall, it is lemon only?" he asked.

"Yes, sir. What a memory you have."

"I have to admit, it is slipping a bit, but nowadays I remember about as much as I really want to. At least I manage to keep fit, though."

"You certainly do. You look downright robust. Are you still running?"

"No, sad to say, my knees have paid the price for those seven marathons. But I work out every morning in the gym. I lift weights and manage to stay in reasonably good shape." He was obviously being modest because he could easily have passed for a much younger man, despite the gray hair. "Now, please, do tell me what you have been doing with your fine legal education."

"After I graduated and took the July bar exam, I interviewed for several jobs and joined a small law firm in San Francisco. At first, I mostly did research and wrote analytical memos. A few days before Thanksgiving, I learned I'd passed the bar, and I was admitted to practice in December."

"I had no doubt you would pass on your first attempt at our abominable bar examination. Did you have more responsible assignments at the law firm after that?"

"Yes, I wrote the brief for a fairly important case and successfully argued it in the First District Court of Appeal. Unfortunately, my boss and I came to a parting of the ways. Actually, not long after that, he came to a more definite parting—he was murdered, which was a shock, of course."

"Murdered? My goodness, who was he? Would I know the case?"

"He was Bernard Kahn, and he was killed along with two other lawyers in Marin County a few months ago."

"Ah yes, I do remember now. It was a rather unusual case. But I do not recall the outcome."

"The killer was identified, and then there was an accident in which the killer was killed. So justice was served, although not through due process of law."

Clara didn't explain that she was the one who had identified the killer, and she had come close to being killed herself before a twist of fate intervened.

"It happens that way sometimes, but all's well when there is justice in the end."

"What about this new beginning for you? Are you looking forward to retirement?"

"Indubitably. After all these years of preparing lectures and grading examinations, I can hardly wait to be able to do what I really want to do."

"And what is that?"

"To start with, I'm going to travel with my darling bride of over three decades. We're making the grand tour. Every trip we've made to Europe before had time constraints, encumbered by my having to make some sort of boring presentation at some sort of dreary educational institution. This time, travel will be for pure pleasure. We will eat, drink, and be merry, for who knows what tomorrow may bring."

"Good. I hope it'll be everything you want it to be."

"I am sure it will be. Now, tell me, you did not come by to chat about my retirement plans, did you? What is on your mind?"

"Am I that transparent or are you that perceptive? Yes, there is something I want to ask you about. Or maybe I should say, someone."

"And who might that be?"

"Vivian Hall. She was a student of yours a couple of years ago."

He paused thoughtfully for a moment. "Yes, of course—Ms. Hall. Terrible tragedy. I saw the item on the news last night. I cannot imagine why such a lovely young woman would kill herself. Or perhaps it was some sort of dreadful accident. She was an excellent student and seemed to have every reason to live. Were you friends with her?"

"No, I never even met her, but I can't help being curious about her sad end. I thought you might be able to tell me a little about her."

"Most of what I can tell you is academic, but I do remember her quite well. Even in a huge lecture hall, she stood out, although she was actually rather petite."

"Was she about my size then? I'm just two inches over five feet."

"Yes, now that you mention it, perhaps even an inch or so shorter. But she had a big personality for a petite person."

"You say she stood out? In what way?"

"I would venture to say she was among the best students I ever had. I do not believe I ever called on her in class without receiving a well-thought-out answer, and I feel sure she never came to class unprepared. Even when I probed her responses, she was quite imperturbable."

"I remember very well how daunting you could be when you probed. I might even be inclined to say you had a tendency to annihilate a student at times rather than merely probe."

"Ah, but the good ones were never the worse for wear. I do not recall that you showed any ill effects from my hypothetical questions."

"Your hypotheticals were the bane of my existence,

but I was determined not to show it. Maybe Vivian felt the same way. I assume her grade in Constitutional Law reflected her class performance?"

"I am reasonably sure it did. Let me think. Yes, if I recall correctly, she and the young man she was seeing seemed to jockey up and down to determine who would come out on top, if you will pardon the double entendre. Sometimes he made the top grade on exams, and sometimes she did. Now that I think of it, that is the way it ended across the board. I have been to so many commencements I am not quite sure, but I think one of them was first and the other was second in the class that year."

"I think you're right. She was second in the class. But I didn't know she had a relationship with the man who was first. Who was he?"

"Oh, dear, now you are taxing my memory. Wait a minute, and I can check it for you."

Professor Murdoch rifled through papers on his cluttered desk and then rummaged through two drawers of a file cabinet. "Here it is," he said triumphantly. "I keep all of the commencement programs. Vivian Hall was the salutatorian, and the valedictorian was Peter Susskind. They were quite competitive."

"That doesn't sound like much of a recipe for romance. How did you know they were going together?"

"One notices subtleties after long experience observing students. They sometimes arrived at and left class together, but at other times I got the impression they were deliberately avoiding each other. Maybe it was no more than the ups and downs of star-crossed lovers."

"What do you mean by star-crossed lovers?"

"Perhaps that is too strong a term. Perhaps I'm merely waxing poetic. I got the impression they had differences because he seemed intent on pursuing a high-powered money-making career, and Ms. Hall seemed to be more public service oriented, especially issues related to juveniles. What about you? Do you have any romances in your life?"

"You may not recall, but I've been married twice. My first husband was a professor here at Cal in the history department, but he was killed in a robbery that went bad. I never thought I'd find love again, but I married a wonderful man who was considerably older. He had a heart attack and died. After that, it was a long time before I could even think about romance. Instead, I went to law school."

"That's usually a sure way to kill romance. I don't recall seeing you with anyone in your law school days, but did you ever find love again?"

"A few months ago, when I was working at the law firm, I became interested in a doctor who was the son of one of our clients. The relationship seemed promising for a while, but it gradually faded after he took a job at the UCLA medical school. Commuting back and forth on weekends didn't work out very well, and I had the feeling he might be rekindling an interest in his ex-wife who lives in Los Angeles."

"So does that mean you are available again?"

"I wouldn't quite say that. I guess you'd say I'm cautious at best. And right now, I'm focusing on what I want to do next in my career." She was growing increasingly uncomfortable answering personal questions, and she wanted to return to a more professional subject.

"I have no doubt you will figure it out. You always seemed to have a level head on your shoulders."

"I'll keep you posted on where I'm headed, but I'm a bit at loose ends right now. Back to the subject of Vivian, though, do you happen to know what her significant other did after law school?"

"No, not really. I think Mr. Susskind went with one of the big firms in the city. I may have written a letter of recommendation for him, but I've written so many over the years I have no specific recollection of doing so."

"Did you know either one of them very well outside of class? I understand it's hard to know every individual in a large class."

"True, I suppose I knew just a small fraction of my students. Over the years, most of them tended to blur into one another. A few stand out. For example, I had a knack for choosing excellent research assistants, and you were certainly one of them."

"You were a demanding taskmaster, but that was part of what I liked about working for you. You demanded the best from me." It was nice to receive a long overdue compliment from Professor Murdoch, but she well remembered the grueling hours she had spent chasing down esoteric legal research to help him with his lofty law review articles.

She still wanted to learn more about Vivian and changed the subject back to Peter Susskind. He warmed her tea. "I do not recall ever having had any meaningful conversation with Mr. Susskind. He struck me as one of the rather arrogant students who fancies himself above seeking the assistance of a professor. But it was not unusual for Ms. Hall to come by after class to ask for clarification of a point under discussion. She seemed intent on doing everything she could to assure her understanding of a subject, not simply to get a good grade."

"Is there anything else you can tell me about her personality?"

"Nothing in particular, I'm afraid. She was quite intense as a student, but she also seemed like a reasonably pleasant person."

"I truly appreciate your sharing your observations with me, professor. If you happen to think of anything else, here's my card. And I do hope you'll let me know how you like your new lease on life. When are you going on your trip?"

"We want to wait until the weather cools down a bit. So, we plan to leave in mid-October."

"It sounds like a wonderful time of life for you and your wife. I hope it lives up to your expectations."

"Thank you, Ms. Quillen. I trust your next venture will be gratifying as well."

❦❦❦

As soon as she got back to her car, Clara called Travis. She was always pleased with herself when she could give him new information relating to a case. Her self-congratulation for learning about Peter Susskind was short-lived, however, as she was disappointed to learn Travis already knew about Vivian's former boyfriend. He told her he had just left Vivian's roommate and was on his way to see Susskind.

"You stole my thunder. I called to tell you what I learned about Susskind in a conversation with my Con Law prof in Berkeley." She filled him in on the rest of what Professor Murdoch had told her and asked, "Did you find out if she and Susskind were still together?"

"No, apparently they weren't. Marilyn Aiello said they had broken up and made up several times in the past year, but he hadn't been around for at least a couple of months or more."

"What else did you learn?"

"Aiello was very cooperative, and she was more composed today. Her eyes were red and puffy, but she didn't cry while I was there. She struck me as a genuinely caring person, and she seemed to have had a sort of big sister relationship with Vivian. She came close to tears when she said she was sorry she hadn't looked after Vivian better than she did."

"How did they come to be roommates?"

"About a year ago, a friend of hers at work mentioned she knew someone who was looking for a roommate and wanted to live in the city center because her boyfriend lived in that area. Aiello looks to be in her early forties, and she said when she first met Vivian, she was reluctant to consider living with someone in her mid-twenties. But she liked her upbeat personality, and it turned out they were compatible, even though their schedules were very different. Vivian was an owl, and Aiello is a lark."

"That can actually be helpful for roommates. Sometimes it's more convenient not to keep the same hours."

"It was in this case, Aiello said, because they shared a bathroom, and they rarely bumped into each other. And it seems they were friends, but they respected each other's privacy."

"What's the apartment like?"

"Very homey, nicely furnished, although Vivian's bedroom was still a little sparse. Aiello gave us full access to everything, but we only turned up a couple of things in Vivian's bedroom. I was surprised to find her handbag and car keys on the dresser. The handbag was one of those huge things women are carrying these days. It contained the usual excess stuff, but not her cell phone."

"That's odd, but it explains why there was no handbag when you found the body. Did you find anything else significant?"

"We'll analyze everything on her laptop, and I have a small leather date book that she seemed to have used regularly. The day before we found her she had noted 'Pick up dry cleaning, etc. Go to BASL to organize office.' The next day the only note was 'Dinner w/ LTS' with just the three capital letters."

"So do we have a pretty good idea of what she did on the last day of her life?"

"Yeah, pretty much. Aiello had asked if Vivian wanted to go with her to the Asian Art Museum, but she said she had errands to run. She did pick up her dry cleaning late in the morning, and she ran a couple of other errands, with stops at a car wash and an office supply store for a new reading lamp. When Aiello got home from the museum about five-thirty, Vivian told her she'd meant to go to BASL earlier, but she got busy with research on the internet and lost track of time. So they had some dinner, which was grilled salmon, half a baked potato, and a salad, with one glass of white Zinfandel wine. That's consistent with the findings of the stomach content from the autopsy."

"Did she go to BASL as planned?"

"Yes, Aiello said she asked Vivian why she was going there on a Saturday night, and Vivian said she might as well since she didn't have a date. She took BART to the Glen Park station, which is an easy walk to the law school on a well-lighted street. She said Vivian often took BART when she didn't feel like driving, and she didn't like driving in the city at night."

"That makes the lack of a handbag even odder. Wouldn't she have taken it with her to the law school?"

"Aiello explained that. She said Vivian had already taken several boxes to her office to update the books in her office and was carrying the last box. It was pretty bulky, and she didn't want to bother with a big handbag. So she just put a few essentials in her pockets, including her Smartphone."

"Did she remember what Vivian was wearing?"

"She said she was wearing dark jeans, a V-neck sweater, and sneakers. She was also wearing a sturdy gold chain with a V on it that she wore most of the time, but the necklace wasn't on her when we found her. She said Vivian sometimes told people the V stood for victory."

"Why didn't Aiello discover her missing before Vivian was found in the bay?"

"She went to bed about ten p.m. She was a little surprised Vivian hadn't come home yet, but she knew that sometimes she'd do things with one of her colleagues from the law school and thought she'd probably gone out with someone. When she went out for a walk the next morning, she didn't realize Vivian wasn't in her bedroom."

"Have you found out if anyone saw Vivian at the law school?"

"The only one we know for sure is the security guard. There are three of them, but they're on duty alone on eight-hour shifts. His shift was eight p.m. to four a.m. He makes his rounds and then mostly snoozes in his office, although he didn't admit that, of course. He knew Vivian and saw her in her office a little before ten."

"Wasn't it unusual for a faculty member to be on campus on a Saturday night?"

"He said it was unusual, but faculty members have access to their offices any time. Some of them showed up at odd hours. There were no cars in the faculty parking lot. He asked her about that, and she said she'd taken BART. She was hanging some framed things on one of her walls. They chatted a minute, and she said she thought she wouldn't be too much longer. There were one or two boxes still unopened on the floor. Then he went back to his office in another building and made rounds again about midnight. The place was deserted at that point."

"Did he check her office?"

"He said there was no light on inside. He routinely tried all of the doors, and hers was locked, as were all the doors in the faculty offices."

"And he didn't see her leave?"

"No, and he said he didn't have any idea about where she might have gone after leaving her office. So far, there's no trace of her till her body was discovered the next morning."

"I assume you examined the office thoroughly. Did you find anything useful?"

"After the dean identified the body at the morgue, I asked her to meet me at the law school. She took me to Vivian's office, and I opened the door with her own key. Everything was neat and orderly: books on the bookshelves, pictures on the walls, desktop computer and monitor set up on the extension of the desk. The dean said the tech people had already set up the new computer, but it hadn't been used yet. There was a stack of flattened cardboard boxes leaning against the wall by the door, apparently ready to be discarded."

"Were there were any signs of foul play in the office?"

"Not that we could find. In fact, it was pretty clean because the security guard said the custodian did his work in the faculty offices early in the morning. The usual routine was vacuuming, dusting, and emptying the trash, and once a week, he polished the brass nameplates on the doors, which he had done on Saturday."

"Did you retrieve any trash?"

"The custodian said he didn't remember collecting much trash because most of the faculty members weren't using their offices yet, but whatever he collected

would've been put into a big dumpster. Our search didn't
turn up anything significant."

"Was there anything unusual in the office?"

"I looked over everything pretty thoroughly, so we
assume she went somewhere else after that. We don't
have any idea where. The security cameras at the BART
station didn't show any signs of her."

Clara started to ask another question, but Travis cut
her short. "I just pulled up in front of Susskind's office at
Safer & Morrison. I'll have to get back to you later."

"Okay, call as soon as you can. Wait a minute—
Safer & Morrison. My lawyer's a partner there." But
Travis had already hung up and didn't hear her.

∞∞∞

It wasn't the first time Travis had been in a big law
firm, but he never ceased to be amazed at the palatial surroundings. He went through three levels of receptionist-
secretaries and had no doubt it would have been even
more complicated if he hadn't shown his SFPD badge
and ID.

He waited, not very patiently, as each well-groomed
receptionist scrutinized his ID and logged in his name
and badge number.

Peter Susskind's office was small, not palatial, but it
was well appointed with polished dark wood and thick
carpeting. He was also well appointed: about six feet tall,
well built, and attired in a dark gray suit, white shirt, and
repp tie with tiny heraldic shields. Not a hair was out of
place above his chiseled face and square jaw.

Susskind's first words as he glanced up from his
desk were, "I've been expecting you. I saw the news
about Vivian online."

"I'm sorry for your loss, Mr. Susskind. I'm Detective Travis, SFPD," he said, as he flashed his badge and ID once more.

"Yes, I know. My secretary always informs me before admitting anyone."

Travis thought the comment was pretentious because the secretary who announced him was obviously serving several associates and wasn't his personal secretary.

"I'm sure this must be difficult for you. I understand you were close to Ms. Hall."

"I don't know how you define close. You might say we had been, but we were no longer close."

"Can you elaborate on that for me?"

"We were part of the same study group in law school, and we dated for a few months after that. I haven't seen her for some time."

"What was the last time you saw her?"

"I'm not sure, perhaps a couple of months ago, maybe more. We'd decided to go our separate ways."

"Why was that?"

"We didn't seem to want the same things out of life."

"And how would you describe that?"

"As you might guess, I'm laying the foundation for a significant career here at Safer & Morrison. I plan to make my mark here and become a partner. I hope eventually to head one of our foreign offices in Europe. I speak three languages in addition to English, and my specialty is international law."

"Do I take it your plans weren't consistent with Ms. Hall's?"

"That's approximately accurate. My career is on track, but Vivian said she didn't want to leave San Francisco. In fact, she took the teaching job at that insignificant law school to stay here even though she was offered more money and more prestige at two law schools back east. You might say she lacked substantial ambition."

"I need to ask you something else, Mr. Susskind. I'm sure you understand this question is purely routine, but where were you Saturday night between eleven and one a.m.?"

"I'm surprised it took you this long to ask it. I was in my apartment with a young woman with whom I had dinner followed by a few drinks. I've printed out her name and contact information so you can check for yourself." He lifted a heavy brass paperweight shaped like a gavel and handed Travis a computer printed sheet of paper. He waited for the next question, but when it didn't come immediately, he asked, "Is that all you want to know?"

"Do you have anything else you think I should know about Vivian?"

"I suppose there isn't much else to tell. I think her pet project the last time I saw her had something to do with helping the children of the homeless. She had a penchant for lost causes. If you'll excuse me now, I have a meeting to go to."

Without another word, he picked up his briefcase and walked out of the office. Travis had a lot more questions for Susskind, but he decided that asking them at this point wasn't worth the effort.

He had no doubt Susskind was well aware he was being investigated as a potential suspect and also well aware of his constitutional rights. Travis was pretty sure he wouldn't provide pertinent information if pressed further, and antagonizing him wouldn't be productive. He hadn't expected to get much out of Susskind, and Susskind didn't disappoint him.

c/ɔc/ɔ

Clara was surprised to get Travis's call so soon.

"What a prick!" said Travis. "Even if she's a *former* girlfriend, he could have the decency to show *some* emotion. He has the kind of personality that gives heartless lawyers a bad name."

"I take it the interview was less than productive?"

"You might say that. I had the distinct impression that if I'd pushed him at all, the next thing, he would've lawyered up."

"Would he need to? Do you consider him a probable suspect?"

"I'm sure Susskind knows, when an ex-girlfriend dies under suspicious circumstances, we take a hard look at romantic relationships. It was clear he was downplaying his relationship with her. Of course, he was aware of Vivian's death before I arrived, but he didn't even ask any questions about how she died. That could mean he didn't care, or it could mean he already knew."

"Did you learn anything at all?"

Travis described the interview in detail and added, "But it wasn't even so much what he said that was offputting as how he said it. It wasn't exactly that he was cold, but sort of indifferent, almost like their relationship had meant nothing."

"I don't know how helpful it would be, but I know one of the partners at Safer & Morrison. Marvin Morrison has been invaluable helping me with my late husband's philanthropic trust. He's been a good friend to me as well as an advisor. Would you like for me to see if I can find out anything else about Susskind from him?"

"Sure. You know I always want every scrap of information I can scrape up."

"Okay, I'll give it a try and get back to you if I learn anything. What's your next step?"

"I have a grim duty. It's one of the toughest parts of this job. After Vivian's parents are picked up at the airport later this afternoon, I have to meet them at the morgue. They told me on the phone they want to see their daughter, and I asked the pathologist to make her look as presentable as possible."

"I don't envy you. Do you know what they plan to do?"

"I told them we should be able to release the body in a couple of days, barring any unforeseen obstacles. They plan to take her back to Massachusetts for burial there. Her mother said she always hoped Vivian would come home, but she never imagined it would be like this."

Clara wasn't surprised to hear the sadness in his voice. She knew he was a soft-hearted father. It made her feel a little better thinking she might be able to help him with the case.

Chapter 3

Another New Beginning

As soon as she finished talking to Travis, Clara called Marvin Morrison. His secretary said he was on another call, but would call back as soon as he could. About fifteen minutes later, he returned her call.

"Good timing, Clara. I was going to call you anyway. I have a few recommendations about your charities to talk over with you and a couple of papers for you to sign."

"I always enjoy getting together with you, Marvin, but I actually called about something else. I want to ask you about something."

"Fire away. What's on your mind?"

"There's a fairly new associate working at Safer & Morrison, and I was hoping you could give me some information about him."

"I'll try. Who is it?"

"His name is Peter Susskind."

"Yes, I know Peter. I was on the reviewing committee that hired him. He had an excellent academic record and struck me as quite ambitious—almost too ambitious for my taste, but my partners probably wouldn't be happy to hear me say that. What's your interest in him?"

"First, I need to tell you this may involve a criminal investigation, and I may pass on relevant information to Detective Travis. Do you remember him?"

"Yes, of course—good man. He was the one you worked with on the case concerning your former boss who was murdered, wasn't he? I know you mentioned having become friends since then."

"That's right, and that's how I got involved in this case. Anything we discuss about this case must be kept strictly confidential."

"Of course. It will be treated as if it were privileged information in the course of consulting an attorney. What's the nature of the case?"

"Did you happen to see the news about a young woman whose body was found in the bay yesterday?"

"No, I must've missed it. Tell me about it."

"Her name was Vivian Hall, and she graduated from Berkeley law a year before I did. Travis first called me because he thought I might have known her. I didn't, but since then we discovered her former boyfriend is an associate at your firm."

"Oh, dear, I wonder if she was that pretty little blonde woman he brought to our reception for new associates right after he was hired. She was short and shapely, and I think she said she had graduated from Boalt. She was charming and also very bright."

"That sounds like her, and I think they would've been dating about that time."

"She was quite different from the one he brought to the firm New Year's Eve party. Good looking, but that one struck me as a bit ditsy. So what's the story on Vivian Hall?"

"The evidence seems to suggest it was homicide."

"Am I correct in inferring you think Susskind might be implicated in her death?"

"Not necessarily, but of course Travis will pursue every angle. He's very thorough."

"I'm not sure how much I can help, but let me check Susskind's personnel file and get back to you."

"That would be great, Marvin. I'd appreciate hearing from you as soon as it's convenient."

ᏋᏍᏋᏍ

Within the hour, Marvin called back. "Normally, personnel files are confidential, but it's easy to glean the most significant information I found from other sources anyway. And I can also tell you some of my own personal reaction from my notes when we hired Susskind."

"Anything you can tell me could be useful. Travis always says 'You never know' when I ask him if something might be relevant. Please, go ahead."

"Okay, here goes. Susskind is twenty-seven, has a BA from USC and a JD from Berkeley law, where he graduated first in his class a year ago. At USC, he majored in Economics, and he took a fair number of computer courses. We thought that could come in handy, as technological knowledge can be useful in a big law firm where some of the older partners tend to be Luddites. Between college and law school he spent a year at an entry level job with a financial institution, but in one of his interviews he said he decided it didn't have the lucrative potential of a career in law."

"Is there anything special from law school other than his class standing?"

"He was on law review and wrote an article on the efficacy of stock option plans and the related legal requirements for compliance with government regulations. I read it before we interviewed him and thought it was erudite, but dull. The rest of his résumé is about as impersonal, although one unusual qualification is that he has a working knowledge of French, German, and Spanish. He told us he took some languages in school and also studied on his own."

"Do you have anything personal to add, Marvin?"

"I can give you my own impressions, for whatever they're worth. I always keep my notes from hiring reviews, in case I need them at some point to help me make a decision about an associate. I noted that I thought Susskind was impressive, but maybe not as impressive as my colleagues seemed to think."

"How did you differ from their opinion?"

"What they saw as self-confidence, I saw as bordering on arrogance. My grandfather was one of the founders of this firm, and I noted that he would've turned over in his grave at the thought of how brash young attorneys have become. I even made a little doodle of Grandfather turning over in his grave. He was a gentleman of the old school."

"Did you recommend hiring Susskind anyway?"

"Yes, I did. I thought he'd be an asset to the firm in international law, especially taking advantage of his foreign languages. The plan is to groom him here and see how he develops. I definitely didn't want him in my department, though. I've always considered working with philanthropic trusts a calling, the kinder, gentler side of practicing law."

"That's one of the reasons I appreciate your good counsel. I'm always pleased with how you handle matters for me."

"Aw, shucks, ma'am, glad to be of service."

Clara smiled. "You remind me of my Southern roots, Marvin, but you can't quite manage the drawl. Thanks for getting back to me so soon. You've helped flesh out the picture a little more, and every detail is potentially useful."

❧❧❧

Clara called Travis and reported the little she had learned from Marvin. She'd barely finished when abruptly he said, "Sorry, I'll check with you later, but I've got to go now. Just had a buzz the Halls have arrived, so I need to go meet them."

She couldn't help thinking about Vivian's bereaved parents and could only imagine the anguish they must be suffering. As she puttered around her penthouse, she kept picturing them in her mind, recalling the countless scenes she'd seen on television when parents had to view their adult children in the morgue. Parents are not supposed to outlive their children.

She knew she was hooked. It was no longer a question of *whether* she would be willing to help Travis find Vivian's killer. Now she was thinking about *how* she could help him. She'd sleep on it, and maybe she could come up with some ideas.

She tried unsuccessfully to read for a while, listened to music for a while, watched television for a while, and surfed the internet for a while. Then what she should be doing hit her, and she retrieved her DVD of *Vertigo* and started watching it.

She had forgotten a lot of the details of where the scenes took place in the Bay Area, and she made notes on the places she decided to visit: the site of the old Ernie's Restaurant, the apartment where Jimmy Stewart began to follow Kim Novak, the flower shop, Mission Dolores, the

Palace of the Legion of Honor, the fictional McKittrick Hotel, Jimmy Stewart's apartment, the fictional Empire Hotel, and the Palace of Fine Arts.

Those nine sites were the most memorable of the San Francisco locales where Kim Novak's character was filmed. Eventually, Clara might even drive down to Mission San Juan Bautista, but she knew she wouldn't go to Fort Point for a while—she'd have to get much more inured to the idea of Vivian's death before she could face that.

Finally, about eleven, she was tired enough to go to bed, and she soon fell into a deep sleep. A few hours later, Clara began to dream and had disturbing dreams of the locales she had seen in *Vertigo.* In place of Kim Novak, she saw Vivian visiting the locales in the film, and she felt she was the one following her as she drove a large 1950s car.

She was driving on the road down to Fort Point when she awoke with a jolt. It read two twenty-two a.m. on her digital clock. She could think of nothing but Vivian as she lay awake until the numbers became three thirty-three. She suddenly sat bolt upright and thought, *I've got it!* She went straight to her computer and composed an email to Dean Penner at BASL, with the subject line Juvenile Law Course at BASL.

Dear Dean Penner:

You may recall our conversation after a recent meeting on Juvenile Law at the San Francisco Bar Association. As a result of your inspiration, I have been pursuing this area of the law and have been appointed to the juvenile dependency panel to represent children in the Court of Appeal.

Yesterday I learned of the tragic demise of Vivian Hall, and it occurred to me that you might need someone to help cover her classes due to start next month. If I can be of service, please let me know. My Curriculum Vitae is attached.

Sincerely yours,
Clara Quillen

After she attached her CV and hit Send, she found it hard to go back to sleep, but finally drifted off. She was awakened by sunlight streaming into her room, not typical for the usually foggy summer mornings in San Francisco. Deciding whether to go back to sleep or get up, she succumbed to her habitual craving for her morning coffee.

In a minute, her single cup Jamaica Blue Mountain coffee was ready, and she walked out on her balcony to enjoy the bay view she never tired of. She strolled back in and woke up her computer. She was surprised to find she had a reply from Dean Penner.

Yes, I do remember talking with you, Clara, and I'm glad to know you followed through on dependency law. In fact, that bodes well for the possibility you may be a good fit to cover one of Vivian Hall's classes this fall. Can you come in to talk about it this morning at 10:00?
Britt Penner

The time on the dean's email was five-thirty. She obviously started her day early. At seven, Clara replied: *Certainly, I'll see you at 10:00.*

სამⴿ

She retrieved her morning *Chronicle* from her front door. There, she found the latest news about Vivian's murder. She read the headline:

Law Professor's Death Found
Probable Homicide, Not Suicide

The article embellished the skimpy facts that forensic investigation had indicated Vivian's death appeared to be a homicide rather than an accident or possible suicide as had been suspected before. It described the pathologist's report as concluding it was more likely the physical evidence was indicative of wounds inflicted by someone other than herself. It provided no specific information about the exact nature of the blow or blows that killed her, the possible murder weapon, or the probable place she had been killed.

෴

As she chose her outfit for the day from her closet, Clara winced as her hand passed over her gray blazer. It looked very similar to the one Vivian had been wearing in her faculty photo on the BASL website. In fact, it even resembled the gray suit Kim Novak had worn in *Vertigo*. Instead, Clara chose her navy pantsuit and paired it with a light blue blouse.

Google Maps indicated it would take twenty minutes without traffic to drive from Clara's home in Pacific Heights to BASL, two blocks from Bosworth Street in Glen Park. To be on the safe side, she doubled the time and added five minutes. She drove her year-old Prius out of her parking garage when her dashboard clock showed nine-fifteen.

She pulled into a visitor parking slot in front of the BASL administration building as her clock showed nine forty-three. The flowing fountain in front of the building had a small sign that read, "Recycled water only used in this fountain."

She waited till five minutes before ten to appear at the desk of the dean's secretary. "Good morning. I'm Clara Quillen," she said with a pleasant smile. "I have an appointment with Dean Penner at ten."

"Yes, go right in. She's expecting you."

The dean's office was not excessively large, but it had an expansive feel because of the big window looking out onto the quad of the law school. The other three buildings facing in toward the quad included the faculty offices on the left, the law library directly across, and the classroom building on the right. Except for the small parking lot in front of the administration building, the additional ones were behind the other three buildings.

The quad was beautifully landscaped, and students dotted the benches among the flowers and hedges. In deference to the California drought, all of the foliage consisted of drought-resistant native plants.

They were the kind of vegetation sometimes referred to as "freeway plants" because they were hardy enough to survive along heavily traveled freeways. The grassy areas had been replaced with realistic-looking artificial grass, and the hedges were edged with smooth dun colored stones.

When Clara entered, the dean looked up from her desk and laughed as she said, "I see you got the navy pantsuit memo."

They were both wearing navy pantsuits with light blue blouses.

Clara chuckled, too, and extended her hand to meet the dean's across the desk. "Maybe it's an omen. It's a pleasure to see you again, Dean Penner."

Both handshakes were firm, which pleased Clara, who was annoyed when she sometimes received a limp handshake from another woman.

"Let's not be formal. Call me Britt, Clara. Let's sit

over here on the sofa. Would you rather have coffee or tea?"

"Coffee would be lovely, thanks. I take it black."

"Me, too, so that saves Kathy the trouble of bringing in cream and sugar." She hit the intercom button and said, "Coffee usual, please, Kathy."

Britt Penner was in her early fifties, pleasantly plump, and she had the beginnings of the kind of wrinkles at the corners of her eyes and mouth that suggest an amiable personality. Her hair was neatly coifed, a natural-looking (though probably not natural) shade of strawberry blonde. Her make-up was understated, but it was clear she had made an effort to maximize a face that still could be considered pretty.

"This is a very nice campus," Clara said. "I've never been here before and didn't know quite what to expect."

"We've been extremely fortunate with this property. The land was endowed to us thirty-five years ago by a local developer who had always wanted to be a lawyer, but he was rejected by the big law schools in the Bay Area. He wanted to build a law school that would be more flexible toward nontraditional students in the less affluent parts of San Francisco. We've tried to be true to his vision, while at the same time developing a law school with high standards. Since I've been dean these past nine years, I've focused on both goals."

"They sound like worthy goals. I was a nontraditional student myself, starting law school as a second career in my mid-thirties."

"So was I when I started at Southwestern. You were lucky to attend Boalt law school, but not all of our students would qualify. Yet we've had a number of housewives and truck drivers who've turned out to be very good lawyers, and even a couple of judges. But some of our more traditional students come here because they like having greater personal attention than they'd receive at one of the large law schools."

"I can certainly relate to that, and I'm pleased to know more about your law school. I'm glad for this opportunity to meet with you again, but I'm sorry for the circumstances that brought me here. Please accept my condolences for your loss."

"Thanks, the loss of Vivian was both personal and professional. She was an extraordinary young woman, and she had such a promising career ahead of her. She'll be missed by students and colleagues as well. We're preparing a memorial service for her that will be at four tomorrow afternoon. It's open to everyone, and I hope you can join us."

"Yes, I'd like to. Even though I never met her, I'm beginning to feel as if I knew her."

"I wondered about that when I got your email. I thought maybe you'd been friends at Berkeley."

"When I first read about her death, I was aware only of having graduated from the same law school a year apart. But when I learned more about her, I discovered we had some professors in common, and we both had an interest in juvenile law."

"That's one of the main things that attracted Vivian to our law school—our emphasis on the law related to children's rights. And that's what drew me to your email, of course."

"Will you find it difficult to cover her classes?"

"We'll be able to split the students in Vivian's Torts class and add them to other sections because we have a relatively low enrollment for the first-year class this year. And we've used a juvenile court judge before as an adjunct to teach the Juvenile Delinquency course in the spring. But I was concerned about covering the Juvenile

Dependency course this fall. Do you think you'd be able to do it?"

"Frankly, I'd prefer having more practical experience first, but I feel sure I wouldn't have any trouble covering the relevant law for the course."

The dean's secretary came in with a small tray with coffee and a plate of blueberry muffins. The mugs had the letters BASL with an appended depiction of a sprig of basil.

"Thanks, Kathy," the dean said.

As Clara picked up her mug, she commented, "I wondered if you referred to the school as basil."

"We figured it wasn't a bad symbol for the school, a hardy flavorful herb that's been cultivated for thousands of years." She picked up a print-out of Clara's CV from the coffee table. She had highlighted several items, which they discussed in more depth. Clara didn't know the dean had already called two of her references and skimmed her law review article, which analyzed the implications of a recent Supreme Court opinion in a juvenile law case.

"Your academic credentials are impeccable, Clara, and I'm especially pleased to see you have teaching experience as well. You taught in high school before you became a lawyer?"

"Yes, I was a high school English teacher for several years. I always enjoyed working with kids." She tried not to get muffin crumbs on the carpet as she sipped her coffee.

"You said you'd been accepted for the juvenile dependency appellate panel, but have you started any cases yet?"

"No, but I have my first appointment to a case. I expect to receive the record from the court any day now, as soon as it's ready."

"Good luck. It's tough work, but I think you can handle it."

"Thanks, I certainly hope so. It would also make a nice complement to teaching the Juvenile Dependency course here."

"Yes, but I have to admit, the pay is pretty low for both of kinds of work. Are you willing to work for so little?"

"I can get by all right for now, and the experience will be invaluable." Clara sometimes forgot she should ask about money, considering that her own affluence made it of virtually no concern to her. She made an effort to avoid letting others know she was independently wealthy.

"In that case, welcome to the faculty, professor."

"Just like that? Are you saying I'm hired to teach Juvenile Dependency Law?"

"Yes, just like that. When we hire full-time tenure track faculty it's a long, complicated approval process, sometimes dragging on for months, with presentations to the faculty, multiple interviews, voting by the faculty and the board of trustees, and so on. But I have the authority to appoint adjuncts, subject to faculty approval at the next faculty meeting. That's merely a formality, though, as the full-time faculty never trouble themselves with looking into the adjunct hires."

"That's great. And I still have a little more time to do some research in this area of the law. I'd also like to attend the proceedings in the juvenile dependency court. I understand they're generally closed to the public, so do you know if I'd be able to attend some sessions?"

"It's usually easy to arrange. I have connections with several juvenile dependency court judges, and I can set it up for you. The judges are always glad to have visitors for valid academic purposes. They have to get permission from the parties in the cases to allow observers, but that's generally not a problem."

"That sounds good. I'll want to get organized here first. What do I need to do now to formalize my status as an adjunct?"

"Kathy will print out an adjunct appointment letter for both of us to sign and then take you over to your office. I hope you won't be bothered by having Vivian's old office, but it's the only one available. We don't have much extra space on this campus. After the police finished their work, our facilities department went in and packed up everything Vivian left behind. They'll repaint in a few days, but you're welcome to go ahead and bring in anything you want to get started."

☙❧

As Clara and the secretary walked over to the faculty office building, Kathy commented, "I've never seen the dean make such a quick decision about hiring someone, even an adjunct, so she must be pretty sure about you. She's under a ton of pressure right now. She always is when the new school year starts, but it's worse this semester with Vivian's passing. She's been fielding a lot of calls from the press and answering a lot of questions from a bunch of other people."

"You'd never know it. She seems to take everything in her stride."

"Yeah, but she's like a duck. She looks like she's gliding smoothly along the water, but underneath she's paddling like crazy."

Their first stop was the faculty services office where Clara was introduced to the three faculty secretaries, Rosalind, Sunny, and Wesley. They were cordial and told Clara they'd be glad to help her in any way they could.

Then Kathy took her to her new office, number one-thirteen.

It was an outer office facing the parking lot instead of the quad, but there was a lovely old olive tree right outside the window that created a see-through veil between her office and the parking lot. Clara wondered if she would sense any presence of Vivian, but inside there were no traces of the former occupant except for the nail holes in one wall. Everything had been boxed up and stored until Vivian's parents could let them know what to do with it. The furniture was basic: a desk with an ergonomic chair, two guest chairs, a file cabinet, and a bookcase that extended the length of one wall.

On the left side extension of the desk sat a phone and the monitor for the new computer, which was ready to be plugged in. "You should check your faculty email regularly," Kathy said. "I'll set up the address in the system, which will be your first initial and the first four letters of your last name, so you'll be 'cquil@law.BASL.edu.' If you need any help getting set up with the computer, you can give tech a call." She gestured to a list of law school phone numbers that sat beside the phone.

Kathy handed her the office key, saying, "This key also works for the secretaries' office, the photocopy room, the mailroom, and the outer door to this building. I'll get a parking gate opener for you and put it in your faculty mailbox by tomorrow. Whenever it's convenient, you can stop by the registrar's office and get a copy of the list of students who are registered for your course. Do you need anything else?"

"Not that I know of, thanks, you've been very thorough."

Kathy smiled as she said, "You're welcome. Now, if you don't mind, I'll be getting back. I don't want the dean to think she can get along without me for long."

As her new situation began to sink in, Clara sat in the desk chair and looked around her. She picked up the phone and heard a dial tone. Without hesitation, she programmed Travis's phone numbers (office, cell, and home) in to the frequently called numbers feature of the phone, just as she had on her cell phone. Then she punched in his cell number, and he picked up with a slightly grumpy sounding "Travis."

"Hi, Mr. Sunshine. You'll never guess where I am. You'll be amazed."

He perked up a little. "Okay, I'll bite. Where are you?"

"I'm in my new office. It was Vivian Hall's old office."

"You're right. I'm amazed. How did that happen?"

She told him the whole story about how she came to be hired to teach one of Vivian's courses at BASL.

"Ya done good, kid," he said. "Even I wouldn't have thought of doing that. It's obviously a good place for you to gather information about Vivian and the people who knew her."

"I hope so. We'll see."

"Did you pick up anything new on her when you talked to the dean?"

"Only that there's going to be a memorial service for her here on campus tomorrow at four. Did you know about it?"

"Yeah, her parents told me. They plan to be there because it's in honor of their daughter. I'll be there and assume you will, too."

"Yes, I'll be there. I'm sorry—I was so caught up in my own stuff I forgot to ask. How did it go with the parents?"

There was an audible sigh before Travis answered. "About as well as can be expected, I guess. It's never easy. They're pretty broken up, but that's about par for the course."

"I feel for them—and you, too. Is there a chance we could get together before the memorial service tomorrow? I plan to come into the office a little after noon and get some things organized."

"Yeah, I'm not sure what time I can make it, but I'll drop by sometime before four. What's your office number?"

"It's one-thirteen."

"I should've remembered from when I was in Vivian's office."

"Yeah, it's a little strange being here. See you tomorrow."

Clara walked over to the administration building and found the registrar's office. She introduced herself to the registrar and got a list of her new students. She had the maximum enrollment of twenty, with thirteen women and seven men. The gender ratio for the law school was about fifty-fifty, but she wasn't surprised that nearly twice as many women as men enrolled in a juvenile law course.

She returned to the faculty office building to take another look around. She strolled along the hall and looked at the faculty offices, recognizing the names she had seen on the BASL website. Each one had a shiny brass nameplate with the professor's name above the words "Professor of Law." On a small cork bulletin board beside each professor's door, the office hours were posted, along with whatever else the professor chose to tack up.

She first noticed the one for Professor John Knox MacArthur because it was directly across the hall from her office. For office hours, he had posted "By appointment only" and beneath that was a gilt-edged list of his academic publications and scholarly honors he had received. There was also a photo of a short man shaking hands with George W. Bush and another one of the same man sitting on a dais with Arnold Schwarzenegger speaking at the lectern. She tried, unsuccessfully, to imagine the occasion for the photos.

MacArthur's office hours contrasted significantly with those of the two legal writing professors, who held regular office hours every day. The only other office that had comparable hours displayed the nameplate for Professor Paula Kelley. Her office hours were *Daily 9-10:00 a.m. & 5-6:00 p.m.* Clara appreciated the rest of her bulletin board, which was covered in cartoons—some political ones about US Supreme Court decisions, some regarding other legal idiosyncrasies, but none bashing lawyers.

દ⁄ગ૯⁄ગ

Clara grabbed a fast food cheeseburger and chocolate shake—which she wouldn't want to admit to anyone else—and spent the rest of the day exploring the San Francisco sites she had noted from *Vertigo.* Earlier she had researched filming locations for the movie and found a list of thirty-two locations, some of which were beyond San Francisco.

She decided to stick with the nine she had noted when she watched the film: Ernie's Restaurant, Kim Novak's apartment, the flower shop, Mission Dolores, the Palace of the Legion of Honor, McKittrick Hotel, Jimmy Stewart's apartment, the Empire Hotel, and the Palace of Fine Arts.

She started with the site for Ernie's at 847 Montgomery Street. In the film, an old friend of Stewart's character told him he would be dining there with his wife, played by Novak.

The object was for Stewart to be able to recognize

her and later follow her, as her husband said he was concerned because of her recent peculiar behavior.

Clara knew there was no more Ernie's Restaurant, which had been an iconic landmark for over sixty years, because it had closed in 1995, before she had even come to California. She regretted never having had the opportunity to dine at Ernie's, savoring haute cuisine in the elegant red silk interior. It was now just a historic brick building, without even the stylish crested canopy that had led to Ernie's entrance.

Next, she drove about a mile to the summit of Nob Hill, across from the Fairmont Hotel, to see The Brocklebank at 1000 Mason Street, the location of the fashionable apartment where Stewart began to follow Novak, at first intrigued, soon entranced, eventually smitten, and finally obsessed with her. In *Vertigo,* he followed her green 1957 Jaguar in his white 1956 Desoto.

Less than a mile away was the Podesta Baldocchi flower shop that in the film was at 224 Grant Avenue, where now there is a clothing store. The flower shop is still in business, although no longer at that same location. In the film, Novak mysteriously emerges from an alley into the shop, where she buys a nosegay of forget-me-nots.

About two and one-half miles from there, another mysterious locale was the cemetery of Mission Dolores, the sixth of the twenty-one California missions. Clara parked and walked through the cemetery, but, of course, did not find the fictional tombstone Novak had visited. Still, the atmosphere gave her an eerie feeling of a presence that evoked the emotion of the scene.

The Misión San Francisco de Asís, named for the forefather of the Franciscan Order, was founded in 1776, but it had long been commonly known as Mission Dolores because of a nearby creek called the Creek of

Sorrows. The cemetery was a burial place not only of no-
table San Franciscans, but it was also the final resting
place of more than five thousand Ohlone, Miwok, and
other early Californians who built the missions. With the
brooding statue of mission founder Padre Junipero Serra
hovering over the now restored traditional plantings of
the late 1700s, the cemetery gardens were the perfect
place to showcase Novak's melancholy character.

From there, it was about six miles to the Palace of
the Legion of Honor, where Novak sat contemplatively in
front of a fictional painting of an enigmatic woman. One
of San Francisco's finest art museums, the Legion was
the brainchild of Alma Spreckels, wife of a sugar baron,
and modeled on the Parisian original built in 1782. Clara
walked between the fine colonnaded wings of the treas-
ure-laden museum, past Rodin's bronze sculpture of *The
Thinker* that graced the entrance.

Clara couldn't resist looking for the painting from
the film, even though she knew it didn't exist. She also
couldn't resist spending a little more time in the museum
looking at a few of her favorites, a fine fifteenth-century
Spanish ceiling from the Palacio de Altamira, El Greco's
St. Francis, and several outstanding works by the French
Impressionists Monet, Renoir, Degas, and others. She
would have to come again soon and spend more time.

Another five miles or so took her to 1007 Gough,
although there wasn't much to see. The McKittrick Hotel,
where Novak enters but then disappears, was fictional.
The spectral Portman Mansion used in the film, built in
1890, was torn down in 1959. The district had since been
redeveloped, and even a historic church that could be
seen in the background in the film had since been de-
stroyed by fire.

The next stop was about six miles away, the Russian
Hill apartment where Stewart took Novak after she made

her ominous plunge into the bay at Fort Point. The building was about a block from the foot of the famous hairpin bends that give Lombard the name of "The Crookedest Street in the World." Looking eastward, Clara could see Coit Tower, the crowning glory of Telegraph Hill.

The plot of the film takes a number of twists and turns, but there were two more places she wanted to see, the next one less than two miles away. Toward the end of the film, Stewart reconnects with Novak, and she is then living in Room 501 in the Empire Hotel at 940 Sutter Street. Clara could hardly believe her eyes when she saw it. While it was still recognizable, despite the stylish makeover since the film was made, it had a new name— Hotel Vertigo. Clara couldn't help smiling.

She'd purposely left one of her favorite places for last, the Palace of Fine Arts, a beautiful structure built for the 1915 Panama-Pacific Exposition, and the only one to survive in its original location. Architect Bernard Maybeck said he wanted the palace to evoke a sense of "the morality of grandeur and the vanity of human wishes" and to be a "grand classical ruin with a cloister enclosing nothing..." As such, it had both majesty and mystery that allowed it to be preserved, even though it was not intended to be a permanent structure.

The crumbling palace was demolished in the mid-1960s and, much later, was reproduced in concrete and steel to render it safe from subsequent earthquakes. The 2011 restoration had been a fine job, anchoring to the building statues of lions and giraffes, diaphanously clad maidens, and angels. She parked and took a long stroll around the building and admired its reflection in the lagoon, where Stewart had strolled with Novak toward the end of the film, before the dramatic climax.

As she sat on a bench and mused about her *Vertigo* tour, she asked herself whether these sites could possibly have anything to do with Vivian's death. The thought that continued to recur was the image of the most significant site she wasn't yet ready to visit, where Vivian's body had been found at Fort Point.

From the Palace of Fine Arts, she was glad to head in the opposite direction, only a couple of miles to her Pacific Heights home. She loved her home, a perfect place to reflect on the myriad thoughts cluttering her mind.

Chapter 4

Moving Memorial

Clara spent the evening and next morning gathering up the books and materials she thought she'd need to teach the Juvenile Dependency Law course. She transferred some files to a flash drive so she could put them on the new computer. She was somewhat surprised and pleased to see how much material she had already accumulated on the subject.

She reviewed Vivian's syllabus that she found on the BASL website. Fortunately, she was already familiar with the textbook Vivian had used and planned to use the same one. She filled one box with teaching materials and another one with a few decorative items. For a moment she thought about buying a plant for the office but decided against it. Hard as she tried, she had a very bad track record of keeping plants alive.

Aside from her excitement at the prospect of possibly being in a position to learn more about Vivian's murder, she hadn't realized she'd also be excited at the prospect of teaching again. She didn't know how much she'd missed it. She wondered how different it would be teaching law students. No doubt they couldn't be any tougher to handle than a bunch of typically bored and often hormone-hyped teenagers.

After a productive morning, she had lunch, showered, and dressed in a black pantsuit with a pearl gray blouse. When she arrived at BASL, she retrieved the parking gate opener from her faculty mailbox and moved her car from a visitor parking slot to the faculty lot. She found it hard to believe all of this had fallen into place so fast, but she didn't realize how many balls Dean Penner had been juggling and thus how glad the dean was to get this one little problem resolved so easily.

It didn't take long to put her books on the shelf, and she turned her attention to setting up files on the computer. Her back was to the door when John Knox MacArthur stuck his head in the office. His head somehow looked too small for his body.

He was on the short side, probably about five-six, but when he entered, she could see it was his legs that were short, not the rest of him. He had a well-developed torso and a barrel chest with a paunch to match. He had a slightly receding hairline, made even more noticeable by a less than artful comb-over.

The dark shade of his hair struck her as incongruous in comparison with the approximate sixty-plus age of his face. His features were small: small eyes, small nose, thin lips, and even smallish ears. He was wearing a black mock turtleneck and slacks with a gray-and-black herringbone jacket.

"Hello, I don't think we've met," he said.

"No, we haven't. I'm Clara Quillen. I'll be teaching Juvenile Dependency Law this semester."

"Welcome to our inner sanctum. I'm John Knox MacArthur." He took a seat in one of the guest chairs. "My office is across the hall. I have a nice view of the quad—a shame you're stuck on the parking lot side. I gather you're replacing Vivian. Terrible tragedy, isn't it?"

"Yes, so I understand, even though I didn't know her. But I wouldn't say I'm replacing her. I'm only teaching her juvenile law course for the fall. I understand students in her Torts section are being divided up and added to other sections."

"I know. I'm one of the unlucky ones who'll have additional students as a result, with that many more exams to grade. I haven't been in such a large law class since I was at Harvard. The small classes at Princeton undergrad were so much nicer."

She ignored the gratuitous reference to his Ivy League schools. "So you're teaching Torts?"

"Yes, and Contracts. I've been teaching those courses so long I could give the lectures in my sleep. Unfortunately, since my classes always consist of first-year students, it's like trying to fill completely empty heads every year."

"That must be challenging, even with long experience."

"You might say so, as the understatement of the day. How about you? Have you been teaching long?"

"I taught for several years before I went to law school, but this is my first opportunity to teach law students. It promises to be interesting."

"I'm sure it will be, although you may find law students uniquely difficult. I well remember my first year of teaching."

He launched into a few anecdotes, and Clara soon realized there was no point in trying to compete with his self-centered stories.

She fell back into her old Southern belle role of listening to a man talk about himself.

He was showing no signs of winding down when another visitor appeared.

"Hello, John. I thought I heard your voice. Do we have a new neighbor in our community? Hi, I'm Paula Kelley," she said, her velvety smooth voice contrasting with her hefty handshake and large frame.

MacArthur's rigid demeanor belied his honeyed words as he said, "It's my pleasure to introduce the newest member of our little family, Carla Quillen. She'll be teaching Vivian's juvenile law course."

"Hi, Paula, but it's Clara, not Carla."

His face reddened. "Do forgive me. I'm not very good with names," he said with mock apology. "Now if you'll excuse me, I have a few things to do before the memorial service this afternoon. I suppose I'll see you both there." He made a hasty retreat without waiting for a response.

Paula Kelley had a ready smile in a moon face that might once have been pretty, topped with short, wavy gray hair. She had a substantial body—not overweight, but more what some people called big boned. She had towered several inches over MacArthur, and he had seemed diminished even more when she spoke. She wore a longish black linen tunic over charcoal gray slacks, adorned by some sort of amulet around her neck.

She didn't look like a typical law professor, even a female one, but she looked very comfortable in her own skin. When Paula heard MacArthur's office door close, she said in a low tone, "I would've rescued you sooner, but I didn't know he was here already."

"Did I need rescuing?"

"After a few more visits from him, you'll understand what I mean. He's the most loquacious member of our faculty. He doesn't normally bother with greeting lowly adjuncts, but I suspect he was curious about who'd be covering Vivian's classes. He was probably hoping they'd gotten someone for Torts so he wouldn't have extra students. He tries to do as little work as possible."

"Yes, I picked up on that."

"So how long did it take for him to mention Princeton or Harvard?"

Clara laughed. "About thirty seconds, I think—both of them."

Paula chuckled as she said, "That may be a new record."

"I'm curious," Clara said. "Does the dean have any problem with faculty members who have prestigious academic credentials since she didn't go to a top tier law school?"

"She dispelled that from the beginning. She had a good record as the dean of academic affairs at the University of San Diego School of Law when she applied for the deanship here. She started her presentation to the faculty by saying if they had a problem with her lower ranked law school, she hoped they'd remember that Justice Stanley Mosk also got his law degree from Southwestern in Los Angeles. He was the longest serving justice on the California Supreme Court, thirty-seven years."

"So I gather that even won over John Knox MacArthur."

"I doubt it, but I suspect he's chastened at least a little because he's not very well regarded by his students. He may be aware he's often referred to as General MacArthur, and he might even have caught a glimpse of someone saluting or snapping to attention behind his back. I think that may lead him to even more braggadocio, unfortunately, but I don't have to be bothered with it because I almost always beat him at tennis."

"Really? That must be tough on somebody with his ego."

"No doubt, but we keep playing, maybe because I don't gloat when I win. Even so, we're fierce competitors, and I suspect he's determined to reach a point where he can beat me consistently."

"You look as if you can handle that with no trouble."

"Yes, in my youth, I even toyed with becoming a professional tennis player, but I knew I could never hold a candle to Billie Jean. Anyway, academics won out. While my upper body strength is pretty good, I was beginning to have occasional twinges of tennis elbow back in my college days. But enough about me—how are you settling in? I'm amazed the dean found someone so quickly for Vivian's juvenile law course."

"I was amazed myself, but it seems I happened to make contact with her at the right time. Were you close to Vivian?"

Paula's pleasant smile faded, and her voice had a distinct catch in it as she replied. "She was an absolute dear, a rare gentle soul, unusual for one so young. She was a truly beautiful person, and I miss her every day." She cleared her throat. "Did you know her?"

"No, but I knew of her. She graduated from law school the year before I did at UC Berkeley. Of course, I was much older when I went to law school as a second career."

Paula asked about Clara's first career, and they continued to chat. They talked about Paula's academic subjects, which were Constitutional Law and Women and the Law. Finally, Paula said, "I'd better be going, or I'll soon overtake John's title for MGP—Most Garrulous Professor. If you like, I'll drop by a few minutes before four, and we can walk over to the memorial service together."

"Thanks, I'd like that. I'll see you later."

After Paula left, Vivian realized that her pleasant conversation had not included any reference to Paula's academic credentials. She thought she remembered but looked her up on the website to be sure—she'd gone to Columbia undergrad and Yale law, with additional study at the Inns of Court in London. She was even more amused then at MacArthur's touting of his own credentials.

About half an hour later, Travis showed up. Except for his brief stop the day before, Clara hadn't seen him since she'd had him and his wife Jo Anne over for dinner a month or so before. He closed the door behind him and sank wearily into a chair.

He still looked every inch a cop—beefy build, craggy features, close cropped salt-and-pepper hair and all. Still, Clara envisioned traces of the Oklahoma farm boy he had been before he became a big city detective. No one else would see him that way, however, as he now wore a well pressed dark blue suit, white shirt, and dark blue tie with small, slightly lighter blue diagonal stripes.

"What's new, Travis?" She meant it as a genuine question.

"Not much, I'm afraid. We're following up on some leads, but nothing has panned out so far. Vivian had a lot of friends, a lot of students, and as far as we can tell at this point, no obvious enemies."

"Same here—everything I've heard about her is exemplary. She sounds almost too good to be true."

"Yeah, every time I encounter that sort of person, I wonder what's hidden beneath the veneer of a perfect person."

"You're getting cynical in your old age, Travis. Isn't it even possible that the only thing hidden is a truly decent person?"

"I'll let you know if I ever find one—present company excepted, of course. Enough of this idle chitchat, though. I've got to put on my funeral face. I'm not looking forward to seeing Vivian's parents again, but with luck, I won't have to have any direct contact this time."

"What's the plan?"

"I understand the dean is having someone bring them to the service, and they'll be sitting in a shielded spot off to the side in the front. I saw people beginning to arrive already, so I'm going on over to see what I can see. Of course, it's better if you don't come with me. We don't need to have anyone connecting you with the investigation."

"Yeah, that's what got me into trouble last time. I'll be going over with another faculty member just before the service starts. Anything in particular I should be looking for?"

"Sure, watch for some guy big enough to lug a small dead body into a vehicle and hope he stands up and says, 'Stop everything. I did it!' Seriously, though, keep an eye out for anything unusual, though I admit I don't expect any big revelations. It's only in the movies that the cops spot the perp looking guilty at the services."

"Okay, I'll do my best. Do you want to meet at Take Five after the service and see if we come up with anything?"

"Sure, it's not far from home for me anyway, and that's where I really want to go."

e/ɔe/ɔ

A few minutes before four, Paula stopped by for Clara, and they walked out to the quad where a small flower-laden stage and hundreds of white chairs had been set up. Clara was astonished to see so many people fill the chairs, with more standing in the back and on the sides.

Fortunately, Paula led her to a section near the front

that had been reserved for faculty, and they took the last two seats in the section.

On each seat was a five-by-seven-inch linen-stock card edged in purple and gold. Beneath the name Vivian Faith Hall at the top were the years of her birth and death and the program for the eulogies. At the bottom, in elegant script, were the words, "Departed from us, but not from our hearts."

A string quartet was playing "Amazing Grace" as two students entered with an ashen-faced older couple between them and led them to their seats behind a screen at the front.

Dean Penner mounted the small stage and began, "Today we are here to remember and honor our friend and colleague Vivian Hall. However warranted words of tribute may be, no words can adequately convey the sense of loss we all feel today." Her opening words were borne out as she continued to speak eloquently about Vivian's life and contributions to the law school.

The dean introduced the next speaker, and each speaker introduced the one who followed. The eulogies could not have been more superlative. The memories were warm and heartfelt, with the solemn mood occasionally relieved by humor.

The president of the student body said, "I was a typical anxious new law student when I entered Professor Hall's classroom for my first class. But my anxiety was greatly relieved when she started her first lecture by saying 'If you think you're nervous, imagine what it's like for me. I'm beginning my first class as a law professor with all of you out there waiting to hear me say something profound. Of course, I have the obvious advantage because, instead of expecting you to admire my erudition, I require only that you laugh at all of my jokes, no matter how lame.' After that, throughout the semester, Professor

Hall made frequent seemingly off-the-cuff jokes, and only in retrospect did her students realize the jokes were designed to help them remember the material they were supposed to learn."

While Clara listened as the service progressed, she also looked around her at the other faculty members as subtlely as she could. John Knox MacArthur was glancing surreptitiously at his Smartphone. Paula was rigid, her only movement the occasional clenching and unclenching of her hands. From her review of the BASL website, Clara could attach names to most of the other faces. All of the faces looked sad, and most people held tissues that dabbed at eyes and noses from time to time.

One face that drew her attention was handsome and the color of coffee with cream. He wore a coal black suit, white shirt, and black tie with small dark gray dots. His dry-eyed expression was stony, but it also gave the impression of extreme control. As Clara watched him, however, she detected deep breaths and an almost imperceptible trembling of his full lips. She recalled his name as Lyle Sheldon or Shelton, but she couldn't remember what he taught. She couldn't help wondering if there might be some significant emotion hidden beneath the stony exterior.

The final speaker was Vivian's roommate Marilyn Aiello. She called to mind their friendship and the good times they had shared, going to concerts and taking in the sights of San Francisco. They had appreciated the great variety of restaurants in the city and joked about collaborating on a book of restaurants with cuisines from A to Z. But they had gotten only through Armenian, Basque, and Cuban, and they were considering whether they should consider Deli a cuisine when Vivian became too busy with her work at the law school for them to continue going out to eat regularly.

Marilyn said her only regret with regard to Vivian was that she had felt a twinge of guilt because, much as she'd always hoped she would see Vivian fulfill her fondest dream of being married and having children, she also knew she selfishly did not want to lose her as a roommate. She had never imagined she would lose her roommate in such a brutal way. It was the only reference to how Vivian had died.

She changed the tone then, reminding students not to forget to laugh at Vivian's jokes, no matter how lame. She predicted that one day they would be sitting in the bar exam and remember some elusive point of law because Vivian had told them not to confuse the Statute of Frauds with a Statue of Frogs. She ended on an encouraging note, saying she hoped the high ideals of Vivian's life would inspire her students to be the best that they could be.

On those words, the music for "Going Home" began, with the string quartet accompanying a fine baritone. He sang purely, deeply, and without embellishment. The dean then joined the two escorts for Vivian's parents as they led them off to a waiting black sedan.

After the last note of "Going Home," no one moved for a while. The audience began to leave as the musicians played an arrangement of Samuel Barber's "Adagio for Strings." Gradually, the only sounds came from the soft rustling of departing guests, punctuated with sniffles and an occasional whisper. Clara had never seen a more moving service.

She couldn't help feeling a little guilty for scanning the crowd to look for anything that might look suspicious, and in a way, she was glad not to see anything unusual. Besides the faculty, she saw only one face she thought she recognized, a quick glimpse of Professor Murdoch as he headed out to the parking lot. She was touched that he had come to pay his last respects to a former student.

Travis drove his police-issue beige car into the parking lot of his neighborhood bar, Take Five, a few minutes before Clara pulled in a few spaces away. When she got there, he was sipping bourbon and branch water, and a glass of Pinot noir was waiting for her in their usual corner booth in the back. It was nice to hear the cool jazz in the background.

"Wow, you're actually off duty?" she asked, knowing he never drank when he was on duty.

"It's about time. I haven't kept track of how many hours I've been on duty since I first got the call about Vivian."

"Let's hope you can go home at least till tomorrow. Is Jo Anne cooking something wonderful?"

"Of course, and you're invited, too."

"Not on your life. She's entitled to a little alone time with you for a change."

"Leave it to you to think like that. Not bad for somebody who hasn't had a love life lately."

"My record with men hasn't worked out very well over the years, so let's talk about something more productive, if you please. I didn't even see you at the memorial service. Where were you?"

"In the far corner, as usual—this is my invisible suit."

"I hope you meant it's a suit that makes you invisible, not an invisible suit. I really don't want to picture you in your underwear."

"I stand corrected. Why do you have to be so literal?"

"It's all those years teaching English, I guess. Anyway, did you see anything interesting at the memorial service?"

"I can't say I did. A lot of people and a lot of sad faces, but nothing really stood out."

"Did you see Peter Susskind? I didn't see him anywhere."

"I scanned almost everybody, and I caught a glimpse of him sitting on the aisle in the back. I didn't get any particular read on him, and he dashed out as soon as the service was over. Did you see anything noteworthy in the faculty section?"

"I don't know if it was anything worth noting, but there was one person with a sort of interesting reaction. I got the impression he might have been holding in a lot of emotion."

"Who was that?"

"I'll double check, but I think his name is Lyle Shelton. He's a very good looking African-American guy."

"Why don't you see what you can find out and let me know? Anything else?"

"I've met a couple of faculty members already, and I'll try to meet the rest as soon as I can without being too obvious about it. The day after tomorrow is a specially-called faculty meeting, so they should all be there. Adjuncts don't go to faculty meetings, but maybe I'll have a chance to meet a few people before and after the meeting."

Clara felt an uneasy twinge at the thought of the effort to meet new people. She still suffered from the insecurities that had resulted from her father's constant criticism of her as an adolescent. To this day, when she tried to become acquainted with someone new, she assumed she would be rejected, and she was always somewhat surprised when she realized she was in fact a reasonably likeable person.

They chatted a few more minutes about inconsequential things, and Andy came by to see if they were ready for another round.

"No thanks. We're driving, and I'm about to head for home anyway," Travis said.

"Nice to see you again, Clara," said Andy. "It's been a while. I knew you'd be coming in, though, when this guy ordered the Pinot noir. I keep a good bottle on hand with your name on it."

"Thanks, Andy, I noticed. It's a lot better than the stuff you had when I first came in."

"We aim to please," he said, as they each left some money on the table.

She anticipated a relaxing evening at home, but as usual, she hadn't predicted the unexpected tasks that would await her.

Chapter 5

Juvenile Dependency

When Clara got home, she found a Post-it note stuck on her mailbox, which held only a few pieces of junk mail. It said, *We have a big package for you. M & M.*

She knew, of course, the note was from Marge and Matt, the older couple in the other penthouse that occupied the top floor of her building. She had been so glad when they moved there from Southern California to live near their grandchildren. They were very pleasant people, with one of her favorite characteristics—they were quiet. That wasn't always the case, however, when they babysat for the boisterous six- and eight-year-old sons of their daughter, who was a harried single mom. Danny and Kenny were clearly a handful.

She rapped on the door, and it was a minute before Marge opened it as she wiped the residue of cookie dough from her hands onto her apron. "Sorry to keep you waiting, but I just put cookies in the oven. My daughter is supposed to take them to a bake sale at the boys' school tomorrow and didn't have time to bake. I would never

have known, but when I called her, she was about to go to
a bakery to buy cookies. I can't seem to get it through her
head that I actually like doing stuff like this for her. She
won't even let us help financially, except when the boys
need something extra. She has a good job, but I wish
she'd let us do more. I admit I'm proud of her independence, though."

Marge obviously had a tendency to ramble on about
her daughter and the grandkids. Clara didn't really mind,
but when Marge took a breath, she wedged in, "You have
a package for me?"

"Of course, where is my mind? It's right here."

As soon as Clara saw the bulky box, she knew it was
the appellate record for her juvenile dependency case
from the court. "Thanks, Marge. I don't know what I'd
do without you. Say hi to Matt for me."

"Will do. He's out for one of his long walks—should
be back soon."

"The cookies smell great. See you later," she said, as
she reached for the heavy box.

"Wait, let me give you one for the road. The first
batch is cool." She wrapped two big cookies in a napkin
and placed them on top of the box, which Clara lugged
across the hall to her place.

She put the cookies on her kitchen counter and took
the box to her study. She slit it open with the small Swiss
Army knife on her key ring. It made her smile every time
she used it because it had been given to her by her stepson, Jake, who had recently gone back for his junior year
at Cornell after a short visit with Clara. The box held six
large volumes, each more than an inch thick, fastened
with long brads.

The aroma of cookies had made Clara hungry, and
she decided to fortify herself with a hearty *croque mad-
ame* sandwich and a bowl of French onion soup before

beginning her huge task. She was still munching on the second cookie when she opened the first volume and looked at the cover.

The caption read *In re K.M., A Person Coming under the Juvenile Court Law,* and beneath that were the words *San Francisco Family & Children's Services, Plaintiff and Respondent, v. Gretchen M., Defendant and Appellant.* The judge in the lower court had been the Honorable Gregory Hart, but it was another name that jumped off the page. All of the attorneys in the case were listed, and the attorney for the minor in Judge Hart's juvenile dependency court had been Vivian Hall.

Even though Clara knew Vivian had done some legal work through the law school's children's rights center, she didn't know Vivian had actually represented children in the dependency court. It was ironic because she had been given a checklist of things appellate attorneys were supposed to do, and one of them was to contact the children's attorney in the lower court to see if they could add any insight to what was in the record. Of course, she would never be able to reach Vivian Hall now.

Clara then perused the table of contents. The first item in the list was the Juvenile Dependency Petition, followed by periodic social worker reports, transcripts of hearings held every six months for a year and a half, and a variety of other relevant reports and court documents. Clara started with the petition, comparable to a complaint in a civil case, and steeled herself for what was to come.

Even so, she was appalled at the allegations of abuse and neglect of the two-year-old girl who had been born drug-exposed and six months later taken to the hospital with a broken arm. The child's name was Krystal in the record, but Clara already knew she was to be referred to by her initials K.M. in the briefs to protect her identity in the appellate case. K.M.'s mother, Gretchen Miller, had shown signs of being under the influence of a controlled substance when she took the child to the hospital, and after the doctor examined the baby, he reported burn marks on her arms, malnutrition, and severe diaper rash in addition to the broken arm. K.M. was detained in the custody of Family & Children's Services and temporarily placed in a shelter for children.

At the first hearing, Gretchen had testified that K.M. probably had broken her arm in a fall from the sofa, but she claimed to know nothing about the burn marks. She said she had left K.M. with her boyfriend while she went out for cigarettes and found the baby crying when she got back. The boyfriend could not be located.

Gretchen said the boyfriend was not the father of the child and she didn't know the identity of the father for certain. She said the father could be any one of several men, for whom she could not provide names, and subsequent investigation indicated Gretchen had most likely been a prostitute to support her drug habit before K.M. was born. Her primary drug of choice was methamphetamine, although she had apparently experimented with cocaine and others as well.

The social worker's first report described the squalid conditions of the cheap hotel room in the run-down Tenderloin neighborhood of San Francisco. The room was filthy, strewn with litter, and unsafe because of fire hazards from multiple electric plugs, mounds of flammable material, and no working smoke alarm. It seemed unbelievable the child had lived only a few blocks from the pleasant apartment near city hall that Vivian, a law professor, had shared with a roommate who was a member of the staff of the California Supreme Court.

As she pictured this child's start in life, she was already in tears. She had read a wide range of dependency cases before, but this was the first one in which she represented the abused child. Thus, it was far more moving than the published cases she had read. Now she had actual responsibility for this child.

She sat for a while, trying to absorb the enormity of what she had gotten herself into. This was only one case, and she was barely twenty pages into a record of hundreds of pages. How could she endure such grim facts in this case and maybe even worse in cases to come? How would she ever be able to do this? Why should she even try?

Serious questions demand thoughtful answers. How could she answer these questions for herself? But after a while, the answer came. Finally, she realized, *if a tiny child can endure such horrors, how can I be so weak that I can't represent her best interests in court? She deserves no less than the best I can do for her.*

So, Clara continued. The dependency court judge found the allegations of the petition true, and on the social worker's recommendation, he ordered K.M. placed with her Aunt Benita in Oakland. The aunt lived with her mother, who was mildly disabled, in a small two-bedroom house in a working-class neighborhood. To regain custody, the judge ordered Gretchen to complete a drug treatment program, submit to regular drug testing, and take a parenting class. She was also to maintain weekly visitation with K.M. in the home of the aunt.

Clara plodded through reports and transcripts of hearings that showed ups and downs in the mother's compliance with her case plan. She seemed to make progress, at times, but had several relapses. At one point, the social worker reported Gretchen was seeing the same boyfriend again, and the judge ordered her to stay away from him or risk losing her child permanently. Meanwhile, K.M. was successfully bonding with her Aunt Benita and grandmother.

Another downturn came, however, when the grandmother's condition deteriorated, and she became more
seriously disabled. Benita tried to keep it from the social
worker, but home visits showed substantial problems in
her ability to care for K.M. The social worker concluded
that despite the aunt's apparent good intentions, K.M.'s
well-being was again threatened by neglect. She informed
Benita that if circumstances did not improve, she had no
alternative but to locate a foster home for K.M. In addition, an on-going problem had been Gretchen's failure to
keep up with the visitation schedule. Even with transpor-
tation passes provided by the court, she claimed it was
impossible to visit across the bay every week.

Throughout the case, Vivian had apparently kept
close tabs on the progress of everyone concerned with
caring for K.M. and informed the judge of what she
deemed to be in the best interests of the child. At the
twelve-month hearing, she agreed with the social worker's decision to place K.M. in a foster home, which the
judge ordered. It was clear from the transcript that
Gretchen was furious with the decision, and after several
of her outbursts in the courtroom, the judge warned her to
compose herself. Finally, she had screamed, "It's not fair!
I tried to do everything you ordered, but it's just too
much. Nobody can do all that stuff."

The judge had considered adding an anger manage-
ment class to her case plan before because of previous
outbursts, and he did so at that point.

By the eighteen-month hearing, Gretchen had completed some, but not nearly all, of her case plan. Especially troubling, though, was her continued sporadic visitation. She had little excuse for that failure, however, as
visits then took place in the play area of the Family &
Children's Services building, which wasn't far from
Gretchen's meager apartment. The address of the foster

parents remained confidential for the protection of the child.

K.M. was bonding with her new foster parents, who said they wanted to adopt her, and she sometimes cried when Gretchen tried to hold her. K.M. was also thriving in the care of the foster parents. They had submitted to a stringent background check and home study, and the social worker assessed them as excellent candidates to become the adoptive parents of this child.

The purpose of the final hearing was to order a permanent plan for the child. The evidence was thorough, and from the judge's questions, he seemed to have listened thoughtfully as it was presented. Several of his questions focused on how Gretchen proposed to support and care for K.M. considering her past record, and he expressed serious concern that she was inadequately prepared to take on the responsibilities of parenthood.

Gretchen displayed bursts of inappropriate anger at various points, but the judge seemed to be reasonably tolerant. He was well aware that the potential for losing one's child can be traumatic, and he was not surprised when a parent objected vehemently. He reminded Gretchen's attorney to control his client and finally quieted her only by warning her that if she spoke out of turn again, she would be charged with contempt of court.

In closing argument, Gretchen's appointed attorney made as strong a case as he could, given the facts, and requested more time for Gretchen to fully comply with the judge's previous orders. Vivian, on behalf of K.M., and the attorney for Family & Children's Services noted the mother had already had more than the statutorily required time to complete her case plan. They recommended termination of Gretchen's parental rights and adoption by the new foster parents as being in the best interests of the child.

Ultimately, after considering all of the evidence, the judge agreed with the recommendation and ordered termination of parental rights, followed by adoption of K.M. by the foster parents once all legal formalities had been observed. He advised Gretchen of her appellate rights and informed her that K.M would be adopted unless she filed an appeal within the time set by statute. The mother's last words in the transcript were her final outburst: "You can't take away my baby. I'll get you all for this!" but the judge did not respond. He said simply, "Court adjourned," and then headed toward his chambers.

The final document in the record was Gretchen's notice of appeal of the lower court's judgment filed on her behalf by her attorney. It was past midnight when Clara finished reading. She was tired but hopeful. From everything she had read, it appeared that the judgment was correct. It looked as if one little girl might have a better life than she ever could have had with her biological mother. It was comforting to know the system worked—at least in this case.

Since there was, of course, no way to consult the child's attorney, Clara's only remaining duties before preparing to write her brief were to speak with the social worker and visit with K.M. in her foster home. She would make arrangements for that tomorrow.

Clara slept later than usual, waking after eight in the morning. She decided to make the most of her time by working on the case in her new office at BASL. It probably would be a quiet place to work, since it wasn't likely many faculty members would be there till the meeting the next day.

By late morning, she had made notes based on her telephone conversation with the social worker, Vanessa Delgado, who provided more detail on both the mother and the foster parents. After Clara introduced herself and the purpose of her call, the social worker said, "I'm sorry, but you'll have to give me some time to call you back. I have an active caseload of well over a hundred cases at any given time, and I can't say I really remember this one by name. Over the years, I've had so many thousands of cases the names blur together, and I don't try to rely on my memory alone anymore."

Vanessa called back sooner than Clara expected and first said, "I didn't realize this is the case where Vivian Hall represented the child. Now I remember it clearly, and I was very sorry to hear of Ms. Hall's tragic death. Did you know her?"

"No, I didn't know her, but I've heard a lot about her since I was assigned to this case."

"All of it was good, I expect. She struck me as very diligent and devoted to this work. I think this was her first dependency case, and she handled it like a pro."

"I understand Ms. Hall agreed with your final recommendations, and I'd like to hear whatever impressions you might have had about the case."

"Sure, I know it's hard to get a complete feel for it just from written reports and transcripts. I have the file in front of me now, and it helps me recall my views at various stages. First of all, the mother is a real piece of work. Gretchen was extremely difficult to deal with from beginning to end."

"Were you able to help her situation at all?"

"The more I tried to help her, the more she resisted. She had spotty success with her drug program and seemed not to take seriously the possible loss of her child until the last stages of the case, even though at every step both the judge and the court documents had cautioned her about the potential for termination of her parental rights."

"Why do you think she reacted that way?"

"It isn't unusual for parents to be in denial till the reality finally hits them, and sometimes then they become angry at me and everybody else in the system. Gretchen had become increasingly heated in her reactions as the case progressed, blaming everyone but herself for having her baby removed from her."

"Can you give me an example?"

"There were plenty. One of her most explosive outbursts toward the end came when she found out the foster parents had been calling Krystal by the name Kristen and intended to change it legally when they adopted her. Gretchen said she had named the baby Krystal because she always felt so good when she used crystal meth, and the foster parents had no right to change her baby's birth name. She irrationally claimed she'd fight it all the way to the Supreme Court."

"Did you think her anger indicated any danger to herself or others?"

"I never saw any signs of suicidal ideation, or I would've recommended a psychiatric evaluation. But she did threaten the foster parents. It was pretty vague, though, just something like she'd make sure they would never keep her child. But it made us all the more certain we'd done the right thing in keeping their address confidential."

"I see in your reports that you gave the foster parents very high marks."

"Yes, the result of the home study was exceptionally good. The foster parents had both worked at a tech company in Silicon Valley till the previous year when the wife had quit her job, hoping to get pregnant. When she'd been unable to conceive, they'd considered fertility measures, but decided instead they wanted to adopt a child who needed a good home."

"And they were firm in their commitment to adopt?"

"They had previously fostered two children and were

disappointed when the children were returned to their biological families. But they strongly believed Kristen was the child they were meant to have. They are financially stable, assessed as not being affluent, but fully capable of providing for her both physically and emotionally."

"So you don't have any reservations about them as parents?"

"None at all. My only concern is that if for any reason the appeal doesn't turn out well, we could lose them as foster parents. After being disappointed twice before, they told me they weren't sure they could go through that again."

"Do you have any opinion about prospects of the appeal?"

She chuckled. "I'm not a lawyer, of course, but I always have opinions about the legal process. In this case, it seems pretty straightforward to me. I can't see any reason at all the appellate court will not affirm. We did everything by the book, and as far as I can tell, there's no doubt there was plenty of evidence to support the dependency court judgment."

Clara thought about the dozens of appellate court dependency cases she had already read to learn more about this area of the law. She had also read the applicable parts of California Welfare and Institutions Code, starting with section three hundred. So far as she could tell through her research, she thought the social worker was right.

"I appreciate your insight, Vanessa," Clara said. "If you happen to think of anything else, let me give you my contact information."

"That's good, but if you don't mind, send it to me in an email. That way I'll have the information, and we can easily communicate by email if it's something that requires a written record."

"Thanks, I'll send it right away."

Clara decided to use her newly assigned faculty email address, and she sent the follow-up email as soon as she hung up. Then she remembered another email she'd meant to send, to ask the dean if she could help her set up a visit to the juvenile dependency court, as she had offered. She received a quick response saying the dean had already made a call arranging for her to visit Judge Gregory Hart's courtroom. All she had to do was call and give her name to the bailiff, who would be expecting to hear from her.

When she called the bailiff, she arranged to go to court the following Monday, subject only to approval of the parties in the cases. She could come as early as eight when the proceedings began and stay for as long as she wanted.

She had one more arrangement to make—an appointment to visit K.M. in the home of the foster parents. It was set for two days later, and she wondered what she could learn from a child who was probably barely talking yet.

Chapter 6

Scene of the Crime

As she was beginning to look through the appellate record again, Clara was interrupted by a muscular young man in a dark green work shirt with the BASL logo embroidered over the pocket. He introduced himself as Ron and said he was from the facilities department.

"We're ready to repaint your wall, professor, and the sooner we can get to it the better. Things have a way of stacking up the closer we get to orientation the week before classes start."

"No problem. I'll be glad to get out of your way, and it'll be nice to have the nail holes patched and painted so I can put up something pleasant to look at on that wall."

"Yeah, it's really a shame the way all this happened. Only last week, Professor Hall unpacked the rest of her boxes, the ones with her pictures and diplomas. She said she'd meant to get around to it all year but somehow didn't seem to make time for it. She just got all the framed stuff up on the wall, and we had to take it all down and pack it up again after we got the news about her. She borrowed a hammer from us, and now we have to use the claw end to pull out all of the same nails we gave her."

The word hit her like a—well, of course—like a hammer!

"You mean she was using a hammer only a few days ago?"

"Yeah, I'm not sure which day it was. I think she kept the hammer a few days, but it was okay because we have at least half a dozen of them besides our own."

"Do you know what happened to the hammer she was using?"

"Sure, it was here when I came in to check on the phone connections. All the framed stuff was up, so I took it back to the facilities office."

"Do you remember what day that was?"

"Now that you mention it, I guess it was in the morning of the day they found her. But I didn't know about it then, of course. That was really a tragedy, wasn't it? Imagine something so terrible happening to a nice person like her." He continued talking about how nice Vivian had always been, not like some of the snooty professors who didn't have the time of day for him.

Clara didn't want to seem like one of the snooty professors, but she was eager to let Travis know what she was thinking and said, "Ron, is it okay to hold off on the painting till I check my schedule? I'd like to have you take care of it at a time convenient for both of us."

"Sure, in fact, I thought maybe we could do it the beginning of next week, if that's okay with you."

"That works for me. I won't need to be in the office at that time."

Ron was a chatty fellow, and Clara could hardly wait to get rid of him. She finally asked him to excuse her as she had some work to do.

"I've got work to do, too," he said. "Otherwise, I'd be standing around yakking all day."

Clara was glad she had put Travis's numbers on speed dial. He was out of the office, but he picked up on his cell.

"What's up, Clara?"

"Maybe nothing, but maybe a lot. I could be wrong, but I might have discovered how and where Vivian was killed."

಄಄಄

Travis was at BASL within twenty minutes of when Clara had told him about the hammer. Two plain clothes crime scene investigators were there soon after. Travis went with them to the facilities office, and he questioned Ron about all of the hammers in the department. Most of the facilities staff had their own hammers on their tool belts, but there were several in the facilities office. As far as Ron knew, they all seemed to be accounted for, because he couldn't recall any faculty members requesting a hammer since Vivian had used one of theirs and kept it.

The hammers varied in age and condition, but they were all basic heavy-duty all-purpose hammers. The crime scene investigators, wearing protective gloves, examined each one carefully. None had any visible traces of significant extraneous matter, but special detection methods revealed a minute trace of blood between the wood handle and the metal head of one hammer. It was dusted for prints, then bagged, marked, and taken straight to the lab.

The only prints were determined to be Ron's, and he readily admitted having picked up the hammer in Vivian's office and taken it back to the facilities office. Travis put a rush on the analysis of the tiny blood sample, and within a few days, the lab confirmed a DNA match with Vivian's blood.

They had their murder weapon, and now they had the crime scene. Clara had been immediately ejected from the office while a thorough forensic inspection was made. Although no bloodstains were visible, with special equipment a few small traces of blood were detected on the carpet and a couple of minute ones on the wall.

They appeared to have been sponged with water, judging from the barely discernable lighter areas in the carpet.

Clara was surprised no yellow crime scene tape had been put over the door to the office while they were investigating. She asked Travis about it, and he explained he'd decided not to release specific information about the crime scene.

Even if some people noticed the police activity, he didn't want to acknowledge officially that the murder had been committed in Vivian's office because, if only the killer knew for sure, it could help to eliminate potential false confessions and might ultimately be useful information with the real killer. They'd already had one regular "confessor" say he had tossed Vivian onto the rocks.

Travis was kicking himself for not calling in the crime scene investigators to go over her office before. But when he had first gone to BASL and checked out the office, there had been nothing visible to indicate a need for further investigation.

"I should know better," he told Clara. "I'm the one who always says never assume anything, but when I saw her office looking so normal, I assumed she had been killed somewhere else after leaving her office."

"Even when you make a mistake, it's a very reasonable mistake, Travis. Don't beat yourself up over it."

"I'm not supposed to make mistakes, but you're

right. It doesn't do any good to fret about what I did wrong. But now I have to try to make up for lost time."

As it developed, however, knowing the apparent murder weapon and crime scene didn't provide much insight to suggest a particular suspect. But it did turn Travis's thoughts to who might have been in Vivian's office and why. Other faculty members, staff, and possibly students were the most obvious suspects, but that didn't do much good when there were so many possibilities.

Upon questioning the security guard again, however, Travis learned that anyone could have walked onto the campus and entered the faculty office building. The outer door to the parking lot was locked from the outside at six p.m., but the inner door from the quad wasn't routinely locked until midnight because faculty members liked to have easy access if they wanted to work in the evenings.

So were they back to square one? Maybe not quite, because it was unlikely some random person would enter the campus from the street, go in through the inner door, and find Vivian in her office. The most likely killer was someone connected with the BASL campus, or at least someone who knew Vivian and where to find her.

❧❧❧

Despite the large number of possibilities, knowing even a little more energized Clara. She had all the more reason now to find out everything she could about who might have had connections with Vivian. After the crime scene investigators finished their work, she had her office back, and she could go to work in earnest.

Even with her renewed energy, however, Clara was feeling somewhat silly for thinking there could be any possible connection between the *Vertigo* sites and Vivian's murder. She was glad she hadn't told Travis about her little Hitchcock tour and imagined he would have gotten a huge chuckle out of her naïve police work. But even if Vivian had been murdered in that very office, did that necessarily mean there was no connection between her being found at Fort Point and any other scene from the film?

ᥱᕽᥱᕽ

Her dreams that night went beyond *Vertigo.* She found herself weaving in and out of Hitchcock plots, starting with some of his early English movies and going to his last one, *Family Plot.* Clara had not seen all of his fifty plus films, and her dreams focused primarily on the ones from the 1950s, which were her favorites. Unlike some of the disquieting aspects of her previous dreams, except for *Vertigo,* these were not particularly disturbing. After she awoke once in the wee hours, she was able to get back to a peaceful sleep.

The next morning, Clara got to her office before nine. She knew the faculty meeting was at noon, but she assumed some faculty members would come in early to work on whatever it is faculty members need to work on. When the first professors didn't begin to show up until about eleven, she was reminded of Travis's admonition never to assume anything.

Clara made a couple of trips to the faculty lounge for tea and introduced herself to whoever was there. She wasn't surprised that Vivian was a prominent topic of conversation, and she tried to pick up on any untoward comments. But generally, the mood seemed somber, and although this gave her an opportunity to match names with faces, she didn't learn anything she considered particularly useful.

At noon, the offices were deserted, with the dean and faculty members all meeting in the large conference room.

Clara ambled down to the faculty services office to get a few office supplies and found the secretaries in good humor, laughing about something as she entered.

"It seems very cheerful in here," she said.

Rosalind replied, "We're enjoying the peace and quiet before the storm. This afternoon, we'll be swamped with new tasks of all kinds. Half of the professors think their work is more important than anyone else's, and the other half get stuck trying to get their syllabuses typed, copies made, and so on after we take care of the entitled ones."

"Who are the entitled ones?"

"They're pretty much the old guys, except for Professor Greenburg. He's easy to work with. The students think he's a terror in class, but he's actually a real sweetheart. They'd be amazed if they knew he plays Santa every year at San Francisco Children's Hospital."

"Really, Professor Greenburg? The one with the big white beard?"

"Yeah, he says the kids don't know he's Jewish, and he can ho, ho, ho with the best of them. He says his wife isn't Jewish, but she's the best Jewish mother he knows, so he thinks he can be the best Santa at the hospital. But the students don't know the most significant thing about Professor Greenburg."

"What's that?"

"He and his wife adopted two disabled children that apparently nobody else was willing to take on. Now they're adults, leading productive lives, and Professor Greenburg and his wife help with their children's children. The grandchildren have turned out to be really good kids, and one of them is getting ready to go to college next year. Most of the faculty members know about it, but the students don't have a clue."

"I've always believed the most admirable acts of generosity are the ones people don't try to get credit for. It's nice to know they've kept a low profile about their good works."

"We know a lot about the professors' private lives, good and not so good, and a lot in between."

"Like what?"

"You'd be surprised what the profs tell us. We even get a whiff of office romances now and then. I guess that's my favorite part of office gossip."

"Any you care to share?"

"I guess I'd better not. We wouldn't want it to get out we're telling anybody's secrets."

"Do the faculty members tell you their secrets?"

"Not exactly. It's more like they seem to let their hair down in here, maybe because they stay on their guard so much with other profs, especially the difficult ones."

"So who are the difficult profs to work with?"

"The worst is the little guy with the Napoleon complex."

"Would you be referring to General MacArthur by any chance?"

"I wouldn't want to name names, but you're obviously on to him already. He has mountains of handouts he uses over and over every year, and we spend hours in the copy room while everybody else has to wait. He also has us copy stuff from law books from the library, and we suspect he reads a lot of it to the students in his lectures. I think he's had tenure longer than anyone here but Professor Greenburg, and he seems to think he can do whatever he wants to, no matter who is inconvenienced."

"That certainly doesn't make your job any easier."

"I don't mean to complain. It's really kind of fun trying to keep everybody happy. Most of the newer profs are pretty easy to get along with, especially the ones hired since Dean Penner took charge. But some of them get frustrated when we get backed up."

"I don't expect to need much from you, fortunately. I've always done my own typing on the computer, and I can make my own copies if I need them. I taught in a high school before I became a lawyer, and I'm used to doing my own work."

"Sounds good, but really, don't hesitate to ask if you need anything. We can always manage to do whatever needs to be done."

"I appreciate that, Rosalind. Mostly, right now all I need are some paper clips, Post-its, a stapler, a legal pad, and a few colored pens."

"Sure, help yourself from that cupboard over there. Take anything you need."

"Thanks, that should do it."

のみの

After she got back to her office, it was quiet for a while until faculty members started streaming back from the meeting. Before long she heard an argument from the office across the hall. The voices weren't loud, but they were intense. She recognized them as belonging to John Knox MacArthur, a couple of other professors she had met briefly, and Paula Kelley.

The other professors left, and Paula popped into Clara's office. "Got a minute?" she asked.

"Sure, come on in."

"Mind if I close the door?"

"Of course not. What's up?"

"My blood pressure, probably."

"What was the argument about?"

"Same old stuff. The newer profs hired since Britt became dean have a different vision from the old guard. Well, not entirely. I'm old guard myself, and I've had tenure almost as long as John. But there are times when I wonder about the value of tenure. There seems to be a movement affront in higher education to do away with tenure."

"Wasn't the theory of tenure to protect the professor's academic freedom?"

"Yes, and I admit I have a hard time with that principle. It's an important purpose, no doubt, but it also has had unintended consequences. Too many professors publish and teach well only until they get tenure, and then they rest on their laurels, or worse, contribute nothing further to scholarship and become lazy teachers."

"I see your point. I've observed that sometimes, too."

"John was even more snide than usual today because he was irritated by having to go to a faculty meeting on a Friday. The dean called this one because she thought it was important to bring us together after Vivian's death. I'm sure John was mainly annoyed about having his long weekend spoiled. All of his classes are scheduled on Tuesdays and Thursdays, so he has to be on campus only a couple of days a week."

"I gather you and John have a tendency to lock horns on more than the tennis court."

"That's for sure. Another argument I've had with him is analogous with regard to tenure—the length of appointments to the United States Supreme Court. John completely agrees with lifetime appointment for justices simply because it's now conferred under the Constitution, based on the premise of guaranteeing that the justices can't be swayed by outside influences.

"Are you saying you don't agree with the constitutional provision?"

"I think it's time we should consider amending the Constitution to limiting the term of appointment, because when the Constitution was written, justices didn't serve such long terms. They generally were not very young when they were appointed, and they had shorter life spans than now. These days justices may well wind up serving for decades and keeping the Court from seeing issues though fresh eyes."

"I haven't considered questions like this since I was in law school," Clara said. "It's interesting to be back with people who think about things like this."

"The trouble with people like John is that they never seem to think about such concerns in any way except how they've always thought about them. For him, there doesn't seem to be any such thing as thinking outside the box."

"That may be largely true of people in general. Anyway, I'm glad to see the questions being raised."

"Sorry to dump on you like this. You're easy to talk to. Hope you don't mind my venting."

"Not at all. I'm interested to know what you think, and I welcome your views."

Clara was eager to establish a reputation as someone who is easy to talk to. Almost from the time they first met, Travis had said that was one of her strongest—and most useful—qualities.

"I almost forgot to tell you," Paula added. "In the faculty meeting, the routine list of adjuncts for this year sailed through without a hitch. So welcome aboard. You're official now."

"Thanks, I'm glad there was no problem. Was there anything else of significance in the faculty meeting?"

"No, it was mostly the usual beginning of the academic year stuff. So I guess that's about all the news from Lake Wobegon, and I'd better be going. I have a meeting of my young women lawyers this afternoon."

"What's that about?"

"They're not technically all young, but it seems to have worked out that way. Most of the group members are women who took my Women and the Law course, and now they're in practice. We meet to share experiences, often to talk about problems they have as women practicing law. Maybe you'd like to join us."

"I don't think I can make it today, but keep me in mind. I had some doozies of weird experiences when I worked for a law firm."

"Great, we meet more or less once a month, but not always at the same time. I'll let you know when we get together next time."

With that, Paula dashed out, and a few minutes later, Clara looked out her window and saw her drive off in her blue Honda hybrid. Shortly afterward, she saw John Knox MacArthur leave in his polished black Mercedes.

Gradually, the cars departed from the faculty parking lot. By three, the only one left besides her Prius was silver Infiniti that looked to be a couple of years old. Curious to see who was still on campus, Clara walked down the hall. She looked through the window into faculty services, the only office that had an inner window facing the hall. She saw Rosalind with her fingers flying over the keyboard and Wesley sorting piles of papers into stacks. Across the hall, Sunny was busy at work in the copy room.

At the far end of the hall, the only door open was to the office with the nameplate for Professor Lyle Thurgood Shelton. Beside John Knox MacArthur, his was the only one with his full middle name on the nameplate.

༄༅༄

Lyle Thurgood Shelton was sitting motionless in the chair behind his desk, his back to the door, facing the window out toward the quad. His close-cropped black curly hair showed above the back of his chair. Clara stood at the door trying to decide whether she should interrupt him.

She was still watching him when he finally turned and looked a bit startled. "Hello—may I help you?" he asked.

"I'm sorry. I didn't mean to disturb you. I was just walking by and saw you. We're apparently the only ones left here today except for the secretaries." She extended her hand and said, "Hi, I'm Clara Quillen. I'm a new adjunct here."

"That explains it. I doubt that any of the full-time faculty are ready to be back at their offices yet. Glad to meet you. I'm Lyle," he said, as he stood and shook her hand firmly. "Have a seat."

He was wearing a crisp blue shirt and equally crisp khaki trousers that didn't seem to wrinkle as he took his seat again. On a coat rack in the corner was a navy-blue blazer beside a pale yellow tie with small blue diamonds.

"Thanks, I'm looking forward to getting acquainted with everybody."

"Don't count on it. Adjunct professors tend to get lost in the shuffle around here, but I happen to think our adjuncts are excellent. They often add some valuable real-life experience to the ivory tower."

"What about you? Are you more scholarly or real life?"

"I like to think I'm a little of both. I teach Real Property and Environmental Law. My special interests are human rights, racism, discrimination, and sexual orientation issues. I happen to be straight, though. 'Not that there's anything wrong with that,' if you'll pardon the twist on the old *Seinfeld* line."

Clara laughed, remembering the episode she'd seen several times in reruns. "So do you suppose feeling guilty about being homophobic is any better than being homophobic?"

He chuckled. "Good question. Discrimination comes in all sorts of forms. Then there are those of us who confuse a lot of the bigots and racists. Me, for example. My racial characteristics are mixed, and sometimes people aren't sure how to treat me."

"Do you mind telling me what the mix is?"

"No, in fact, I appreciate the up-front question. Most of the time people are self-conscious about asking— they're too concerned with political correctness."

"I'm all for political correctness when it serves a reasonable purpose, but it's nice to meet somebody who doesn't seem overly concerned with it. So what's your story?"

"I'm a reverse Obama. My father is white, and my mother is black. But I have nicer ears than he has. They were a boon to the political cartoonists."

"You have a nice middle name, too. Did your mother choose it?"

"No, surprisingly, it was Dad who insisted on Thurgood. When he was young, he participated in the civil rights movement in the South in the sixties. That's where he met Mom, but they moved to Chicago after that."

"I always find ethnicity interesting, but I hope not in a prejudicial way."

"Is there anything of special interest in your ethnic background?"

"Not much. I'm sort of mongrel, I guess. There's some Irish, which may explain the auburn hair, and some other British Isles mixed in, with probably some European stuff thrown in as well. I started tracing it once, but got sidetracked when I went to law school."

"I know what you mean. Nothing else exists when you're in law school."

"It seems a little strange to be back in law school again, but at least it's nice to be on the teaching side."

"So what are you going to be teaching here?"

"I'm teaching Juvenile Dependency Law this semester."

Lyle looked disconcerted. He took a deep breath and paused before he murmured under his breath, "Vivian's course."

She was about to respond when Lyle got up abruptly and said, "I'm sorry, but I just remembered an appointment. I'll be late if I don't leave right now."

He grabbed his jacket from the coat rack and left the tie dangling as he ushered Clara out of his office. By the time she reached her own office at the other end of the hall, her Prius was the only car left in the faculty parking lot.

She looked again at the profile for Lyle on the faculty listing. Before his JD at Stanford, he had earned a PhD in Sociology at Northwestern. He had already contributed to a textbook on environmental law, written several articles published in prestigious law reviews, and participated in numerous presentations on human rights and related subjects.

He had an impressive background, but he struck her as unpretentious. Most of all, she was impressed that he hadn't tried to impress her.

Chapter 7

His Honor

Clara figured she might as well go home before calling Travis. She wasn't sure what to make of her conversation with Lyle, but it did seem somewhat strange the way it ended. She wanted to get Travis's take on it.

He listened to her description without interruption. "I don't want to read too much into it, but it seems pretty clear he had a definite reaction to Vivian."

"I think so too, but I'm not sure. He's hard to read. At first, he appeared to be very open, even about sensitive subjects like race and sexual orientation, but then he seemed to shut down completely."

"You'll have to see if you can get closer to him. There may be something there."

"Okay, but tomorrow I'm heading off in a different direction, and I'm excited about it. I'm making my first visit to dependency court."

"Good for you. I know you've been developing an interest there, and I'm glad you're pursuing it. Meanwhile, I've got my own work to do. We have a bunch of leads to follow up."

"Let me know if you find anything promising."

"Will do—talk to you later."

Things seemed to have been happening so fast for Clara that she felt good to be able to relax at home. She enjoyed her penthouse and always felt grateful for her late husband's fortune that made it possible for her to live there.

She put on a CD with the Brahms *Fourth Symphony* and took a glass of Pinot noir out to the balcony. She stood by the railing (but not too close, considering her borderline acrophobia, though not nearly as bad as Jimmy Stewart's wooziness in *Vertigo*) and watched the fog roll in. She stretched out in a lounge chair and pulled a wool afghan around her, remembering the words attributed to Mark Twain, "The coldest winter I ever spent was a summer in San Francisco."

Yet that was one of the very things she loved about San Francisco. The fog was an amorphous specter, casting a spell of white magic over the already magical city. In summer, it formed at the headlands of the Golden Gate, as moisture-carrying Pacific winds merged with the chilly waters of the bay, causing the moisture to condense like droplets on a glass of cold lemonade.

The resulting fog poured though the Golden Gate at ten to twenty miles per hour, sucked inland by the high temperatures of California's Central Valley. But even in the fifteen years she had lived in the Bay Area, she had noticed the effects of global warming. There were many more warm days than she could recall from when she had first arrived, and she might even have to break down and install air conditioning, much as she preferred the fresh air.

The natural air conditioning of the fog was in effect

today though, and soon she began to hear the low moan of the foghorn in the distance. Some people said it sounded mournful to them, but Clara had always found it comforting. For her, it was the perfect reminder that she was where she wanted to be.

After having had only a light lunch at her desk, she was feeling hungry and went to see what she could find in the fridge for dinner. There was a leftover piece of salmon she could warm up, and she could add a baked potato and salad.

She shuddered as she remembered—that was Vivian's last meal. So instead, she cut up the salmon, tossed it into a bowl with a can of clam chowder, and heated it in the microwave. Sometimes she wound up with odd combinations, depending on what she happened to have on hand. She had some grapes and strawberries for dessert, and unusual for her, a second glass of wine, this time a crisp Chardonnay.

The weekend dragged, even though Clara spent much of it making preparations for the course she was going to teach. She ran a few errands on Saturday and caught up on her laundry. In the evening, she watched an old movie and thought nostalgically about the days when she used to go out on a Saturday night.

On Sunday, she somehow wiled away the day, first reading the *Chronicle* more thoroughly than usual, as well as selected articles online from the *New York Times*. She surfed around the internet, cleared out some old emails she'd meant to delete, and organized a few photos she'd intended to get around to before. When she watched *60 Minutes,* it psychologically signaled the end of the weekend, as it used to do when she was in law school, but she had seen most of the segments on previous broadcasts. There wasn't even a new *Masterpiece* to watch on PBS. She was eager for the workweek to begin.

She, of course, didn't know it would be far more interesting in a way she hadn't anticipated.

ℰℐℰℐ

She slept well Sunday night and woke early Monday morning. She chose a taupe pantsuit with an ecru blouse, feeling that would help her appear unobtrusive when she went to the juvenile dependency court. Small pearl earrings and a gold brooch set with pearls on her lapel completed the outfit. She arrived at the court at seven-fifty, found the courtroom, and gave her name to the bailiff.

Her first surprise was the lack of formality, not even an "All rise" when the black-robed judge entered. Her second surprise was how attractive he was—tall, good features, a nice touch of gray at the temples, and a few crinkles at the corners of his dark brown eyes. He called for the first case and smiled at the fidgety four-year-old child sitting by his lawyer. The judge leaned down to hand a teddy bear to the little boy with nut-brown skin and neatly cropped afro hair.

"Good morning, young man. I understand we're here this morning to see about letting you go home with your mom today. That's good news." The little boy looked up, wide-eyed, at the judge and then at his lawyer, who smiled and squeezed his hand.

The judge sat back in his big chair, looked at the people seated at the tables in front of him, and continued, "But first we have some business to attend to. We have a law professor visiting with us as an observer." He indicated Clara in the back of the small courtroom. "If anyone objects to her presence, please let us know now." He paused as the attorneys for the mother, the child, and the county muttered, "No objection, Your Honor."

"Good, then let's get started. We're here for the disposition of this case involving the minor C.J., who was detained after he was allegedly found unsupervised in the courtyard of his apartment complex. According to the social worker's investigation and subsequent reports, his mother left him in the play area with instructions to stay there till she returned. She reportedly went for a job interview and came back approximately two hours later."

He looked straight at the mother and said, "Mom, is that true?"

Hanging her head, the mother responded, "Yes, sir. I'm ashamed to say so, but it's true."

"Tell me more about how you feel about what happened that day."

"Mainly, I was scared to death when I got back, and my baby wasn't there. A neighbor came out and said she'd been watching for me because she'd called the department of child welfare to come pick him up. She gave me the phone number to call, and that started everything happening."

"These reports say you didn't object when the social worker thought C.J. should stay with his grandmother for a while till you could get your job situation worked out. Is that correct?"

"Yeah, my mom and I had our differences in the past, but she stepped up and offered to help. She used to say she wouldn't help me because I wasn't married when I had my baby, and my troubles were all on me. But now I want to move in with my mom, and I think we can get along okay. I didn't get the job I went to see about that day, but I've got me a job now, cleaning up at a beauty school, and I can pay my share of the rent and everything with my mom's help."

"Does C.J.'s dad give you any help?"

"No, sir. I don't even know where he is. He split before C.J. was born."

"Do you think you'll be able to support yourself now?"

"Barely, but they told me at the beauty school they think I'm a hard worker, and they've offered to give me a break on the cost to take the course at the school. I'm hoping to save enough to train to be a beautician and get me a better job."

"Who will be taking care of your little boy while you're working and going to the beauty school?"

"My mom will look after him whenever I'm not home. We may have to go from paycheck to paycheck for a while, but at least I have a paycheck now. And my mom has a little income that helps. I'm doing okay now. I'll never leave him by himself again."

The judge turned to the social worker, as well as the attorneys for the child and the county, to get their take on the case, and they agreed it appeared that the circumstances were stable enough to safely return C.J. to his mother.

Then Judge Hart declared judgment: "While I find the allegations of the petition true, I also find that circumstances have sufficiently improved to make it safe for the child to be returned to the custody of his mother."

He looked directly at the mother and said, "Mom, this was a serious situation that might have had a very much worse outcome. Do you understand that?"

"Yes, sir, I do."

"Good. Luckily, instead of a bad outcome, today we have a happy ending. Let's keep it that way, okay?"

"Yes, sir, don't worry. I'll take good care of my boy from now on."

"I'm glad to hear it. You and your lawyer will have to check with the bailiff for the paperwork you need to have before you can take your son home with you." He added a smile as he said, "I wish you well, but hope never to see you in this courtroom again. Next case, please."

Clara was amazed that the case had taken only a few minutes, and there was not even a pause before going to the next one. As the morning progressed, some cases were more complex and took a little longer, but all went through in rapid succession with only a ten-minute mid-morning break. At noon, the judge recessed the court until twelve forty-five and asked Clara to come to his chambers.

She followed the judge and when he gestured toward a chair, sat opposite him across his desk. They exchanged pleasantries as he reached into the small fridge behind him and took out two sandwiches, an apple, and an orange. "Sorry not to be able to offer you more for lunch, Ms. Quillen, but this is about all I have time to eat on days when court is in session."

"It's far more than I expected. Thanks for thinking of me."

He poured coffee for each of them and said he hadn't thought to get cream and sugar so he hoped she could drink it black. She assured him she preferred it that way.

Clara briefly told Judge Hart about her interest in juvenile law, and the rest of the conversation focused on his observations about the morning's cases. Then he asked, "Are you able to stay for the afternoon calendar?"

"I wouldn't miss it for anything. Today has been a real eye-opener for me. Will there be so many cases this afternoon?"

"Not quite. The ones calendared for this afternoon are farther along the line and more complicated, and the last one will most likely be a termination of parental rights. Those are the toughest ones, for a number of reasons."

She was about to ask him to explain when he looked at the clock and said, "We have only five minutes to get back in the courtroom. I'll see you there."

She dashed out to the ladies' room and got back just when Judge Hart entered and called for the next case.

The afternoon cases seemed even more intense than the morning ones, and the judge had been right about the last one. The father in the case had been incarcerated for burglary, and the mother was an alcoholic who had failed to complete her court-ordered program and maintain sobriety. Their five children ranging in age from three to twelve had been split up, with the paternal grandparents caring for the three oldest children, who were school age, and the two youngest placed in a foster home. The children were named alphabetically: Audrey, Billy, Charley, Denny, and Elly.

The oldest child was present, but the other two school-age children had chosen to stay in school instead of coming to court. The judge asked Audrey, the twelve-year-old, questions about how she was doing in school and what she did with her friends, and then some questions like what were her favorite subjects and what did she like to do for fun. Finally, he asked about what it was like living with her grandparents.

She rolled her eyes. "They're sort of old fogies, and sometimes they're too strict." Then her face softened. "But they take good care of me and my brothers. I love my mom and all, but she isn't always there for us the way Grandma is."

"So do you feel okay about staying with your grandma?"

"I'm okay with it if I can still see my mom, at least as long as she's not drinking."

The mother was in tears as she said all she needed was a little more time to get her act together. She claimed to love her children, and she said she finally understood what she needed to do. Other evidence concerned the welfare of the two pre-school children and the qualifications of their prospective adoptive parents.

The mother's attorney argued for more time for the mother to complete her case plan, and the father's attorney argued that he would be able to care for his children when he was expected to be released from prison in about a year.

County counsel argued that the children had been removed from their parents two years before. Thus, time had run out for the children, and they needed the stability of a permanent home.

The attorney for the children said his independent investigation and consultation with all five children supported the social worker's recommendations, as stated by county counsel.

Judge Hart summed up the evidence succinctly and rendered judgment: he ordered legal guardianship for the three oldest children with their grandparents and termination of parental rights and adoption for the two youngest children. The mother broke into tears again and barely heard the judge advise her of her appellate rights before court was adjourned.

Clara had, of course, followed every nuance, and she caught the judge's subtle gesture inviting her again back to his chambers. It was a little after six o'clock, but she felt as if she'd been in the courtroom for a week instead of merely a day.

When she entered the judge's chambers, he was already removing his robe to reveal a white polo shirt and jeans. She hadn't noticed before he was wearing black running shoes.

"You survived your first day in dependency court," he said. "How do you feel?"

"Mostly I feel drained. Is every day like this for you, Your Honor?"

"No day is like any other, because every case is unique. But yes, nearly every day is as full of emotion and sometimes drama. But you can drop the 'Your Honor' bit now. It still makes me feel as if someone is addressing my father. Call me Greg."

"Thanks, that's a lot easier. And I'm Clara. I have a few thousand questions for you."

"Fire away."

Some of her questions were legal ones, but many focused on the dynamics of the parents, children, and attorneys she had observed throughout the day.

He answered patiently and thoughtfully, until at last he said, "I'm really sorry to break this up, but I need to get going. I have to grab a bite to eat before I give a presentation for some other judges at a continuing education session tonight."

"I'm amazed you have the energy to do more work tonight after the day you've had. I'm exhausted just from watching, and it must've been much more tiring for you."

"I can't say I'm not tired, but this work is so absorbing it's hard to think about much else."

"I still have a lot of questions for you, if you can spare some other time."

"I always have time for people who are really interested in this work. Why don't you give me a call before the weekend, and maybe we can find some time to pick up where we left off."

"Thanks, I'd like that very much. I appreciate all the time you've given me already."

"My pleasure," he said with a bright smile that seemed to reveal genuine pleasure.

∽∾∽

As she drove home, Clara's mind was filled with thoughts about everything she had observed that day. Permeating it all was Judge Gregory Hart. She didn't know what she had expected in a judge, but whatever it was, it wasn't Greg.

When she got home, she made herself a tray with an odd assortment of nuts, yogurt with cucumber, and sour dough bread, followed by the rest of the grapes and strawberries left from the night before. She savored her glass of Pinot noir as she sat on the balcony watching the final touch of the sunset behind the fogbank. The background music was Dave Brubeck, some of the last recordings he made before he died.

She found a couple of other things to munch on in the fridge and decided she was too tired to make anything more substantial for dinner. How could she be so tired when she'd been sitting all day? Obviously, that was part of the problem. At thirty-eight, she was already feeling debilitated if she didn't get enough exercise, and she'd been far too sedentary the past few days.

So it was yoga time, and after almost an hour of poses and stretches, she felt much better. But she had been ignoring the longing inside that what she really wanted was to soak in a warm bubble bath. How could she justify a tub full of water in this drought? Would it be okay, as long as she felt guilty about it?

Finally, she took a quick shower and decided that would have to do. She stretched out on her sofa with a good reading light and a good mystery, but she felt herself drifting into the Land of Nod when Travis called.

"Hi, Clara, I meant to get back to you sooner, but I've been completely tied up. I wanted to let you know we've finished with Vivian's laptop, and we found some interesting stuff."

"Tell me about it."

SECOND IN HER CLASS

"Her files and folders were very well organized. A lot of stuff had been deleted, but we were able to recover it eventually. It turned out to be study material for the bar exam and some of her law school notes. One of the files in the Pictures folder had been deleted, too, and we were able to retrieve a few selfies of her and Susskind. The other stuff fell into five main folders: BASL, Boalt, Dependency, Family, Friends, and Miscellaneous."

"What was in them?"

"The most interesting ones were a few files named with initials, but most of them weren't very hard to figure out. PS is obviously Peter Susskind, and the professors in the BASL folder are easy to identify from the website: PK is Paula Kelley, JKM is John Knox MacArthur, and LTS is Lyle Thurgood Shelton. There was also one on a disgruntled student identified only as RP, and maybe you can find out who he is. She had a few other BASL files, including one for the dean, but none of them suggested anything personal. They were mostly comments on issues raised in faculty meetings. The others were on the courses she was teaching and work with the children's rights center."

"So in the files you found interesting, do they imply any likely suspects?"

"Not for certain, although there are a few red flags. I especially want to know what you think about the three BASL professors, since you've talked to them, but read the Peter Susskind file, too. There's also an interesting one in the Dependency folder that may suggest a possible threat. The file is named GM, but we don't know yet who that is. Maybe you can shed some light on that one."

"I'll do what I can. Did you find anything significant in Vivian's email messages?"

"They were pretty consistent with the notes she made in the files for things like social engagements, but there was nothing that really stood out. So maybe she was reluctant to put anything in an email that might come back to haunt her. The notes in the files are much more revealing because they were written informally, like a private journal that she didn't expect anybody to read."

"I can't help feeling a little uncomfortable reading personal things like that, but I'm glad to do it if there's any way it might help find her killer."

"That's the spirit. I'll send them over to you right away as attachments. Some of them are pretty long, so I may have to send some in separate emails. I almost forgot. One that may be pretty large is a picture file. In addition to the LTS journal doc in Word, there was an LTS in the Pictures folder."

"What was in that one?"

"A lot of photos around San Francisco, mostly touristy type stuff: pictures of either her or Lyle at places like the Palace of Fine Arts, on Nob Hill, or selfies with the Golden Gate Bridge in the background, that sort of thing."

"Okay, I'll review everything, but I hope you don't mind if I start on them tomorrow. I'm pretty beat tonight."

"Sure, but get back to me as soon as you can if you have any insights."

"When you send them, use my regular email address, but also send it to my BASL address. It's cquil@law.BASL.edu. That way it'll be easy to access the files to look at when I'm at the law school as well as at home."

"Okay, I'll send them right away."

She waited until several emails arrived with the subject line "Attachments" and the message, "As we discussed, from the VH laptop."

As tired as she was, she downloaded the attachments and took a quick look at the LTS photos Travis had mentioned. It hit her that some of them had been taken at a few of the location sites in *Vertigo*. That didn't necessarily mean anything, as they were common San Francisco locales for a lot of tourists. Still, they made her wonder.

Clara put her computer to sleep because she knew if she started on the other files Travis sent she'd be up all night. Sometimes, she decided, it was okay to be Scarlett and think about that tomorrow.

Chapter 8

Views from the Victim

The next morning, the first thing she thought of was the emails from Travis. She double checked to make sure they had also arrived at her BASL email address.

She made a cheese omelet and toast, washed them down with coffee and orange juice, and dressed for the day. She wasn't quite sure if she should dress professionally for her visit with K.M., but decided she should be comfortable for meeting a two-year-old and chose a simple knit top and casual slacks.

She plugged the San Mateo address of the foster parents into her GPS and headed south on the 101. She followed the directions of the British voice she had named Malcolm (after an excellent guide she'd had on her first trip to London), and he took her right to the apartment where K.M. had been placed with her foster parents.

After ringing the bell, she heard footsteps, followed by a pause that she suspected meant a moment to view her through the peephole. With a small child held snugly on her hip, a slightly nervous-looking young woman opened the door. She was slender, wearing a pink T-shirt, cutoff denim shorts, and low-cut pink athletic socks. Her long black hair and features were distinctly Asian, but she spoke perfect American English. "Hi, I'm Amy, and this adorable little tyke is Kristen. You must be Ms. Quillen."

"Yes, but please call me Clara." She handed Amy her business card.

Amy's next comment suggested she felt that she owed an explanation. "I know Kristen doesn't look like me, but she looks a lot like my husband. He's always proud when we're out and people comment that she looks so much like him."

"These days, I think most people are pretty used to unusual family combinations, especially in this part of the country."

Amy seemed to relax a little as she offered Clara a seat and something to drink, and Clara took a glass of water. She put Amy more at ease by saying she had read the excellent reports on her and her husband and understood Kristen had been doing very well with them. But she explained that she was the child's attorney, and her role would be to represent the legal interests of the child in the appellate court. Her contact with the foster parents would be solely to further that end.

"I understand. Vivian told us the same thing about representing the child. I feel so sad about what happened to her."

"Yes, it was sad, but you have a lot to be happy about right now."

"We really do. We're so fortunate to have Kristen. She's our pride and joy. I have complete faith everything will go through all right with the adoption this time." As she said it, Clara had the sense it was more positive thinking than complete faith.

They began to chat as Kristen played with a few toys

on the floor. She seemed somewhat small for her age, but she was animated and appeared to be healthy. From reading the social worker's reports, Clara knew she was completely up-to-date on her medical check-ups and immunizations.

After chatting about Kristen's development, Amy showed Clara around the apartment, again with Kristen on her hip. She opened the wooden gate that blocked the stairs and took her to Kristen's room. It was small but appropriately furnished, full of children's books and a few toys. Amy explained that they put out only a few toys at a time, and when Kristen became bored with one, they removed it and replaced it with something else. Amy said, "We try to be alert to the delicate balance between keeping Kristen stimulated with new things, but not overwhelming her with too much stuff."

Kristen was shy at first, but she opened up gradually as she became used to Clara, who got down on the floor to play with her. At one point, Kristen ran after a ball and tripped over another toy. She began to cry and immediately went to Amy for comfort. After checking to make sure she wasn't hurt, Amy diverted her with another toy, and soon she was playing and smiling again. She brought a book to Clara and said, "Read me, please," and Clara was glad to oblige.

Kristen nodded off, and Amy explained she was used to having a late morning nap before lunch. After Amy gently tucked her into bed, they went back downstairs, and Clara took advantage of the opportunity to talk with Amy about the case.

Amy described the final permanency hearing. "I was in the back of the courtroom for the last hearing, and I was distressed by how Kristen's mother behaved. On the rare occasions I've ever raised my voice with Kristen, she has looked frightened, and I think seeing how Gretchen acted in court helped me understand why. The social worker had already told us to be on our guard because Gretchen had told her she would never give up her child."

"Did she ever threaten you directly?"

"She called a couple of times when she'd apparently been drinking, or maybe on drugs, who knows. We started screening our calls, but we didn't get many more from her. Of course, she doesn't know where we live."

"Do you have any reason to believe she might pose a threat to Kristen's safety?"

"I'm not sure, but one thing troubles me. After the last hearing, I called Vivian, and she mentioned she'd had a visit from Kristen's mother in her office at the law school. Vivian had a student with her, and Gretchen showed up at the door and started talking loudly. She asked her when she'd be finished because she wanted to talk to her. Vivian told her she had appointments scheduled for the next hour and a half, but she couldn't talk to her anyway. She told her that since Gretchen was represented by counsel, she couldn't speak with her directly, only with her attorney."

"How did she respond to that?"

"She said something like, 'It's all your effing fault I lost my child, and you lawyers are all in cahoots with each other.' She apparently hung around in the hall for a few minutes and then left. Vivian said she called security, but by the time the guard got there, Gretchen was gone. Does she know you're representing Kristen now?"

"Probably. She should've received a copy of the appellate record from the court, and the cover has the names of all the attorneys in the lower court, as well as the ones appointed for the appeal."

"I hope she doesn't come after you. I'm not sure the woman is mentally well balanced. At the very least, you never know if she might be on drugs again."

Clara didn't want to end the visit on a negative note and changed the subject to the foster parents' plans for caring for Kristen. Amy was enthusiastic about the plans they had made, and it was clear they were devoted to her care.

"Thanks for all you've done for Kristen," Clara said. "It looks as if everything is going well, and I hope it continues to go well for your family. You have my business card. Please don't hesitate to call in case anything comes up that you think I should know about. I'll be available to look after Kristen's legal interests till the appellate process is complete."

❧❧❧

As Clara drove back home, she thought about the visit, and the social worker's positive final report seemed to be completely on target. Verbal exchanges during the visit with the child had been minimal, as she was just beginning to formulate simple sentences, but observation had told Clara the most important things. Despite being somewhat small, Kristen gave every indication of being mentally alert and developmentally on track. In every way she seemed to be comfortable in her surroundings. She called Amy "Mama" and had gone to her for comfort when she was hurt. All the signs were good.

When Clara got home, she made detailed notes on her visit with K.M., whom she now knew instead as a cute toddler called Kristen who had an apparently devoted foster mother. Then she started working on the electronic files Travis had sent her. After what the foster mother had told her about Gretchen showing up in Vivian's office, she was reasonably sure the GM file referred to Gretchen Miller. When she opened the file, she knew immediately that was correct.

The notes in Vivian's GM file included a detailed description of the mother and her progress on her case plan, both from the social worker's reports and her own observations of the evidence presented in court hearings. The last part of the file described Gretchen's disturbing appearance in her office. It essentially confirmed what the foster mother had told her, with more detail about Gretchen's incoherent babbling and disheveled appearance.

After finishing the GM file, she decided to try to identify the student Vivian had referred to as RP. She was glad she had introduced herself to the registrar and called to ask her about RP. She said she had found a note Vivian had written about a difficult student, identified only with those initials, and wondered who it might be.

In less than a minute, the registrar had pulled up the names of all the students Vivian had taught the year before. Three had the initials RP, two women and a man.

"Do you have any idea which one it is?" the registrar asked.

"It would have to be the man because the note refers to 'he.' What's his name?"

"It's Richard Piper. Let me see if he's registered for any of her courses this year." In a few seconds, she came back with, "No, he was academically disqualified. It looks like he's no longer a student here. Do you need any other information?"

"It might be handy to have his contact information, just in case anything comes up."

"No problem. I'll zap it over to you. I'll attach a photo of him from last year's student face book, too. Have a good day."

"Thanks, you too."

Moments later, the email arrived with the address, phone number, email address, and photo of RP, Richard

Piper. As long as she was looking at emails, she checked the few others that had arrived. Besides the ones from Travis, two had BASL administrative information, and one from Hartg with a California court tag had been sent at noon, fifteen minutes before, apparently from Judge Gregory Hart.

The message she saw on the screen said, *Hi, Clara. We could continue our conversation over a meal if you can make it sometime this weekend. Let me know: brunch or lunch, your choice. Greg.*

Was it a date or only a follow-up professional meeting? Which did she want it to be? She hadn't dated anyone since she broke up with the doctor who had moved to Los Angeles. Actually, she hadn't formally broken up with him. The relationship just sort of fizzled out. They hadn't communicated for more than a couple of months. She supposed that pretty well qualified as being broken up, formally or otherwise.

She really did have more questions about juvenile dependency court. There was certainly no reason to decline the opportunity to learn more. So she hit reply and wrote, *Brunch is one of my favorite meals. Is 10:30 Saturday all right with you?*

A minute later he responded: *Fine. I'll pick you up. What's your address?*

She replied with her address and cell phone number in case he needed to reach her. They had an appointment, whether or not they had a date.

ɞʝɞ

Before she tackled the files from Travis again, she had a big chef's salad laced with avocados, mushrooms, pine nuts, and Kalamata olives, smothered with a lot of

Roquefort dressing. She rationalized the excess by saying to herself she would benefit from the extra calcium.

As Clara began reviewing the other files Travis had sent her, she was curious about all of them and hardly knew where to begin. Hours later, she knew they filled in a lot of gaps and left a few more. She decided to start where cops typically start, with the significant other.

Peter Susskind was in some ways the ideal boyfriend and in other ways the boyfriend from hell. The PS file, as well as the others, was written informally. It had dates along the way, but not daily entries.

Three days in law school & already I know this is where I belong. I've never felt so intellectually stimulated before. Other kinds of stimulation, too. First guy to volunteer in Murdoch's Con law class was a tall hunk named Peter Susskind. Impressive performance.

Her next entry was two days later.

Murdoch called on me today. I was quaking in my boots, but held my own—after a mere seven hours of study for that one class. It was worth every minute. He didn't put me down, just gave me a curt "Thank you, Ms. Hall" & went on to devastate the next guy.

Peter waited for me after class (he sits in back, I'm near the front) & asked me for coffee. Not Starbucks, but a quaint little place he drove me to in his cliché sports car. He got around to asking if I'd be part of his study group, only three guys & I'd be number four. He said he thought the group could use a female perspective. I hope he didn't mean it in a sexist way, because I think I analyze like a law student, not like a female. Anyway, it took me all of two seconds to say yes.

Numerous entries followed noting the study group activities, but they mostly focused on Susskind. Before long, the comments became less law school, more personal, then intimate.

I assumed it was coming, but can't say I was really ready for it when Peter maneuvered me into bed. I didn't mean to get involved with anyone my first year in law school. But I'm not sure how anyone could say no to Peter. He expects yes to whatever he wants. I can't say I'm sorry though. See the last two words of the first paragraph of this journal.

In various entries, Vivian described differences of opinion with Peter and heated debates on legal issues. She enjoyed standing up to him, but had difficulty coping with their first major fight at the end of the first semester.

We got our first grades today. Peter was furious! I made one point higher on the final in Murdoch's Con law class. He blew up at me, claiming it was because I wasn't ready when he came to pick me up for our date. I knew it was the grade though, but didn't confront him about it. I hate confrontation.

I can't believe I just wrote that. How can a lawyer hate confrontation?

During the next year, Vivian's relationship with Peter was volatile, mostly since they were fierce competitors in class. After taking Professor Murdoch's Constitutional Law class together and juggling back and forth for first and second in the class, they tacitly chose not to take any more of the same classes.

In the third year, their arguments centered mostly on her evolving career choice. Peter had never wavered from his goal of corporate law, and she was impressed because over a period of several years he had learned French, German, and Spanish to prepare for international corporate law. Vivian had been unsure what area of law she wanted to pursue, but she was leaning more and more toward public interest law.

In her final semester of law school, a legal internship clinched it. She interned with a woman judge in juvenile court, and she was sure juvenile law would be her field. She mused about the possibility of becoming a juvenile court judge herself one day.

Her next entry about Peter was telling.

I'm so relieved! Final class standings were announced today. Peter came out first & I'm second in the class. We went out to celebrate & he was euphoric. Being first would've been nice, but I'm glad it worked out this way. He needs it more than I do. We'll both be grad speakers, but he'll be valedictorian.

Vivian and Peter studied for the bar exam together, and neither had any doubts about passing. As soon as the bar exam was over, Peter was hired as a prospective junior associate by Safer & Morrison, where he had had a summer associateship the year before. More permanent employment was, of course, subject to passing the bar.

Vivian was still unsure exactly how she wanted to fit into juvenile law. So she had applied for teaching positions to give her more time to explore the possibilities. With her excellent academic credentials, she received three offers from small law schools, two on the East Coast and one from BASL. Even though the others offered more money, she didn't hesitate accepting the offer from BASL because it was the only one that allowed her to teach juvenile law along with the core curriculum course of Torts.

The added benefit of teaching at BASL, of course, was that it allowed her to stay in San Francisco. She had fallen in love with the city and knew she wanted it to be her permanent home. Vivian and Peter both decided to leave their student digs in Berkeley and find a place in the city. Peter would have a high salary and could afford an expensive apartment not far from Safer & Morrison in the financial district. The next journal entry explained Vivian's choice.

Peter talks about living together, but I'm not so sure. He says if we live together he'll have a better chance to persuade me to go for a high paying job & forget about public interest law. I can't convince him that pay isn't my number one priority. I'll check out a roommate possibility I heard about in the civic ctr. area. He won't like it if I decide not to move in w/ him, but it's a concession to live only about a mile from him when I'm about four miles from BASL, too far to walk every day, which I'd prefer. But it's close to civic ctr. courthouse, which will be convenient for my dependency cases. It's a big decision for me to choose what I want over what Peter wants.

The next entry was three days later.

Success—I agreed to share a place in the civic ctr. area w/ a nice woman who works for Cal. Supreme Court. I really hit it off w/ her, Marilyn Aiello, & it's rare to find a decent, affordable place in this area. It's also rare because it's a little pocket that seems safe, even if surrounded by grungier stuff & it's w/n walking distance of gorgeous city hall, SF library, Asian Art Museum, Davies Symphony Hall, etc. Best of all it's close to dependency court.

Peter blew up, but I knew he would. He's like a spoiled child when he doesn't get his way. His reaction makes me even surer of my decision not to live w/ him. He's been too big a part of my life already.

The next few months showed a definite decline in the relationship. They had occasional dates, becoming fewer and farther between. They celebrated in November when they learned they had passed the bar exam, although he was annoyed because she had scored slightly higher on the multi-state portion of the exam than he did. Vivian went home to visit her parents for Christmas, but by January her relationship with Peter was ostensibly over.

New Year's Eve: home alone. Peter called a couple of days ago & asked me to go to a law firm party w/ him. I fell back into the old pattern & said yes. I didn't have any other plans anyway. I started deciding what to wear in the afternoon & wondered if anything I had would be good enough for Peter & his fancy new law firm. Suddenly I didn't care. It didn't seem worth it to go out w/ him again. I don't see any future w/ him & called & told him so.

I couldn't believe it, even for Peter. He seemed more annoyed w/ the broken date than when I said I doubted we had a future together. He kept ranting about how it was too late to get a date at this point on New Year's Eve. Finally, I just hung up on him. He called back twice, but I let it go to voicemail. I'm sorry I've wasted so much time & energy on Peter, but it's over. The end.

There was one more entry in the PS file.

So much for it's over/the end. I'm still getting calls from him. He even came by my office yesterday. I told him not to show up again. He can't control me anymore. Why did I never notice what a control freak he is? Now it's really over— starting right now—THE END!

Clara found herself silently cheering Vivian. She deserved better.

Then Clara sobered at the thought. *She deserved a lot better, but look what she got.*

ભ્છ

It had taken hours for Clara to read through the PS file, but she was ready to tackle another one. She opened the LTS file and began to read. It was much shorter.

Most faculty members have been friendly to me, but Lyle Shelton has been especially nice. He helped me find my way around & tipped me off about other faculty mem-

bers etc. I wondered about a possible ulterior motive & now that's pretty clear. He finally asked me out for Sat. night. We've had occasional lunches nearby, but this was the first clear invitation for a date.

I had mixed feelings when I had to turn him down because I already have tickets for the symphony w/ Marilyn for Sat. So it was easy to say no & I just mumbled something when he said "Maybe another time." I was sort of glad to have a legit excuse.

It hasn't been that long since I put the kibosh on Peter. Am I still stinging from all that angst? Lyle seems so different from Peter—very laid back. He's clearly attractive, & we have a lot in common. He has a lot of public interest concerns & seems to understand why I want to pursue juvenile law.

Why am I hesitating? I guess it could be complicated getting involved with a colleague, whether it develops into anything or not. But a lot of romances start in the workplace.

I'm hedging on the elephant in the room, of course. Is it racial? I could never think of myself a racist. But could I be? I've hated racism as long as I remember. But it's been said everybody has some racism—it's only a matter of degree. I don't want to believe that, because I wouldn't want to tolerate even a scintilla of racism in myself, though, if I thought it was there.

I think I know what I'm getting at. It's funny how this stream of consciousness writing helps me sort out my own thoughts & feelings. My real problem isn't resisting a relationship w/ someone who's half black for a racist reason. It's the opposite. Down deep, I think I could go for Lyle in a way I never have before & that's the problem.

Do I want all the potential problems related to an interracial relationship? He's told me about the problems his black mother & white father had, even in Chicago. He had his own problems w/ prejudice growing up. What would it be like for our kids?

Good grief, did I really write that? I've got us married w/ kids before we've even had a proper first date. But that's the time to think about it, dammit! If I learned anything from being involved w/ Peter it's that it's better to end something sooner rather than later if you know it's going nowhere.

On the other hand (as Tevye would say), Lyle's parents have weathered all the racial storms. And times really have changed, or at least they are changing.

I have to find out. Maybe if we went on a first date, there wouldn't even be a second date. Maybe we are destined to be just good friends.

I guess we'll find out. I called Lyle & we have a dinner date on Sun. He was very cool about it & didn't let on it was a big deal. I think it is.

The next entry was dated two weeks later.

When I got back from my first date w/ Lyle, I started to continue this journal. But it felt too much like writing about Peter. He & Lyle are light years apart. I've decided not to add to this for a while. I'll let it drift & see where it goes.

That was it. There were no more entries in the LTS file.

Instead of starting to read another file, Clara took a break and checked her emails. One in the BASL email account was particularly fortuitous.

"Clara, it was nice to meet you, but you probably noticed that our chat a few days ago ended somewhat abruptly. I got to thinking that maybe I owe you an explanation. If you're free for lunch tomorrow, do you want to get together? Lyle"

She didn't hesitate and responded immediately. They

decided to meet for lunch the next day at Delancey Street Restaurant. Clara called Travis to let him know.

ఴఴఴ

Clara had known about Delancey Street Restaurant since her late second husband had been a significant contributor to the restaurant training school of the Delancey Street Foundation, a self-help residential organization for people who have hit bottom to rebuild their lives. Named for the street on New York's Lower East Side where many immigrants who came through Ellis Island had settled, the restaurant was a fitting place for downtrodden people of all backgrounds to start a new life.

Clara loved bringing people who didn't know about it to Delancey Street, and she enjoyed watching Lyle read the history of the place on the back of the menu, including, "All proceeds after food costs go to house, feed, and clothe our residents and teach all skills, values, and attitudes needed for a successful drug-free and crime-free life in mainstream society."

She also knew the place would provide an easy subject of conversation before Lyle got around to saying what he had to say. Clara ordered her favorite, a Cobb salad, and Lyle ordered crab cakes with mango papaya salsa. After a bit of small talk, they were served by a solicitous waiter. Clara had always hated those scenes in movies where the characters talked with their mouths full, and she was pleased to see Lyle had better manners.

At last, Lyle opened up with an apology. "It's been bothering me ever since we talked a few days ago. I'm concerned you must've thought I was very rude when I almost threw you out of my office."

She made it easy for him. "You said you had somewhere to go. I didn't give it a second thought."

"That wasn't entirely true. The only place I had to go was out of there. When you said you'd be teaching Juvenile Dependency Law this fall, I was thrown off balance. I didn't want to let myself think about anyone else teaching her classes. The reality of Vivian's death hadn't sunk in, and I guess it still hasn't."

"I thought it might be something like that. I'm truly sorry for your loss. It must've been hard for you to think of someone else teaching her course."

"I shouldn't feel that way. I'm glad her work is continuing because she was passionate about juvenile law. But I'm also glad my office is at the far end of the hall from hers. I still can't bring myself to go near her—I mean *your*—office."

"I gather you were especially close to Vivian?"

"I don't think that was a complete secret. She didn't want to let everybody know we were going together, but on a small campus like ours, there probably aren't many secrets. Has anyone mentioned it to you?"

"No, I suppose people are being discreet, or maybe even considerate, if they knew you were a couple."

"More than likely, the latter. Discretion is pretty rare on our gossipy little campus."

"Her death must be twice as hard on you if you feel you can't talk about her."

"You might say so. I didn't like keeping our relationship a secret anyway, but Vivian was adamant."

"Why did she feel so strongly about it?"

"I know what you may be thinking, but believe me, it wasn't racial. Vivian didn't have a racist bone in her body. All she would say was she'd come out of a very negative relationship, and she wanted to be much more sure of us before we were open about our going together."

"So you think she still had some reservations?"

"Maybe even more than that, but I'm not sure. I have no doubt she loved me, but maybe not enough to spend the rest of her life with me."

"What about you?"

"I was smitten almost from the first time I met her. We had a great conversation about the importance of public interest law. As things progressed, I thought I played it very cool and didn't rush her. But she clearly wasn't ready for a commitment."

When the waiter came by to ask if their food was all right, they said it was fine and continued eating before Clara returned to the same point in the conversation.

"You said Vivian wasn't ready for a commitment, but I gather you were."

"Oh, yeah, big time. I'm four years older than Vivian. I wanted to settle down, get married, and have kids—the whole megillah."

"That's not a word I'd expect you to use."

For the first time, Lyle laughed. "My father's Jewish. I'm entitled."

Clara smiled and said, "Ah, so you're Jewish and black? Double whammy."

"Yeah, although technically I'm not Jewish because it's my father who's Jewish, not my mother, and Jewishness descends through the mother. I still got plenty of flak as a kid. But I'm stronger for it, and that's what I tried to tell Vivian. She said that might be okay for me, but she wasn't sure she wanted to put her own kids through something like that."

"So you were at an impasse?"

"I like to think it was only a temporary impasse." He dipped another bite of crab cake in the fruity sauce. "But I was frustrated at times, especially with the secrecy. Now it doesn't seem to make any difference. I guess down deep I wanted to believe love conquers all."

"It's sad that you'll never know, at least not with Vivian."

"Yes, right now I can't imagine ever loving again."

"I won't give you any platitudes about that. But I can tell you from experience, after the death of my first husband, I did find love again. Sadly, he died too, but it's been a couple of years now, and I'm not so closed off as I was."

"So you do understand. No wonder it's so easy to talk to you. I haven't opened up like this to anyone in so long I can't even remember."

"I hope you'll consider me a friend. We can talk any time."

"Thanks, Clara. I can always use a friend."

The waiter returned to clear their dishes and offer the dessert menu. They eyed it covetously but decided on espresso instead.

She had wanted to ask Lyle a lot more questions about his relationship with Vivian but thought it was better not to push right now. She would probably learn more after she'd had a chance to develop more rapport with him.

Funny, she recalled Travis saying the same thing about his interviews with Marilyn Aiello. She'd first suggested Travis's methods seemed cold and calculated, but, as usual, had bowed to his superior experience, and now she planned to use the same technique.

❧❧❧

When she got back to her car, Clara called Travis and reported on her lunch with Lyle. "It fleshes out what was in the LTS file, and he seems like a very credible person."

"Maybe so, unless he's playing you."

"That's pretty cynical, even for an old cop like you, Travis."

"I didn't mean it quite that way. But you have to develop an elemental detachment when you investigate a homicide. You know, like Sherlock Holmes. I've known killers who were very smooth about covering their tracks. This homicide, for example, looks like it was done on a sudden impulse, not necessarily based on long planning. In a moment of anger, a lover could strike out and then later decide he didn't want to pay for his crime."

"You keep referring to the killer as 'he.' Do you think it's possible it could've been a woman?"

"I have to remind myself you want that 'he or she' grammar when it could be a man or woman. In this case, though, it's probably more likely a man, but it could be a woman strong enough to remove a body and transport it to the bay."

"And you said Vivian was petite. How much strength would it take?"

"You're right. She weighed barely a hundred pounds. It wouldn't take as much strength to carry her as it would for a big heavy body. But somehow he—or she—had to have gotten the body out of the office to a vehicle and eventually lift her out and dump her on the rocks."

"I don't think I'll ever get used to the nonchalant way you refer to dead bodies."

"Sure you will, as soon as it sinks in that the only way to investigate a murder is to detach yourself from the victim. You've got to start thinking of Vivian's dead body as separate from Vivian the person. You also have to maintain a detached distance from anybody who could possibly qualify as a suspect. And that's just about anybody."

"I see your point. I guess that's the kind of detachment you meant when I said you sounded cynical even about Lyle. But I still can't help thinking Vivian's hesitation about commitment would not be enough to drive someone to murder."

"Who knows? There may have been something else going on. Don't forget the adage, Clara: You never know."

Chapter 9

More Views from the Victim

It was early Wednesday afternoon, and she still had three of Vivian's electronic files to review. She thought she would have plenty of time to do that and also work on her appellate case. She was thinking ahead with a plan to get a good night's sleep Friday night before her date (if it was a date) with Greg on Saturday morning. She'd finish with the faculty and then take a look at RP, the disgruntled student.

JKM—John Knox MacArthur—she wasn't exactly looking forward to this one. He struck her as such an oily character, outwardly smooth, even glib, but with a shadow of something else. Maybe the file would help her find out what might be lurking beneath the academic exterior.

Her first hint came within the first couple of paragraphs of Vivian's JKM journal.

I'm settling into my new office & had a friendly visit from the prof across the hall, JKM. He seems very impressive. Excellent academic background, lots of publications, etc. He seems really knowledgeable about Torts, which I'm a little apprehensive about teaching. He of-

fered to help any way he could. Funny, though, when I joked he could help me carry boxes in from my car, he said he was sorry but had a back problem. I wouldn't have really asked for help w/ that, of course. Ron from facilities already said he'd help me carry stuff in. JKM ended the conversation w/ lavish compliments for me, said he knew I'd be a stellar prof.

So much for flattery. I was chatting w/ Paula Kelley this afternoon & happened to mention JKM's back problem. She laughed & said in effect he didn't seem to show any back problem on the tennis court. He's her biggest competitor. Even more interesting was something else she said. When I commented JKM seemed impressive, she said he could seem that way, but just watch out, keep my back covered. E.g. she'd been talking w/ JKM earlier & he told her "I'll be surprised if Vivian lasts the year. She's far too delicate, and law students will eat her alive."

So I'm on my guard w/ him. I'm also determined to prove him wrong. I'm tougher than I look.

Numerous other entries followed, and references to JKM became more and more critical of him. Vivian had often differed on faculty issues with MacArthur, but she rarely expressed her opinions in faculty meetings. As the newest professor, she thought she should get a better understanding of the lay of the land before clashing with one of the longest tenured professors. It wasn't hard to do that, however, because almost always Paula or one of the younger tenured professors would express Vivian's own point of view in meetings.

About a month later, more interesting items began to appear in her journal.

JKM has been popping over frequently. Sometimes he's trying to get my support for one of his positions in faculty meetings. Other times seems to be picking my brain. Not sure what to make of it. Hope the old guy doesn't have a crush on me.

A little later, MacArthur's hidden agenda emerged.

JKM came in today, beat around the bush a bit, & then said he had an offer I couldn't refuse. Hate to admit it, but he's right. Still on my guard after Paula's warning, but JKM told me about his elaborate plan to write a new textbook on torts, making it available only electronically at lower cost to students. Supposed to be quite innovative, as it's interactive w/ students & profs. Showed me his publisher's approval & said he wanted to work w/ some- one more tech savvy than he is. I do like the idea of lower cost because books are outrageously expensive for law students (even if I still prefer real books w/ paper pages). I didn't tell him I'm not especially tech savvy, but I figure I could learn what I need to as I go.

I'm more reluctant because he said he wouldn't be able to credit me as co-author but would include my name in acknowledgments. He also said it wasn't neces- sary for the publisher to know about my work on the book since he's the one with the big name & long list of publi- cations. I have to admit that makes some sense. At least putting me in acknowledgments would help get my name out there.

Meanwhile, I'll keep working on my juv. law article. That's where my heart is anyway. Maybe JKM can help me get it in one of the more prestigious law reviews. But even w/ his long list of pubs, I notice they're not usually in the most impressive law reviews.

In the next few months, the journal entries made it clear Vivian was doing most of the work on the book, while MacArthur interacted with the publisher. She final- ly realized she couldn't maintain the pace and began to doubt she'd ever get the credit she deserved. Between the demands of teaching and working on the book, she was not getting enough sleep and was losing weight.

I can't keep this up any longer. I'm afraid to alienate JKM because he's one of the profs who'll eventually vote on my tenure, but enough is enough. Besides if I'm going to be able to represent even a single kid in juv. court, I've got to cut out something & now I'm well into my first juv. dependency case. Also, I've become suspicious whether JKM will actually give me any real credit for my work. Even if I'm in the acknowledgments, it wouldn't begin to show how much actual work I've put into the book.

The next entry was dated a day later.

I approached JKM about quitting my work on the book. At first, he seemed to be taken aback, then understanding, but said he'd rather discuss it in the evening when it's quieter & told me to reconsider before we talked again.

I had nothing to reconsider, but agreed to meet w/ him in my office tonight. We argued & it got pretty heated. I might've toned it down a little, but nobody else was around so I didn't worry somebody would hear me. I really blew my top when JKM said what a shame it would reflect on my hope for tenure to be a quitter. I'm no quitter & told him the only reason I'd keep helping him would be to get his vote on my tenure & that's the wrong reason to do something.

Then I threatened to let people know who was really doing the work on "his" book. He called me an ingrate, said I was lucky to work w/ someone of his stature & I wouldn't get another chance like that. We wrangled on for at least an hour & finally, he stormed out & slammed the door. Good riddance. What a prick!

A couple of weeks later, Vivian made the last entry for JKM.

I can't believe a guy with an office a stone's throw

away can manage to ignore me so completely. Not quite completely because when others are around he's his usual smarmy self. I make it a point to be ultra-polite whenever I see him whether anyone else is around or not. I love passing him in the hall w/ a cheery "Hi, John, how are you" & watching him squirm. It's fun to watch a wirm squirm.

That last entry was dated a week before Vivian died.

Clara felt she needed to take a tea break at that point. She had seen MacArthur only as someone who was rather full of himself, but she now had a better understanding of how exploitive he could be. She recalled Travis saying three of the main motives for murder involve love, sex, or money, and sometimes they merge in odd ways.

She wondered if ego should be added to the list. On second thought, didn't MacArthur stand to lose a lot of money if his book deal fell through without Vivian? But then killing her wouldn't help that, would it? Or could it if it kept her from revealing her role in writing the book?

ɛ⁊ɛ⁊

After a cup of tea and a scone, Clara thought the PK file would probably be much more pleasant to read. It began just that way.

I think I may have a new friend. Paula Kelley dropped by to welcome me & was so warm & friendly I almost couldn't believe it. She's a big woman & seems to have a big heart to match. She has a mellow voice & gentleness that's inherently comforting. We care about a lot of the same things, with special focus on women's issues. Related to that, Paula also cares about children & families, so we have a lot to talk about.

The next entry was a few days later.

I had a great chat w/ Paula after today's faculty meeting. I wanted to bounce off her my take on personalities & dynamics on issues discussed. Paula has a wicked sense of humor, but mostly she's a sympathetic listener. She's so easy to talk to I sometimes have to remind myself to ask her about her own life.

Most of the continuing entries were about faculty, students, teaching, and other BASL matters. They usually had lunch together once or twice a week. One entry was intriguing, although not fully enlightening. It followed a discussion Vivian had had with Paula about the subject matter in Paula's Women and the Law course.

It's easy to relate to Paula's views on historical treatment of women re legal status. It's not so easy to understand her strident attitude toward men. I can't help wondering if she had bad experience(s) w/ men in the past. I've tried to ferret out info about it, but no luck. She's very open about everything else, but not about men. I don't even know if she's ever been married. I thought about asking straight out, but for some reason, I'm not comfortable doing so when she's never given me an opening. She seems to get along okay w/ male profs, but mainly in an academic way. Her antagonism toward JKM is understandable, of course, as I feel the same.

The entries for PK continued, but they seemed to be either innocuous or cryptic. Clara couldn't help feeling there was more to their conversations than Vivian had included, but she couldn't put her finger on why. Her own interactions with Paula had been nothing but positive, although she had occasionally noticed the same negativity toward men that Vivian had observed.

As Clara thought about her own conversations with Paula, she began to realize Paula had typically diverted attention away from herself. She hadn't given it much thought, but if anything, had only assumed it suggested an admirable selflessness. Big ego wasn't uncommon among highly educated, highly intelligent people, and Paula's apparent lack of ego had seemed refreshing.

The last entry for PK was a simple one-liner, without explanation.

I've decided to stop going to Paula's monthly women's group.

Clara made a mental note to find out more about Paula if she could. She had no perceptible reason to think of her as suspicious, but she always had Travis's nagging "You never know" in the back of her mind. Between her innate curiosity and Travis's little aphorisms, she had a tendency to question everything—and everyone. She wasn't entirely sure that was a good thing.

ᏔᏔᏔ

It was time now to examine the disgruntled student in the RP file—she plunged back into Vivian's journal.

I'm starting this file because of a pattern of disturbance from RP in Torts. He's a thorn in my side. Maybe I shouldn't have made the joke at the beginning about being nervous in my first class. Students generally laughed & seemed to relax, but before class was over RP began to challenge me. Maybe he sees me as a novice, an easy target. In the second class, he started to dominate the discussion. I nailed him & he looked ticked off. Other students seemed to approve though, when I cut him off.

In the next few classes, RP said nothing, but his body language was surly: arms crossed, frequent frowns, didn't take notes, etc. He had spurts of spouting off-the-wall theories in class but shut down at other times. I wonder if he's bipolar.

In class, I looked straight at RP & reminded the class of office hours, encouraged students to come, espe-

cially if they were having any problem w/ the course. I got swamped in office hours w/ students for a few days. Then it dwindled, but still no RP. On the midterm exam, RP made the lowest grade in class. I sent him an email asking him to come see me. No response. I mentioned it to the dean, who suggested I keep a record of dealings w/ RP & said she thought she was seeing a pattern of behavior in him reported in other classes too. So I started this journal on him & will continue as necessary.

Vivian's next entries described more of RP's demeanor in class, although most of it was undefined. She speculated again about possible mental health concerns and wondered whether she should try to find out whether he had any history of mental problems. A week and a half later, she added this note.

Nothing definite for a while, but most days RP looks sullen in class. I've also passed him in the hall near my office. He always turns his head & pretends not to see me. I've even said hello a couple of times, but he still ignores me. I thought I saw him watching me drive off one day, but I'm not sure because he turned away.

Several weeks later, she wrote this entry.

In the week before the final exam, RP finally came in. I could almost see the chip on his shoulder. He was very confrontational, demanding to know how he could pass the final when I had favorites & had it out for him. I assured him that wasn't so & said I wanted him to succeed as much as he did & couldn't have favorites anyway because of blind grading using student numbers instead of names. He said he knew profs could tell the identity of students because of writing style & besides, "You want me to fail so it'll be easier for you to have somebody at the bottom of the curve in your class."

I reminded him there's no specific mandatory curve at BASL as in some law schools. Then he mentioned for the first time that he'd transferred from another law school. He wouldn't say why, but instead started demanding assurance I'd pass him in Torts. I told him if he performed as he did on the midterm he'd probably get a minimal passing grade, but I could make no promises. Again he said I had it out for him & stormed out. I can't decide if his self-defeating attitude shows he's unbalanced or just a spoiled brat.

I looked up his record. It's not clear why he left the other law school a year before. I couldn't find anything re possible mental health problems, but maybe nothing's in the record because of privacy requirements.

Vivian's next entries related to concerns about RP's forthcoming grades. Then sometime after the final exam, she made this note.

Exam grades are out today. As expected, RP is the lowest in his class. I think it's a borderline decision whether to give him a passing grade. Am I copping out if I pass him? I wouldn't admit it to him, but I was pretty sure which exam was his because of his quirky writing style. Did that influence me? Sure it did, but the other way around. I went over his exam twice trying to see if I could justify giving him a better grade. Finally, I decided to give him the lowest passing grade in class.

I wasn't surprised when he burst into my office waving a paper w/ his grades, saying he had tangible proof I was out to get him. He said he'd take it to the administration because it made all the difference & caused him to be academically disqualified. But my grade couldn't have been the cause. His must've had enough failing grades in other courses to bring down his GPA, as mine alone wouldn't be enough to disqualify him.

I contacted the dean & filled her in on recent history w/ RP. She said not to worry, she'd dealt w/ the likes of him before & thanked me for giving her a heads up. She called later & said not to take it personally, as RP had filed a formal complaint against all his profs, asserting all were in a conspiracy to instigate his academic dis-qualification. Not much else to do now but wait for the other shoe to drop (whatever that means in this case).

Clara was surprised when she looked at the time and saw it was almost eight p.m. So she had a little dinner and then spent a couple of hours reviewing juvenile dependency law to prime herself for her brunch on Saturday. She couldn't help wondering what else she might need to know to be ready for Judge Gregory Hart.

Chapter 10

Budding Romance

It was Saturday morning at last. She hated this feeling, but at the same time, she loved this feeling. The closest phrase she could think of to describe it was "ambivalent anticipation." It was not promising she had felt exactly the same way just before her first date with the oh-so-eligible doctor who had eventually ceased to be a part of her life.

Should she be feeling this way anyway? Maybe it really was just a professional meeting with Judge Hart. But she didn't want it to be merely that.

Okay, how do you dress for this? She went to the casual section of her well-organized closet. Should she wear a skirt or slacks? *Skirts may be more feminine, but hardly anyone wears them anymore. Slacks more clearly say casual, I'm not expecting anything in particular—the right message?*

She checked the weather report. It predicted seventy-two degrees for the high temperature on a mid-August day in San Francisco. *How perfect is that?*

She had a nice casual dress she'd bought to wear the

last time her eligible doctor was due to come up from Los Angeles to take her out, and he had canceled on her because of a medical emergency. It wasn't the first time, and, despite the assumption it wouldn't be the last time, it became the last time. She still hadn't worn the dress. So why not wear it today? *Okay, go for it.*

The dress was a soft shade of aqua. It was simple, form-fitting, but not clingy. She checked the rest of her look: hair freshly washed and shiny, make-up minimal, espadrilles to keep the casual look, a turquoise cashmere cardigan in case it turned cool, small handbag. The mirror told her if she wasn't the fairest of them all, at least she would do.

When she was completely ready, her digital clock read ten-seventeen. The doorbell rang at ten-thirty. She, of course, didn't know he had arrived five minutes early and waited before ringing the bell.

He was wearing a muted pastel plaid shirt with the sleeve cuffs rolled up, khaki slacks, and tan boat shoes. He looked younger than his forty-one years, which she had learned when she Googled him and read about his appointment to the bench three years before.

When they got into his Lexus, he asked, "How does Greens Restaurant sound? Have you been there?"

"Not for a long time, but it's a great place. Does that mean you're a vegetarian?"

"No, I'm okay with being at the top of the food chain. I actually don't eat a lot of meat, especially red meat, but I like Greens mostly for the location. I think the view is terrific."

By the time they got to the restaurant and parked by Fort Mason, it was eleven o'clock and Greens was opening. He'd obviously made reservations, as they were seated in the prime spot of the airy restaurant with an exceptional view of the Golden Gate Bridge. The fog was lifting above the top of the international orange towers. He ordered a spicy scrambled egg combo, and Clara ordered a milder dish that included a tasty blend of veggies and poached eggs.

As they sipped good coffee and waited for their food, they began talking about juvenile dependency law and continued as the savory dishes arrived. At the end of the meal, Clara wondered if she should offer to pay half of the tab, but didn't have the opportunity. Somehow, Greg had already paid, and she thought maybe the conversation would end there.

As they left the restaurant, Greg said, "How would you like a stroll around this area? It's one of my favorite places in San Francisco."

"Fine with me. I love this city, here and a few hundred other places."

"You aren't a native San Franciscan, are you?" (She didn't know he had looked her up on the state bar listing and saw that her BA and MA were from the University of Virginia, before she got her JD from UC Berkeley law school.)

"No, I was born in Kentucky and went to the University of Virginia before I came to California. I taught English in a high school in Piedmont, and my first husband taught history at Cal. He was killed in a robbery that went bad. I didn't go to law school till after my second husband died of a heart attack. He was quite a bit older than I am. I can't believe I just told you my whole life story in a couple of sentences. I guess that may be too much information."

"Not at all. I'd like to know more about you, but I'm sorry for your loss. I know how hard it is because my wife died of cancer several years ago."

"That must've been especially hard. Was it a long illness?"

"Yes, she became progressively debilitated over more than a year. I'd been working at a big law firm, and they wouldn't agree to let me work half time to help care for her. Fortunately, we had both made enough money that I didn't have to work for a long period of time. She had been a violinist in the San Francisco Symphony. After she died, I began to reassess what I wanted to do with my life."

They continued to chat as they strolled around Fort Mason, which had been established as a US military reservation after California was granted statehood in 1850. They saw several squatters' houses, constructed by civilian squatters who built houses on land they didn't actually own, and the General's Residence built in 1866, which had housed Army generals before becoming an officers' club.

As they crossed the Great Meadow Park that had been crowded with refugees from the 1906 earthquake and fire, Clara asked, "How did you become a judge?"

"I had a pretty good track record as a lawyer, and I eventually got my appointment to the bench three years ago. I confess I don't think it hurt my chances that my father had been a judge. He had a laudable reputation on the bench. My mother might've become a judge, too, if it hadn't been for me."

"Really, how's that?"

"She was a lawyer herself, a rarity for a woman in her day. But she took time out from her career to have me, and she didn't ever get back to it after my brother was born. She found she liked having the freedom to do the things that were important to her, and she did a lot of good works over the years."

"What kind of things did she do?"

"You name it, she did it. She has boundless energy, and her projects have been very eclectic. They ranged from the arts to the poor. But she said no matter how much she tried to do, there was always more to do."

"Is she still active?"

"Not so much with her projects anymore. She and Dad are in their seventies, and after she finally convinced him to retire they traveled, and they especially tried to spend time with their grandchildren. My brother is a math professor at a small college in Vermont, and he has two kids, boy and girl twins."

"So have you always lived in San Francisco?"

"Yes, born and bred, except for college and law school. Like most kids, I wanted to get away from home. I didn't know I lived in the best place in the world till I left it."

"Where did you go to school?" (She already knew, of course, because she had looked him up in a California judges' directory.)

"NYU undergrad and University of Chicago Law School. I guess I started working my way back west again."

"When did you meet your wife?"

"I came back to San Francisco to work for a big law firm, at first thinking I wanted to make money instead of following in my father's footsteps. I got season tickets to the symphony, and I took my dates there whenever I could find one who liked classical music. Several times I noticed this good-looking woman in the violin section, and then I made a point of looking for her. After a while, I quit taking dates and just looked at her."

Clara chided him good-naturedly as she asked, "So you're one of those guys who fell in love just because a woman was good looking?"

"Ouch—no not quite, although I guess it started that way. I had a friend who played clarinet in the orchestra, and I asked him if he could introduce us."

"And the rest is history?"

"Yep. We were married a year later."

"Do you have any children?"

"That's the biggest regret of my life. Every year we said maybe next year we should start a family. Somehow, we never seemed to get around to it. When she got sick, it was too late. How about you? Any kids?"

"I have a stepson named Jake. He's a junior at Cornell. My second husband was his uncle, and he adopted Jake when he was a baby after his parents died in a car accident."

"Some kids are luckier than others. I wish more kids were as lucky as Jake."

"Does that have anything to do with how you wound up in juvenile law?"

"In a way, yes. Like other new judges, at the beginning, I rotated in assignments, and as soon as I hit juvenile law, I knew that was the place for me. I don't know of any area of the law where you can make more of a difference in people's lives. In juvenile delinquency, sometimes you can turn a kid around and give him a better life. In dependency, you make crucial decisions that affect the lives of whole families as well as children."

"So you're planning to stay with juvenile law?"

"Yes, till my dying day. Most judges are eager to rotate out of juvenile court because it's not a prestigious area of the law. But for me, it's a perfect fit."

As they walked along the waterfront, they appreciated Fort Mason's transformation of wartime warehouses and piers into a lively cultural complex. The view of the bay was spectacular as they walked along the water's edge, and Greg asked if Clara had been to Alcatraz Island.

"Not for years, at least a decade or more."

"Neither have I. Why don't we do that soon?"

Her heart leapt up—just as Wordsworth's did when he beheld a rainbow in the sky. She knew it was a cliché, but it really did. She was surprised herself to realize she was sure she wanted to see this extraordinary man again.

As she looked over the bay toward Fort Point, she became aware she hadn't given a thought to Vivian since she'd been with Greg today. Then she became pensive, and he offered her a dollar for her thoughts.

"A dollar?"

"Yeah, inflation. Besides, you look so contemplative, I assume yours would be worth more."

When she mentioned Vivian, he said he was aware of her murder, having known her briefly when she represented a child in his courtroom. He was very surprised to learn Clara had been assigned to the appeal in the same case.

"I'm not sure what the ethics would be in this situation, but to be on the safe side, we probably shouldn't talk about the case."

"I agree. As you know, I have to take an independent position on behalf of my client who's the child in the appeal, and it should be based strictly on what is in the appellate record."

"Of course, I know the drill. I've had a number of appeals in my cases. So far, none of them have been reversed. I think we're all right ethically as long as we don't talk about the case you're working on."

As if on cue, she changed the subject to her teaching at BASL. It also came as a surprise to Greg that she would be teaching the course Vivian had taught. He said he hadn't known about Vivian's full-time job as a law professor at BASL.

They avoided any further mention of Vivian, but talked about Clara's course for the fall. Greg offered to

SECOND IN HER CLASS   149

have Clara's students visit his courtroom, which she
agreed would be an excellent opportunity for them.

Clara talked easily with Greg except for one other
subject. The most significant thing she didn't tell him was
about Travis or her role in helping him investigate Vivian's murder. She didn't think there was any reason not to
trust Greg, but she remembered how adamantly Travis
had always warned her before: "Don't give anyone even
the slightest hint you're helping law enforcement on a
murder case, no matter how much you trust him. You
never know."

How could she trust anyone with that admonition
ringing in her ears? She knew her life would never be the
same again as it had been before she knew Travis. But it
was certainly more interesting.

Her day with Greg ended late that afternoon when he
suggested a stroll around the nearby Palace of Fine Arts.
It seemed ages since she had been there, but it actually
hadn't been very long ago when she had taken her tour of
the Hitchcock locations for *Vertigo*.

Time seemed slightly off kilter between the 1950s
film and the present. At first, it was slightly unnerving
being there again, but soon she let herself be seduced by
the lovely surroundings.

The ambiance was enhanced by several wedding parties, which were frequently photographed around the
grounds.

Neither Clara nor Greg commented on them. They
simply enjoyed the charming setting until Greg said, "I
hate to end this, Clara, but I have a reception to attend
tonight in honor of Justice Moreno who retired from the
California Supreme Court a while back. I wish I'd known
you sooner, and maybe you could've come with me."

"Sounds nice. I'm one of his admirers."

"Could we make up for it and get together for Alcatraz tomorrow? I guess that's an odd choice for a second date, but I think it would be an interesting outing."

"At least now I know it would be a date. I wasn't sure about today."

Greg grinned. "I wasn't exactly sure myself. I haven't had many dates since my wife died. Maybe now I'll have a few more."

⁊⁊⁊

When Clara got home, she decided to call Travis and fill him in on the identity of the initials in the files for GM and RP. But she was surprised when the first thing he said was, "What did you think of Judge Hart?"

"How did you know about that?"

"I am a detective, you know. We have our ways."

"Are you keeping tabs on me, Travis?"

"Not twenty-four/seven. I just keep an eye out when I happen to be around."

"And when did you happen to be around?"

"It's not as sneaky as it sounds. I was running some errands for Jo Anne and noticed I was near your neighborhood when I went to pick up some sourdough bread at a bakery. As long as I was nearby, I swung by your building and saw the judge picking you up."

"How did you know who it was?"

Travis looked a little sheepish when he answered. "When you said you were going to observe in Judge Hart's courtroom, I checked him out. You can Google anybody these days, and I saw his picture."

"So now my life's an open book, huh?"

"I wouldn't say that exactly, but it never hurts to have somebody looking out for you."

She admitted to herself, though not to Travis, she was pleased to think somebody cared enough to look out for her. She wondered if he had any idea he was like the father she had always wanted.

"As long as you're nosing around, I might as well give you some new information. You read the same electronic files from Vivian's laptop as I did. The two you hadn't identified were GM and RP. I was pretty sure GM is Gretchen Miller because she was the mother in the case Vivian had in the dependency court, and I've now been assigned to in the appellate court."

"Lucky coincidence—so you'll be able to keep an eye on that one, I assume. What about RP?"

"I got the information from the registrar at BASL. He was a student named Richard Piper. You can't really tell for sure from her journal whether she thought he might have been physically threatening, but he wouldn't be the first law student to go off the deep end."

"Good work. Do you know if he's still around?"

"Not for certain. He was academically disqualified from the law school, but I got his contact information from the registrar."

After Clara gave him the information, Travis said, "I'll get right on it. Meanwhile, take care, okay?"

"You know me, Cautious Clara."

"Let's keep it that way."

eↄeↄ

Clara hadn't been to "The Rock" since she'd gone there with her first husband soon after they had moved to California fifteen years ago. As a history professor, he was trying to visit every historical landmark within a reasonable distance, and Alcatraz was high on his list. His dissertation had been on the Warsaw Uprising in 1944, a tribute to his Polish grandparents who had immigrated just before the war, but even though he taught European History, he'd always had a keen interest in the history of wherever he was.

The long afternoon on Alcatraz Island with Greg was a different kind of experience. His interest was less focused on the history of the island and more on criminal law. He had appreciated his rotation in criminal court particularly because of how it had helped him during his time in juvenile delinquency court. Whenever he could, he learned as much as possible about the youthful missteps of the criminal defendants who appeared before him. He said he thought it helped him make judicious decisions about the future of the juveniles whose fate often depended to a large extent on the wisdom of his decisions.

The Alcatraz maximum-security federal penitentiary had held some of the most notorious and incorrigible bad guys, including Al Capone, George "Machine Gun" Kelly, and the killer "Birdman" Robert Stroud. They had all been sensationalized in movies, and especially fictionalized was Stroud, who had studied birds at Leavenworth but had never been allowed to keep them during his seventeen years on Alcatraz. Even on a pleasant summer day, D Block still seemed somehow bleak and cold, a stark reminder of the most dangerous inhabitants who had been kept there in solitary confinement.

The tour of the historic penitentiary was fascinating, but it was the amazing view of the bay that delighted them. They walked completely around the island (she'd followed Greg's suggestion to wear jeans and comfortable walking shoes) and observed the flora and fauna. The old gardens planted by prisoners and staff had fallen into ruin, but in recent years, the Garden Conservancy had revived the gardens.

They took the Agave Trail leading past the fragrant eucalyptus trees where black-crowned herons nested, across the hillside with three types of agaves. The trail led down to the tide pools where they tried to identify the little sea creatures that inhabited them. Late in the afternoon, they began to see a few more birds in the remoter areas, along with an occasional lizard and field mouse.

As they took the ferry back, Greg said, "As long as we're doing the historical touristy stuff, how about dinner at the Cliff House?"

"Do you think we're dressed okay?"

"They cater to tourists who wear anything. Besides, you look great no matter what you're wearing, and with you around, nobody will even see me."

She was pleased at the compliment, of course, but was still glad she'd worn a nice blouse with her jeans. "Have you been there many times?" she asked.

"Are you kidding? I'm a San Francisco native. I've never been there."

"Me either. I guess it's about time we christen it."

Tourists had been going to the Cliff House for more than one hundred and fifty years, since the first one was built in 1863. After earthquakes and fires, this one was the fourth incarnation, not nearly as grand as one built in the late nineteenth century by Adolph Sutro, which was like a French chateau with turrets and an observation tower.

Still, the view was panoramic, and they had a tasty, if pricey, seafood dinner as they watched the sun set over Seal Rocks and the vast Pacific Ocean beyond. They could also see the ruins of the historic Sutro Baths and the entry to the Golden Gate. It was truly a golden moment as they lingered over a good California Chardonnay and learned more about each other's personal lives.

When he took her home at almost ten, Greg apolo-

gized for leaving her so early but said he still had to review some files before the usual early start of his court in
the morning. Much as she had enjoyed being with Greg,
she was glad to let it end at that point. She preferred to
take things slowly.

Slowly? She had met him less than a week before
and had already had two lengthy dates with him in one
weekend. How much faster could it progress? But she
was still glad when he asked her to accompany him to a
formal annual dinner the next Saturday to welcome new
judges to the court.

�''⋯''⋯''

Clara had two more weeks to prepare for her new
course, as the last week of August at BASL would be
taken up with orientation for new students. Her role was
minimal, however, merely to be introduced at a reception
on the first day, but it was also optional for her to sit in
on orientation sessions and to be available in her office
for students who might have questions. Meanwhile, she
decided to be at the office at least part of every day and
see if she could pick up anything that might relate to Vivian.

She was pleased to see the walls of her office had
been repainted and Vivian's nameplate had been removed. Ron from facilities dropped by to see if everything was all right, and she thanked him for his efficient
help.

"Is there anything else I can do for you?" he asked.

"In fact, yes, if you don't mind. I'd like to have my
furniture rearranged a little. The desk is too heavy for me
to move without your help."

"No problem. How do you want it?"

She explained she wanted it set so her back would be to one wall and thus she could see the window to the outside in one direction and the door to the hall in the other direction. Ron said he'd have no trouble moving it by himself, and in minutes it was exactly the way she wanted it.

"Thanks so much, Ron. You're a prince."

He grinned as he answered the vibrating phone in his pocket and took off for his next task. She settled in and was absorbed in her computer research when she was startled by a strident voice at her door.

"Who are you?" the voice said. It came from a thin, wild-eyed woman who was unkempt and had bad teeth. She looked anxious and without taking a breath repeated, "Who are you? Who are you?"

"I beg your pardon," Clara said.

"I said who are you? You're not Hall for sure. What happened to her name on the door?"

"Professor Hall is no longer with us. May I help you with anything?"

"I know damn well she's no longer with us. Good-bye and good riddance to her. God won't forgive her no more than I will. And I never will. It's all her effin' fault. She ruined my life."

"What do you mean by that? Who are you?"

"I'm the mother of the baby she stole from me. I'm her real mother. If it wasn't for her, they woulda given my baby back to me. My baby is all I had. So she took away everything I had. She was trash. She probably thought I'm trash, but she's the one who's trash. I'm Krystal's real mother."

"Are you Gretchen?"

"Yeah, how'd you know? Are you psychic or something? Who are you? Who are you?"

"I'm a new professor here."

"Well, Miss Prissy Professor, what're you doing in Hall's office? There shouldn't be anybody in here but ghosts. Are you a ghost? Are you a ghost?"

Gretchen had moved closer and was leaning over Clara's desk. She was fingering the heavy bronze bookend that braced the books on the corner of the desk.

"Why don't you have a seat and tell me why you're here."

"I don't want no seat, and I don't have to tell you nothing. I don't know who you are. Who are you? What are you doing here? There shouldn't be nobody here."

"I'm a new professor here, and this is my office now."

Gretchen started to pace nervously around the office. She continued to ramble erratically, but Clara couldn't quite make out what she was saying. Meanwhile, when Gretchen's back was turned, Clara punched in the code for security on her office phone.

Gretchen looked confused, walked out of the office, then came back into the office, and said, "Who are you? Who are you?" and turned back into the hallway.

She went toward the outer door to the faculty parking lot, and Clara saw her sprinting in the direction of the BART station just as the security guard came in.

"Thanks for coming, but it's okay now. An agitated woman was in here a few minutes ago, but she's gone now."

"Do you know who she was? Or can you give me a description?"

"Her name is Gretchen Miller. She's thin, white, a little above average height, has scraggly light brown hair, watery brown eyes, and discolored teeth. She was wearing ragged jeans and a faded red tank top, and she was barefoot."

"That all sounds familiar. I think she came in and

caused some commotion for Professor Hall a while back. I can check my log."

"Please do, but I'm pretty sure you're right. I think somebody mentioned something like that happened when Professor Hall was here."

"Do you think that could've had anything to do with what happened to her? Anything you want me to do to follow up? Do you want me to notify the police?"

"No, that's okay. I'm not sure it means anything, but I can give them a call so they'll be aware of it."

"Good, it can't hurt to keep them in the loop."

As soon as he left, Clara called Travis. She didn't reach him but left a message on his cell and office phones. Minutes later, she had a call from the security guard.

"Yeah, it was the same woman. That's the name and general description Professor Hall gave me, even the same clothes. I'll be on the lookout for her and let you know if I see her anywhere around campus."

"Thanks, I appreciate that."

She had just hung up when Travis called back. "Your message said it wasn't urgent, Clara, but I know the tone of your voice. What's going on?"

"It's over now, at least for the moment, but I admit it was a little unnerving." She described Gretchen's behavior and added, "I don't want to overreact, though. She may be harmless."

"What you described sounds like classic meth behavior, and you can't tell when somebody like that could turn violent."

"Now you're scaring me. Do you think she's a threat, and more importantly, could she have been Vivian's killer?"

"Meth addicts can be completely unpredictable. She's definitely worth a look, and you should be on your

guard. It might be worth it to put somebody on you till
we find out more about this woman."

"Thanks, but no thanks. I'm not going to be paranoid
about some drugged-out woman. She didn't seem coher-
ent enough to do much real harm."

"Don't be so sure. Be careful, Clara. If it wasn't her,
we know for sure somebody killed Vivian. We don't
want anybody getting wind of your participation in the
investigation. Remember you can quit any time you feel
like it."

"You know I'm not a quitter, Travis. And you don't
have to remind me you always say not to trust anybody,
no matter how much I trust them."

"That's more like it. Keep repeating it like a mantra.
I almost forgot. I've got a report for you. Actually, it's
non-report, I guess. We followed up on the contact information you gave us for the student Richard Piper. He
hasn't been at that address for several weeks, and the
phone was disconnected. We tried the email address, too,
and it came back as undeliverable. We're trying to find
relatives now. He has a brother, but we haven't been able
to contact him yet. I'll keep you posted."

"Thanks, and I'll do the same."

ᘒᘒᘒ

Within five minutes, she had to do exactly what
she'd just told Travis she would do. After checking her
BASL email one last time before leaving the office, she
realized someone had hacked into her account and had
seen the emails from Travis that had the attachments
from Vivian's laptop.

There was a new email with the subject line, *Life or
death matter!* And the message was: *YUR life or death!
Only 1 way u cd have stuf frm her laptop & besides I saw*

the big cop in ur office. So ur workng w/ cops & Im
watchng U. Any more signs ur a snoop & ur snoopng
days are over—FOR GOOD!!!

She called Travis and said, "I didn't expect to keep
you posted so soon, but I just received an email that concerns me. Shall I forward it to you?"

"No, read it to me first."

After she read it, he said, "Don't forward it to me because the hacker would probably know about that. I'll put
my best tech person on it right away to see about tracing
the email. Go on home now, and keep an eye out around
you."

"Okay, but it looks like it was written by someone
who was pretty spaced out. I wouldn't think Gretchen
could be capable of hacking, but do you think she
could've been the one who sent it?"

"Maybe so, but it's just as possible it could've been
sent by someone who's well educated trying to sound ig-
norant."

"Yeah, I know—you never know. That also means
this could be nothing more than some hacker making a
sick joke."

"Even if it could be taken as a sophomoric prank, it
could just as well be a real threat. The references to Vivian's laptop and your working with the cops are too close
to home. It doesn't pay to ignore it."

"Any advice on how I should react?"

"Go along as if you never received it. From now on,
don't email me about anything on your BASL account,
and don't use it for anything but routine law school matters. I'll have the tech gal make sure your personal email
isn't compromised and check your cell phone, too."

"Good, I'd be lost if I couldn't communicate."

"We need to communicate more than ever now. Report anything unusual to me, no matter how insignificant it may seem."

In a zombie monotone, she replied, "Yes, master. I'm going home now. I'll eat some dinner. I'll listen to the news. I'll go to bed. I'll read a book. I'll go to sleep."

"Very funny, Quillen. I said anything *un*usual. Get it?"

"Got it."

"Good."

She wondered if Travis had any idea they'd just engaged in wordplay from a wonderful old Danny Kaye movie, *The Court Jester*.

Chapter 11

Gauging Colleagues

Clara was a little annoyed with herself for feeling apprehensive when she went into the office the next day. There were no signs that the tech person had been in her office. She called Travis, who told her the threatening email had been sent from a blind address that had immediately been abandoned and couldn't be traced. He reminded her to be cautious with her BASL email and probably her office phone, too. Her personal email and cell phone checked out all right, but it wouldn't hurt to be discreet anyway.

After she hung up, she thought for a while and asked herself if she was being foolish to keep working on Vivian's murder, but she had no sooner asked the question than she knew her answer—she couldn't imagine doing otherwise.

She felt much better when Paula Kelley dropped by to see if she was free for lunch. Even with Paula, however, she had some underlying nagging questions that made her a trifle uneasy. It seemed as if she was suspicious of everybody these days, and she didn't much like the feeling.

They went to a small Thai restaurant within walking distance of the law school. Clara had to make an effort to keep up with Paula, who had longer legs and walked at a brisk pace. "Do you always walk this fast?" Clara asked.

"Sorry," Paula said, as she slowed her stride. "I'm used to moving fast on the tennis court, and it's natural for me to walk fast. I do weight training, too, to help my serving swing. My doctor says with my aerobic exercise I should live to be a hundred."

Paula ordered her entree to be extra spicy, and Clara ordered hers mild. She felt a little wimpy about it for some reason and explained, "It's not that I don't appreciate spicy flavors. It's only that when I eat something very hot, my tongue goes numb and I can't taste anything else for the rest of the meal."

"Maybe that's why I like it spicy. It keeps me from tasting that awful Thai food," Paula quipped.

The food was actually quite good, though, spicy or not. Conversation was good, too, mostly having to do with law school politics and national politics as it related to legal issues. Finally, Clara steered the conversation around to Vivian.

"The memorial service seemed very moving to me. Even though I didn't know Vivian, I felt I knew her better after the service. Did it seem appropriate to you?"

"I guess there's only one thing that bothered me a little, but there's no way to avoid it unless people suddenly start being more truthful in eulogies. I've never been to a funeral or memorial service that didn't heap high praise on the deceased, no matter what kind of scoundrel he might have been in reality. So when someone like Vivian is eulogized, only those who knew her well can know how genuinely she deserved every accolade and then some."

"There was certainly an aura of sincerity in the eulogies for her, though. Somehow, I think most people have a pretty good idea of the truth."

"I hope so. And I hope the monster who killed her gets what's coming to him."

"When you said 'he,' do you have any doubts that it was a man who killed her?"

"It had to have been a man. Any woman would've appreciated what a special person Vivian was. No woman would've dumped her on the rocks like that. It's too crude. It was undoubtedly a man with too much testosterone."

"Do you have any idea how she could've wound up there? It seems like such an unlikely place to find her."

"All the more reason it had to have been a man. It was probably someone who admired all those sexist Hitchcock films like *Vertigo.*"

"That's interesting. I guess I never thought of Hitchcock films as sexist."

"The women are always shown as weak little flowers, subordinate to the men."

"What about Grace Kelly in *Rear Window?* She was pretty gutsy going over to Raymond Burr's apartment to investigate the murder of his wife."

"But as usual, she had to be rescued by a man. Even with a broken leg, Jimmy Stewart came to her rescue. And Cary Grant rescued Eva Marie Saint in *North by Northwest.* Why is it always men rescuing women in those plots? At the very least, couldn't another woman have come to the rescue once in a while?"

"That would be a good twist, I guess, but it wouldn't do much for the romance."

"There's more than one kind of romance. At least in

recent films, we have a few different interpretations of gender on film. Oh, look at the time. I have to get back for a committee meeting."

Clara had the distinct feeling Paula had said more than she had meant to, and suddenly everything clicked. She should've known. The thing that had been nagging all along was the possibility Paula had romantic feelings for Vivian. Was that why Vivian had decided to quit Paula's women's group? How could Clara find out? You can hardly come right out and ask about a woman's romantic feelings for another woman. Or was that an old-fashioned notion?

঩঩঩

When she got back to the office, she thought about how she might get such information. It was worth a try. Anyway, she'd wanted to see if she could learn more from Lyle about his relationship with Vivian. She called him and said, "Hi, we haven't talked for a few days, and I was wondering how you're doing."

"Plugging along. I'll be glad when classes start. Then I'll at least have something else to focus on. I don't expect anything will displace my thoughts of Vivian, but I can use the diversion."

"How about a lunch break tomorrow? My offer of friendship still stands."

"Sounds good. I have a tendency to stay too tied to this desk, and it would be good to get out for a change of scenery."

"Fine. You know the places around here. Do you have any favorites for lunch?"

"My favorite place isn't around here. It's a cozy little Italian restaurant in North Beach I used to go to with Vivian, and I'm not sure I could ever go there again. How about Mexican? There's a pretty good place near here."

"I'm always up for Mexican. How's noonish tomorrow?"

"Let's make if a few minutes before that and beat the crowd. La Corneta Taqueria is a popular place for lunch. It's a no-frills cafeteria, but the portions are tasty and hearty."

"No frills suits me fine. See you tomorrow."

c⁄ɔc⁄ɔ

Clara sat in on some orientation sessions in the morning, and the afternoon was devoted to campus tours for the new students. Students were touring in clumps led by upper-class students, and other strays were milling around taking care of a variety of class registration matters. Occasionally, a new student hesitantly peered into her office and asked where to find something, and she was pleased to be able to point someone in the right direction. She was beginning to feel not so much like the new kid on the block.

She walked around campus, too, getting a look at the new crop of students. Several times she noticed one somber face with sunken eyes that seemed out of place, though, and it also seemed vaguely familiar. His long, thin face reminded her of the painting of St. Francis by El Greco at the Palace of the Legion of Honor. Rather than an ethereal saint, however, he was scruffy looking, even among law students who were often somewhat scruffy looking.

It was a warm day, but he was wearing a dark gray hoodie and had several days' growth of beard.

Back in her office, she was absorbed in reading a law journal when she was disconcerted to see the same austere face appear in her office doorway. She asked, "May I help you find something?"

"No, I already found it. But it's really different now."

"Do you mean this office?"

"If you want to call it that. I would call it her den of iniquity."

"I've been assigned to this office only recently. Have you been here before?"

"Many times—or close by anyway."

The face inched in with the rest of the ascetic body, and he began to wander around as if he owned the place. He ambled back and forth looking at the walls, the bookshelves, and the desk. Clara watched him as he paced, trying to understand what he was doing there.

He seemed oblivious to her or to there being anything odd about his presence in her office. "Are you teaching her classes, too?"

"Do you mean Professor Hall?"

"Professor Hell. Who else?"

"I'll be teaching Professor Hall's Juvenile Dependency Law class this fall."

Clara was making an effort to maintain a tone of normalcy in a conversation that was obviously bizarre. The young man's hostility was palpable, and she didn't want to buy into it.

"I'd be in that class if she hadn't flunked me in Torts," he said matter-of-factly. "I would've taken any class she taught just to be able to give her a hard time."

How could she not have recognized him? Even with the sunken eyes, the face was the same as in the photo from the student face book that the registrar had sent to her, and it belonged unmistakably to Richard Piper.

"What are you doing these days, Mr. Piper?" she asked.

He didn't seem the least bit surprised that she knew his name and didn't skip a beat before he answered, "I'm going to hell. What would you expect?"

She saw a wildness in his eyes that she only thought she had seen at first. Now she was reasonably certain this was a mentally deranged person. She remembered reading in Vivian's journal that she wondered if he was bipolar. If so, this seemed like an extreme case. Maybe it was something even worse, as Vivian had speculated.

"Is this a stopover on your journey?" she asked.

"Only briefly—my route is pretty direct. I won't even pass Go or collect two hundred dollars. I'll go straight to hell. Or is it jail? I can never remember."

"I guess that depends on what you've done. What have you done, Mr. Piper?"

"I can't remember. I must've done something to make her put me in the corner with a dunce hat."

Frantic to figure out what she should say or do, Clara tried to think what might get through to him. All of a sudden, the question became irrelevant as Piper said, "I've got to go now, or I'll be late to class," and he bolted out the door as unpredictably as he had arrived.

She peered out into the hallway and saw him head toward the exit door, soon lost behind a bunch of new students being led into the building for a tour. After her encounter with Gretchen Miller, she couldn't bring herself to call security. So instead she called Travis and told him everything that had happened with Piper.

"I'll dispatch somebody over right away. They can get there before I can."

"No, don't do that. He didn't say anything that was an actual threat, and I don't think it's a good idea to have cops around here scaring new students."

"But we've been looking for him for questioning, and this could be our chance."

"I doubt it. My guess is he's on the next BART train going who knows where."

"That may be right, but we still need to talk to him. I located his brother in Pennsylvania, but he hasn't had any contact with him for many months. He told us Piper had been diagnosed as bipolar with borderline schizoid personality disorder."

"Was he ever treated for mental illness?"

"His brother said he was treated for a little while, but then the insurance company denied further coverage. He thought there was no question Piper needed more treatment, and he wrangled with the health insurer for a while. Anyway, after Piper was released from his treatment program, his brother said they lost touch."

"How long ago was that?"

"More than a year ago, his brother recalled. When he came out to see him, Piper told his brother he was giving up on California. He said he planned to go back to Pennsylvania, but his brother returned home, and Piper never showed up."

"Did you learn anything else about his connection with Vivian?"

"No, his brother didn't even know he'd gotten back into a law school after he'd left the previous one."

"So what do you think? Does he seem to be a likely suspect to you?"

"With the mentally ill, it's almost impossible to know without some forensic evidence. They can be harmless or homicidal. To be on the safe side, though, it's best to assume Piper is potentially dangerous. If you ever see this guy again, do whatever you can to protect yourself, and if you get any clue to his whereabouts, let me know."

"Don't worry. I have no desire to deal with somebody like him without back-up."

"Okay, partner. I'll watch your back whenever I can." And she knew he would.

೭ೞ೭

The next morning, Clara was in the office at her desk when Lyle called about eleven-forty. "Hi," he said, "I can break away any time. Drop by when you're ready for lunch."

"I'll be there in a few minutes. I'm having visions of tostadas dancing in my head already."

She noticed he asked her to come by his office and assumed it was still too painful for him to go to Vivian's former office. She wondered how long that feeling would last. Could there be any more to it than loving, but painful, memories of Vivian?

There she was again with Travis-inspired suspicions of everyone—did she really need that? Lyle seemed so genuinely in love with Vivian. How could she doubt him? But she also couldn't help thinking about Travis's simple list of motives: love, sex, and money. Two out of three might well apply to Lyle. Maybe that would have to be her subtext, but she'd also try to learn what she could about other faculty members.

At the restaurant, Clara ordered her tostada with extra guacamole, and Lyle went for flautas with everything. When they began eating, he ate slowly as they conversed, savoring each bite and pausing between bites. At first, they talked about plans for their new classes about to start, and Clara was able to make a smooth transition into different professors' teaching styles.

"How would you rate some of the professors as teachers, and may I venture to ask where you'd place yourself?"

"Sure, I'll start with me. I don't know exactly where I'd place myself on a scale of one to ten, but I think it's somewhere above a five and less than ten, of course. I pride myself on clarity in teaching Real Property because I try to simplify the subject rather than make it more complex. It can be a dense subject, and I well remember my own professor making it even denser."

"That reminds me of my Real Property prof as well. He was always spouting complicated hypotheticals about Blackacre and Whiteacre till I had a hard time seeing the forest for the trees. I have a theory that the less knowledgeable a professor is about the substance of the material, the more he or she will try to make it difficult for the students."

"I agree. I think it's a common device to cover up one's own ignorance. I work hard to make it easier for my students, not more difficult."

"Do you use the same straight-forward approach when you teach your course in Environmental Law?"

"Essentially, yes, but I'm really privileged to be teaching that subject. Since it's not a required course, the students who take it are self-motivated and take an active interest in the subject. So I'm energized by their energy. The hard part is keeping up with the ever-changing law."

"Okay, what about other professors?"

He mentioned several professors and their various quirks, both good and bad. "One of our most interesting professors is Warner Greenburg, because he's such a wonderful contradiction. He out-Kingsfields Professor Kingsfield in class. Remember him in *The Paper Chase?* Warner is quite intimidating in the classroom and challenges his students to the max. But he's otherwise very unlike Kingsfield, who was basically indifferent to his students. Warner cares a great deal about his students, and he'll bend over backward to help a student who's making a sincere effort to learn."

"Is there anything Professor Kingsfield did better than Professor Greenburg?"

"Only one, or maybe two. Kingsfield was a dapper dresser, and you might say Warner is more vintage Goodwill. I suspect his cut-rate wardrobe may have something to do with his generosity toward charitable causes, though, and I can't very well fault him for that."

"And what is the second thing?"

"Have you seen Warner's office? It looks like a set for one of those hoarder television shows. Books and papers stacked everywhere. He has to meet with students in the library because there's no place to sit in his office. You can't even tell if he's in there because the stacks are higher than his head when he's sitting at his desk."

"Does that affect his teaching?"

"Apparently not. The one thing he does like Kingsfield is his use of the Socratic Method in the classroom, and his technique is also well organized. Even though I happen to think the method is outmoded, Greenburg seems to use it with the utmost effectiveness."

"Are there any professors you'd classify as either the best or the worst teachers?"

"No contest. That would be Paula and General MacArthur."

"Even you call him that?"

"Not to his face, of course, and not to students. But that's the typical way students refer to him. They tend to be pretty open with me, so I get a fairly good idea what they think."

"And I gather they don't think very highly of John Knox MacArthur?"

"I'd say that's an understatement. I suspect he'd be out of here in a nanosecond if he weren't tenured. His classroom demeanor is dictatorial and sarcastic, and he's known for giving the same stale lectures year after year. He claims he would be able to teach in his sleep, and I wouldn't be surprised if sometimes he does. I don't think he's had a new idea in years."

"He sounds dreadful. I feel sorry for the students."

"I do, too. Last year, he started bragging about his innovative new electronic textbook, but he was a fraud even about that."

"How so?"

"It was Vivian who was doing almost all of the substantive work on the book. As far as I know, I'm the only one she ever told about how extensively she was working on it. I warned her not to get involved with MacArthur, but she said she didn't want to cross him."

"Was there any particular reason?"

"She said it was because she expected him to be on her tenure committee, and she thought she needed his good opinion of her. She believed she could show him her scholarly qualities by cooperating with him on the book. But I thought she might've had some even stronger reason for continuing to work with him."

"What sort of reason could that have been?"

"MacArthur could be very vindictive. I've heard rumors about his underhanded treatment of others who crossed him in the past. It's hard to say how much truth there was in the rumors, but I wasn't sure how far he might go if he and Vivian ever had a significant difference of opinion."

"Do you know whether anything like that happened with Vivian?"

"I wouldn't be surprised. I know she was working very hard on the electronic book. Besides the subject matter, she had a lot of work to do on the technological stuff.

MacArthur apparently sought her help based on the stereotypical notion that all young people are tech savvy."

"And she wasn't?"

"Vivian was extremely bright, but she wasn't much more tech inclined than any typical college student. So she was educating herself in that area at the same time she was trying to research new developments in tort law, prepare for her classes, and represent a child in a dependency case."

"And was she having a hard time keeping up with it all?"

"She was barely keeping her head above water. Sometimes she said she was too exhausted to go out. She said she realized she was getting desperate when she considered calling her old boyfriend for help with the tech stuff, but she decided against it. I suggested several times she should tell off MacArthur and get on with her own work. All she'd say was she'd think about it. It's all a moot point now, of course."

His eyes misted as he said that, and Clara decided it was time to change the subject.

"Did you say Paula was the best teacher?"

"On a scale of one to ten, I don't think anyone is quite a ten because there's always room for improvement. But Paula comes closer to it than any other professor I know."

"What makes her such a good teacher?"

"She's a remarkable combination of a deep thinker, a challenging professor, and a compassionate person. She never waters down her subject and always inspires her students to think more deeply than they ever had before. But at the same time she motivates her students to strive for excellence, she completely understands when they come to her because they're struggling. She puts in more individual time with students than anyone else on campus."

"Does she have any special classroom techniques?"

"I've never sat in on her classes, so I can judge only by what I've seen her do in demonstrations. Every year, she does a sample class for new students during orientation week. It's amazing how she can mesmerize a group of first-year students who've never even seen her before."

"How does she do that?"

"First, she introduces a prominent legal issue and gets them to think about it, and then they contribute to the discussion. In the beginning, they're reluctant, but soon they get caught up in it and ideas are flying. Then as soon as someone says something profound, she switches gears with something like, 'But what if...' and causes them to think in an entirely different direction."

"Does that unnerve them?"

"Yes, but in a good way. Even though they're all college graduates, many colleges, even good ones sad to say, turn out students who spout only what they think their professors expect them to say. Many of them have subordinated the ability to think for themselves, assuming they ever had it in the first place."

"That sounds somewhat cynical to me."

"I don't mean it that way. In fact, I think most intelligent people are thinkers beginning in childhood, but somewhere along the way, we lose that. We're indoctrinated to work for grades and passing standardized tests instead of testing our own thinking. Paula has a magical gift for taking students back to that early phase and causing students to think for themselves. She believes that's a fundamental quality of a good lawyer."

"I couldn't agree more. Is there anything else that stands out in her teaching?"

"Two essential points always emerge in Paula's orientation demonstration. One is the uncertainty of the law. After the discussion shifts in different directions, students begin to feel a little off kilter. Someone invariably asks, with all that uncertainty, how it's possible to know what's right or just in the law. Paula then asks how many students chose law as a career because they wanted to promote justice. Most of them raise their hands."

"I would've been one of them."

"Me, too, but over time you and I have learned how elusive justice can be. Paula lets them know right up front the uncertainty of a discipline that they had thought held such a promise of certainty. Some of them are uncomfortable with the concept at first, but all of them are better prepared to study law because of it."

"That's a very good point. What was the second point you said emerges in her demonstrations?"

"It's an essential point, too. The second point she introduces when she asks, 'What is the only tool a lawyer has?' Students are always puzzled at first, and they tentatively make a few stabs at an answer. What would you say?"

"It's an easy question to answer now, but I doubt that I could've answered on my first day of law school. Of course, it's the lawyer's ability to use language, whether oral or written. The only tool any lawyer has is words."

"Bingo. It should be self-evident, but most students haven't given it much thought. So Paula uses examples of how lawyers can use words in positive, manipulative, and devious ways: the good, the bad, and the ugly."

"That's a subject dear to my heart as a former English teacher. When I first started law school, I thought I was at a significant disadvantage with my fellow students because many of them came from academic disciplines I thought were more closely related to law. I didn't think my knowledge of Beowulf or Shakespeare or even modern literature would be much help to me. Eventually, I realized that understanding something about how words are used—and misused—would be a genuine asset."

"That's Paula's point, and Vivian was very taken with Paula's ideas."

At last! Clara had become so caught up in Lyle's comments on legal education, she had lost sight of trying to steer the conversation toward Paula and Vivian. Now she had her chance. "So I gather Vivian was influenced by Paula?"

"Very much so, even to the extent she thought of Paula as her mentor. When Vivian started here, she was painfully aware that, despite her academic achievements, she had almost no teaching experience. She attended all the orientation sessions the week before classes started, and she was as mesmerized by Paula as the students. In a way, you might say Paula became Vivian's Svengali."

"Was her influence that strong?"

"I guess that may be laying it on a bit thick. In any event, Paula had extended the hand of friendship to Vivian, and then they became close colleagues."

"Was she closer to Paula than she was to any other professors?"

"She was close to me, of course, but that's another story. She also talked with almost everyone on the faculty in varying degrees. Sometimes she learned in reverse. For example, when she got wind of how much students disliked MacArthur, she pumped him about his teaching methods and knew she didn't want to be like him."

"I gather she was trying to find her own voice for the classroom."

"Exactly. The first year of teaching is hard for anybody. We're just feeling our way for a while. Vivian was beginning to develop her own style, but she used a lot of Paula's techniques."

"Did they spend a lot of time together?"

"They did, especially at the beginning of the school year. They talked a lot, went to lunch, and occasionally did things on weekends. Vivian even tried tennis, but despite the age difference, Paula way outclassed her, so that didn't last long. After the holidays, when Vivian became more and more involved with MacArthur's book, she had less time to spend with Paula."

"Is that why she quit going to Paula's women's group?"

"How did you know about that?"

Clara suddenly realized she knew that only from Vivian's journal, which, of course, she couldn't reveal to Lyle. But then her white lie came easily. "I think Paula may have mentioned it. I was wondering if she was a little miffed about it."

"Funny you picked up on that, too, because I wondered the same thing. Vivian had always talked to me about almost everything on her mind, including Paula. I didn't even notice she'd quit going to the women's group for a couple of months, and when I asked her about it, she was uncharacteristically reticent. She said she had too many things on her plate already and had to cut something out. But I sensed something else might be going on."

"What did you think it was?"

"I'm really reluctant to say what I think because I don't have any concrete evidence for it. It's more of a feeling, but I think I saw a few nuances, too. There was something very attentive about the way Paula behaved around Vivian. I didn't notice at first because Paula's demeanor generally tends to be attentive to others. It's a characteristic of that compassion for others that's so much a part of her personality. But it seemed to have a different feature to it with Vivian."

"Different in what way?"

"That's the problem. I can't really put my finger on anything definite. Just little things, like Paula holding the door for Vivian, offering to take her places, sometimes a glance…"

"Are you suggesting Paula might've had some romantic feelings for Vivian?"

"That's just it. I don't really know for sure. I even tried to ask Vivian about it, obliquely of course, because I thought she might be sensitive about it. But she only changed the subject. That's what gave me the feeling there might be something to it. I sensed that Vivian knew Paula was attracted to her, but she seemed to want to protect Paula's privacy."

"Why would that be? It's hardly uncommon for women in San Francisco to have openly romantic feelings for other women."

"If anything, I think that may explain it, at least partially. Because Paula had not outed herself, Vivian would never have done so. But there's another possibility consistent with Vivian's personality. She wouldn't want to hurt Paula by letting people think she had rejected her."

"And you think she did reject her?"

"I have no doubt that Vivian wouldn't have been romantically inclined toward another woman. As she and I became closer, she seemed to be separating herself more and more from Paula. I never once saw any sign in Vivian of a romantic interest in Paula, or any other woman for that matter, but only appreciation for Paula's other stellar qualities. My best guess is she may have felt a little guilty that Paula might have misconstrued Vivian's admiration for her."

Now that Clara had a clearer picture of Vivian and Paula, she wanted to see if she could learn more about Vivian and Lyle. "You mentioned becoming closer with

Vivian, but you also said she was hesitant about a commitment with you. Would you be comfortable telling me how your romance developed?"

"In a way, it's difficult to talk about, but in another way, I'd really like to talk about it. I've been afraid to talk about Vivian ever since it happened. Talking about her in the past tense is hard."

"I'm a good listener."

"So I noticed. Well, here goes, the love life of Lyle Thurgood Shelton in a nutshell."

"I can hardly wait," she said with a gentle smile.

"All right, this is the essence. I've never been shy with women, but I've always been very aware of the implication of my biracial identity. Sometimes it's been an impediment, but other times it's been an unexpected advantage. I don't kid myself about having sometimes gotten dates because I was different. After President Obama was elected, all of a sudden I possessed a whole new charisma. I admit I took advantage of it when the opportunity presented itself. But it was completely different with Vivian."

"Different in what way?"

"I've done my share of casual dating, everything from a rare one-night stand to relationships that lasted for maybe a few weeks. But I'd never been smitten with anyone the way I was smitten with Vivian. She had every quality I admire in a woman."

"That's not hard to see from everything I've heard about her."

"Everything you've heard that's good is true and then some. She was beautiful inside and out. She had a remarkable mind, exceeded only by her big heart. She's one of the few people I know who not only meant it when she entered this profession and said she wanted to help people, but she also carried through and did it. In some ways, I was in awe of her, but amazingly, I knew she was attracted to me, too."

"That sounds like a pretty hopeful sign for a successful relationship."

"It might have been, except for the fact that she was holding back. I learned early on she was coming out of a bad relationship with a guy named Peter she'd dated since she started law school. So I took it easy for quite a while as I tried to get close to her without scaring her away. I knew I was crazy about her not long after we first met, but I didn't want to chance losing her."

"How did you handle it?"

"At first, I kept it mostly professional. Since I'd been teaching here for a while, I offered to help her fit into the faculty and gave her tips on developing her teaching skills. I figured if we could establish a friendship first, maybe love would follow."

"Do you think it did?"

"Yes, finally, but I admit it was tough for me to be patient. Then in January, when the new semester began, I saw a change in her, and she was giving off signals that she'd be interested in me more than as just a friend. Since I'd made an effort to keep it casual for a while, I was thrilled when she reciprocated my more romantic efforts. By late March, I was completely head over heels, and it seemed she was beginning to feel the same way. But there was still a sort of approach avoidance thing going on with her. A few days before April fifteenth, everything came to a head."

"How do you remember the date so specifically?"

"I was helping her with her tax return. She said she'd always had trouble figuring out tax law, and I was glad to have a chance to help her on anything. I'd had a short-term job once helping people prepare tax returns. Hers wasn't particularly difficult, but she was grateful for the help."

"So what did you mean everything came to a head?"

"We were at my place when it all flared up. After I finished up her tax return, we were talking about taxes, and I decided to test the waters by saying how much easier it would be to file a joint return instead of having to file two returns. Without any warning, she became defensive. It was the first time I'd ever said anything that even hinted at marriage."

"And did that cause her to react in a negative way?"

"To say the least. It was our first big fight, and it got pretty heated. We both said a lot of things we later regretted. She said things like she wasn't ready even to think about marriage, let alone consider it as a real possibility any time soon, and she certainly hadn't considered marriage to me. In the heat of the moment, I asked her if it was because of my race, and she got really angry."

"What did she say?"

"At first, she was so angry she stammered. She had taken my remark as accusing her of racial prejudice, but she emphatically wanted me to know her only concern was the effect mixed races could have on our potential children."

"So did that tell you she, in fact, had thought about marriage with you?"

"Yes, and I was heartened by that, although I didn't say so at the time. Instead, I immediately apologized for the racial remark, but I still couldn't resist asking her where she thought we were headed. She said she had no idea where we were headed and maybe we weren't headed anywhere. That made me angry again, and I said something like, 'So that's why you don't want anybody to know we're seeing each other. This is just a dalliance for you.' That was a big mistake, because she left in a huff. We didn't speak to each other for about a week."

"But you did get back together?"

"We both felt bad about the whole thing. I figured I'd moved too fast, and she said she'd missed me and didn't want to stop seeing me."

"How did things stand then?"

"We were sort of back to square one. She knew I'd do anything to keep seeing her, and she reinforced the conditions. She said she wasn't ready to go public about us and flatly refused to talk about marriage. I had no choice but to do things her way, but it was very frustrating."

"Did things change over time?"

"We had our ups and downs. One day we were having a great time walking around the Palace of Fine Arts on a beautiful day. Everything was going great till a wedding party showed up for a photo shoot, and suddenly Vivian insisted we leave. So when things were going well, I was on cloud nine, and when they weren't, I was exasperated."

"Your relationship reminds me a little of that old Longfellow poem,

"'There was a little girl,
And she had a little curl
Right in the middle of her forehead.
When she was good
She was very, very good,
And when she was bad she was horrid.'"

"Exactly! That seemed to be what was becoming of my life with Vivian. I don't mean she was ever horrid. She couldn't be. But sometimes the relationship seemed horrid, especially when I was beginning to feel it would be horrid if I couldn't share my life with her."

"Is that how things stood before she died?"

Lyle seemed uncomfortable with the question and mumbled something Clara couldn't quite make out. She decided to approach it in a different way.

"When was the last time you saw her before she died?"

"A few days before. I'd been to a conference in Washington, DC, and as soon as I got back, we made a dinner date for a Wednesday at our favorite Italian restaurant in North Beach. We were happy to be together again, but it didn't seem as if anything had changed with her view of our relationship. We talked again about the implications of marriage, and she repeated her concerns about the negative potential for our children. I couldn't seem to convince her otherwise. It appeared to be a stalemate then, but I want to believe she would've come around if her life hadn't ended so soon."

"So how did things stand at the end?"

"She said she had a lot of things to catch up on to get ready for the new school year, and we made a date for the following Sunday night. It was a date we never kept, of course. That's the day they found her at Fort Point."

The tone of his voice had a weary quality, overlaid with sadness. There seemed to be nothing more for Clara to probe. She didn't want to end on a melancholy note, so she turned again to law school matters. The walk back to campus was pleasant enough, but beneath the conversation, she thought Lyle seemed to be in another world. She wasn't sure what that might mean.

❦

When Clara got back to the office, she passed the

faculty lounge and saw Warner Greenburg in conversation with John Knox MacArthur. It seemed funny to her that she always, even in her own mind, thought of him as John Knox MacArthur instead of simply John or even MacArthur.

His persona somehow seemed to demand his full name. She couldn't imagine that as a child his friends might have called him Johnny. In fact, it was hard to imagine he had been a child or had had friends.

So she was curious about the animated conversation he was having with Professor Greenburg, and as soon as she went to her office and locked her handbag in the bottom drawer of the desk, she grabbed her teapot and cup and headed for the faculty lounge. She puttered in the background making tea and listened to what they were saying.

"I still maintain the loss of Justice Scalia was the worst blow to the US Supreme Court in at least a hundred years, Warner. Whatever you may think of his views on originalism with regard to the Constitution, you can hardly fault him for his rhetoric."

"I don't deny his rhetoric was sometimes superficially clever, but I think he was a blight on the legal profession and more particularly a bad influence on lawyers as well as law students."

"How can you say that? His use of language invariably set a high standard."

"He may have set a high standard for sarcasm and personal attacks, but his biting gibes were hardly an admirable example. I was talking with one of our legal writing professors a few days ago, and she said she knew her students had been negatively influenced by Scalia's writing when they turned in papers laced with derision and ad hominem barbs."

"Of course, you know what I think of legal writing

professors. They're a worthless add-on to the faculty who have nothing of substance to teach."

"There's no point in our having that disagreement again, John. If all we lawyers have to work with is words, what is more important than teaching law students how to use words well?"

"But you've admitted Scalia used words well."

"I've said his rhetoric was sometimes clever. That is not the same thing as using words well. The way he used language all too often amounted to nothing more than nastiness, and thus it became merely a crutch for his inability to use reason or legal precedent to support a cogent argument."

"Nonetheless, Scalia's legal opinions are clearly persuasive, Warner. Isn't that obvious from the very fact that students emulate him?"

"Law students are by definition unseasoned, and the way Scalia manipulated words seasoned them in all the wrong ways. They may find his truculent style amusing, but they receive the wrong message when they see mockery as legal argument. Instead of showing respect for his judicial colleagues, Scalia referred to their rationale with words like gobbledygook and nonsense. He reveled in his own turn of phrase, and his attitude, like his legal theory, had a negative effect on the legal profession."

"Maybe you should be a bit more tolerant of Scalia, like Ruth Bader Ginsburg."

"You've got me there. Other than their mutual admiration for opera, I'm totally mystified by that friendship. I have no idea how a brilliant logician like Ginsburg could have tolerated a bombastic Machiavelli like Scalia."

MacArthur picked up his coffee cup and, typically, had the last word. "Well then, I suppose we shall just have to be like them and agree to disagree."

When the door closed, Clara sat down with her tea. "So do you agree to disagree, Professor Greenburg?"

He laughed. "No, I wouldn't even agree with him to that degree. I just allow him to have the last word. He has impeccable timing with his exit from the stage, and it doesn't seem worth the effort to demolish the man when he's already so diminished."

"I gather you're not bosom buddies then?"

"Hardly. I doubt that I'd even say we're friendly enemies, as I might have said in the past. That ended a couple of years ago when one of our colleagues retired. Sitting in that exact same spot, John said, 'Alas, it's truly a sad day. My very last WASP colleague is leaving us.' He didn't even realize how offensive the comment was to me personally, as well as to the world at large."

"So even if you're not a WASP, do you think he'll lament you as his last white male colleague on the faculty?"

"The good news is, it won't happen that way. He'll go before I will. I may look older than John because of my white beard, but in fact, I'm two years younger."

"That's a lovely thought, professor. I hope I'll still be around to see him go."

"I hope so, too. You might even be around long enough to retire from the faculty yourself. Some of our adjuncts have become permanent members of the faculty."

"If nothing else, this taste of teaching will help me decide if this is the career I want for myself."

"I'm a great believer in doing what you really want to do in life. I've been fortunate in that respect."

"That's refreshing to hear. I don't know many people who can say that."

He looked a trifle shy as he said, "I guess it's the Mr. Chips in me."

ოჩლა

Clara realized she'd been sidetracked by the conversation, but even so she didn't think any additional information was wasted, even if it turned out to be irrelevant to her primary purpose. She was reminded, however, that she needed to update Travis on her progress. She called him on her cell phone to report everything she'd learned about various faculty members during her lunch with Lyle.

She focused on the ones who seemed closest to Vivian, but she included the others as well. Travis had often told her not to leave out seemingly irrelevant details. "You never know when one of them might trigger the solution to the crime. Why don't you come over this weekend, and we can go over everything we have so far? Jo Anne said she'd fix us an old-fashioned Sunday dinner like my mother used to make."

"That sounds good. I always enjoy Jo Anne's cooking."

And it was also comfortable to be in a home where she felt so safe, considering that lately she'd been feeling on edge.

Chapter 12

Possibilities

Clara had a productive week as she prepared for her class, but she was running out of ideas for ferreting out information for Travis. She figured it was just as well, probably, as she gave more thought to her Saturday date with Greg. For her, it couldn't come soon enough.

Friday night, he called to make sure of the plans for the next night. He sounded tired, but assured her he'd be up for a festive evening at the formal dinner for the new judges.

It suddenly hit Clara—the pressure was on. Greg had mentioned he hadn't had many dates since his wife died. That also meant he might not have taken a date to the annual judges' dinner since that time. Clara knew very little about his wife, but she couldn't help wondering if Greg's colleagues would be comparing her to his wife. Would she measure up? Did she have to? It was only a date, for heaven's sake, so why was she agonizing?

At least the new judges probably wouldn't have known his wife. Good grief, how much could she overreact about a simple date? Maybe he hadn't even gone to the dinner for years since his wife had been ill. Could she possibly think of more ways to feel insecure?

But she couldn't help it. She had had too many years with her father pointing out all of her flaws in excruciating detail. She had to try to be perfect, knowing full well it was impossible to be perfect.

So naturally, she spent most of the next day trying to look perfect. First, she manicured her nails, shaping them to be tapered and feminine, but not claw like. She chose a subtle natural shade of nail polish that blended with her skin tone. She did deep breathing exercises as she relaxed on her balcony while her nails dried.

The big question, of course, was what to wear. In the back corner of her large walk-in closet, she still had several formal gowns from the days when she and her second husband Jon used to attend opening nights at the symphony and the ballet. The slinky black one looked great, but maybe it was too much (or too little, since it showed a tad of cleavage).

After weighing pros and cons of several gowns, she finally decided on a silk one in a muted print with varying shades of earth tones, primarily burnt sienna accented with gold. She was pleased to find she still had the comfortable mid-heel gold satin pumps and matching bag she had bought to go with the gown. She hadn't worn spike heels for years, since she'd observed the damage they had done to her mother's feet by the time she was forty. The shoes were only a little out of style, but what would a bunch of old judges know? Her long gown would hide most of her shoes anyway.

She allowed herself one more minute in the shower than usual. After drying off, she applied a spritz of the light but expensive perfume her most recent former boyfriend had given her when his medical work had once again trumped their date. She held up the gown in front of a full-length mirror and felt pretty confident about the overall look. The gown went well with her auburn hair, which she wore simply and softly to frame her face.

Her face: she spent nearly an hour applying make-up that she intended to make her look as if she was not wearing make-up. The final touch was her jewelry. Two small gold butterflies fluttered from her earlobes, and a slightly larger one hung from a well-wrought Italian gold chain around her neck. Three small multi-colored jewels comprised the segments of the butterfly's body. Her second husband had bought the jewelry for her on the Rialto in Venice on their first wedding anniversary.

Her first husband Steve hadn't had the means to give her expensive gifts, but the ones he gave her were always thoughtful. She put one of them, a lovely monogrammed Irish linen handkerchief, in her evening bag. He'd given it to her after she had once mentioned that she'd always carried one since the days her Southern mother had said, "A lady always carries a freshly laundered handkerchief."

She thought about her two husbands and how happy she had been with each of them, in quite different ways. Steve had been her young love, her hope for a long future together, building a family together, neither of which had materialized after he was murdered by two thugs.

Jon had been her mature love, opening a world of travel to her and giving her a world of thoughtful gifts she would never have had with Steve. Above all, Jon had given her a fine stepson, as well as his own caring and companionship beyond her greatest expectations.

As she thought of them, she wondered about Greg's wife. He had spoken fondly of her, but it was typically difficult to fully understand anyone else's relationships. That thought, of course, led her to Vivian's relationships—Vivian and Peter, Vivian and Lyle. Should she include Vivian and Paula, Vivian and MacArthur, anyone else? Relationships, after all, aren't only romantic relationships.

She was still mulling that over as she applied her finishing touches and looked at herself again in the full-length mirror. She was pleasantly surprised by the glamorous woman looking back at her. Even if she wasn't the fairest of them all, she thought she'd be able to hold her own.

She retrieved the gold lamé wrap from the back of the coat closet and couldn't think of anything else to do in the next half hour before Greg was due to pick her up. She put the wrap around her shoulders and, through the open balcony door, watched the fog roll in and erase the Golden Gate Bridge. She drew the wrap tighter, still a trifle chilly, but it was a good feeling. Looking out at the city view below her, she knew she was where she wanted to be.

When the bell rang, she answered and said she'd be right down. She was dazzled when she saw him waiting for her, resplendent in his tux. Before she could say anything, he said simply, "Wow."

"I might say the same for you," she said.

"A woman's best accessory is a well-dressed man."

"Then you certainly fill the bill."

"I wasn't quite sure. I've worn this thing about once a year for the past decade. I didn't know if I'd still pass muster."

The evening was elegant in every way. They arrived at the Palace Hotel to be greeted by a uniformed man who parked the car and a doorman who directed them to go past the opulent Garden Court Restaurant to a small banquet room upstairs. When they passed a large mirror, Greg paused a moment and said, "Pretty good-looking couple, don't you think?"

Clara smiled.

As they continued walking, they talked about the glorious history of the hotel, including the destruction by fire following the 1906 earthquake.

"You remember the story about Enrico Caruso, don't you?" Greg commented. "He had appeared as Don Jose in *Carmen* just a few hours before the earthquake struck. It was rumored he checked in with forty pairs of boots and checked out wearing only a bath towel."

"But did you ever read his own version of the story? He wrote a first-hand account that was published later, saying he was sleeping in a room on the fifth floor when he was awakened by the shaking of his bed about five a.m. His valet gave him some clothes, and after he dressed, they managed to get a cart that took them and his many trunks to the Oakland Ferry. He said he was frightened but did not lose his head and certainly was not half crazy with fear as some rumors had reported."

"The truth may lie somewhere in between, although we'll never know for sure. But we do know he immediately took a train for New York and vowed never to return to San Francisco."

"And he didn't, which was his loss, of course. It was only three years after the earthquake that the hotel was rebuilt, grander than ever."

When they entered the ballroom, they were greeted with champagne and hors d'oeuvres, followed by a gourmet dinner without a rubber chicken in sight. The fine food was matched by excellent service. As the crowning touch, Clara especially liked the chocolate mousse dessert.

Mingling with the other guests was pleasant as well. During the social hour at the beginning, Greg ushered Clara around the room, introduced her, and participated in pleasant but lightweight conversations. She enjoyed the ambiance, and commented, "You're pretty good at this small talk stuff."

"It goes with the territory. It isn't the conversation that matters in a situation like this. You can hardly be expected to work out a plan for world peace with a glass of champagne in your hand. But it gives us all a chance to renew old acquaintances and make new ones. We don't have much time to socialize when we're working."

Once in a while, Clara caught glances from other women that roused her curiosity. Were they wondering who she was, sizing her up, or did they just happen to be glancing in her direction? Sometimes she thought she caught a glance from her to Greg and back again, particularly from one attractive female judge who wasn't wearing a wedding ring. In addition to the judges, most of whom were accompanied by their spouses, other guests included some of the court personnel. She couldn't help thinking there might be some women present who were considerably less than thrilled to see the court's most eligible man with a new date.

Clara had also been wondering about the extravagance of the occasion, considering her awareness of how tight the current budget was for the judiciary at all levels in California. A brief speech before dinner by the presiding judge of the San Francisco Superior Court explained. She was a regal-looking African-American woman, wearing a plum-colored gown with a matching swirl of feathers in her hair.

"We especially want to welcome our new judges this evening, and we'll introduce each one after you've had some more substantial food, but we also want to welcome our friends and guests now. If you haven't attended this annual function before, I want you to know that it's possible only because of a generous benefactor who will not allow us to identify her. There's no way we could pay for this out of our already stretched budget. We'll have a few more words to say about that later, but now on with the dinner."

During dinner, Clara and Greg chatted with their fellow guests who were close enough for conversation, but they also enjoyed each other's company. Although Clara had been to comparable functions with both of her late husbands, she couldn't recall ever having enjoyed herself more at a formal dinner. She was reminded once again how glad she was to be part of the legal profession.

The after-dinner speeches might have been long by some measures, but Clara was fascinated. She not only got to know who the new judges were but also much information about the current state of the courts. One thing she already knew was that practically every judge there made less money than he or she would have made in private practice.

One reason there were new judges every year was that some left the bench because they couldn't sustain their preferred lifestyle on a judge's salary. She knew of at least a couple of judges who had others dependent on them and therefore needed the more lucrative income of the private sector.

The ones who stayed on showed a sense of dedication that was extraordinary in the legal profession. She couldn't help wondering if she might have had hopes of becoming a judge if she had started sooner in her legal education. As it was, she felt that by the time she had enough experience to be a good judge, she'd be almost old enough to retire.

It was nearly eleven by the time the festivities ended, and Greg drove Clara home. She was wondering if she should invite him up when he said, "It's getting pretty late. I forgot to ask you out again, and I guess I was presumptuous thinking you'd be free the whole weekend.

Can we get together tomorrow? Would you be interested in the J.M.W. Turner exhibit at the de Young Museum?"

"Yes, I'd love to see it, but I can't tomorrow. I have plans with friends."

"Can you make it next Saturday then?"

"Sure. How about a picnic? I can bring a loaf of bread, and you can bring a jug of wine."

"It's a deal. As long as you also bring thou."

He was counting on her smile and followed it with a kiss. "Mmm, nice," he said. "Chocolate mousse."

She smiled again before turning to go inside.

⌥⌥⌥

Sunday dinner with the Travises was as enjoyable as the other meals she'd had with them. Clara never quite got used to hearing Jo Anne call him Roy, let alone the various endearments she used for him. Travis was a different person at home, not a grizzly but instead a big teddy bear.

Clara had gotten used to the gentle German shepherd named Molly who politely followed Jo Anne around and remained at her feet when she was sitting. Clara had teased Travis once about Molly's obvious preference for Jo Anne, and he said it was only natural since Jo Anne was the one who fed and walked her all the time.

But one incident had told her there was more to Molly than met the eye. Once Clara had been sitting at the dining table with them when the doorbell rang. She heard a low growl and saw Molly bare her teeth, poised in a position ready to lunge. Jo Anne gave her a quiet command, and Molly completely relaxed, but still followed Jo Anne when she went to answer the door and sign for a package delivery she was expecting.

When Jo Anne rejoined them, they talked for a while

about the value of a protective dog, and Travis said he knew he could find a good one for Clara. She had always wanted a dog, ever since her father had denied her any kind of pet as a child, but the time had never seemed right. She was tempted, but she still believed her desire for travel and having complete freedom to come and go as she pleased indicated she was better off without the responsibility of a dog.

Today, as usual, Molly was placidly in her place by Jo Anne under the table. The food was excellent, but Travis complained good naturedly, "This isn't quite like my mom's Sunday dinners in Oklahoma. She'd send my sister and me off to church while she cooked. It was years later I found out Mom stayed home because she didn't like the fire and brimstone sermons. She sent us because she wanted us Bible Belt kids to learn Bible stories so we wouldn't feel left out around all the church-going folk. But she was never really religious."

"Is that why you're not religious, Travis?"

"Partly, but I didn't like the sermons either and thought a lot of the Bible stories were silly or worse. I especially disliked that story about God asking Abraham to sacrifice his son. What really clinched it, though, was being a cop. I've seen too much bad stuff to believe there's a compassionate deity up there somewhere watching over us. But I always loved Sundays after church and especially appreciated my mom's fried chicken. It was the best meal of the week, when our other meals were often skimpy after my so-called father left her."

Jo Anne interjected, "Unlike his mother's chicken, however, *my* chicken is skinless breasts simmered in a low-fat wine sauce. Roy's cardiologist would never approve of fried chicken."

"He'd also probably disapprove of your delicious mashed potatoes," Travis said.

Jo Anne pretended to whisper to Clara. "Don't tell Roy, but they're healthy, too—my own secret method. He wouldn't like them if he knew they're low-fat."

"Aargh, it's a conspiracy, like the sides of nice fresh veggies and fruit for dessert," said Travis. "Even my mom made apple pie for dessert. I picked the apples right off the trees."

"There's nothing wrong with the apples. It's the pie that's the forbidden fruit," Jo Anne said.

"Okay, okay I give up. I have to admit, dinner was outstanding, even if it was on the healthy side."

"I have to do something to counteract all the junk you eat when you're on the job. I don't want you known as the Donut Detective. Now you and Clara go sit and talk while I clean up. I'm dying to hear all about the case, and I can listen to every word from the kitchen."

"No, please let me help," said Clara.

"I wouldn't dream of it. Roy usually does his share, but I'm letting him off the hook because I'd much rather hear how you two are putting the case together." Jo Anne admitted she had already heard Travis's view of the case, but she was eager to hear Clara's take on it and how they played off each other with their theories.

Travis sank into his leather recliner, and Clara sat opposite him on the sofa. Then despite the comfortable chair, he leaned forward. "You start off, Clara, and I'll fill in as we go along. How do you see the case shaping up from your angle?"

"I've identified some moderately suspicious links between people at the law school and Vivian, but frankly I'm not sure if what I've learned shows any motive strong enough for murder."

"What about the two weirdos who came to your office?"

"They really may be the most likely suspects if for

no other reason than their unpredictability. Gretchen Miller has had her ups and downs with drugs. So she might be capable of anything. Have you investigated her?"

"Yeah, right after she came to your office we thought she was definitely worth a look. I had one of our female officers interview her, and she took the social worker, Vanessa Delgado, with her."

"How did it go?"

"She was very hostile. She ranted and raved about her baby being taken away from her, and she blamed the social worker, the judge, the foster parents, Vivian, and everybody else but herself. She said they stole her baby's identity by changing her name and claimed that was a crime."

"Did she have an alibi for the time of the murder?"

"Not only did she *not* have an alibi, she couldn't even tell us where she was that night. She kept saying stuff like, 'I musta been at' so-and-so, or 'I musta been with' so-and-so. She couldn't give any real account for her whereabouts at the relevant time."

"Do you think she was smart enough to get into the faculty office building late at night and strong enough to dispose of the body?"

"She'd been to Vivian's office before, so she at least knew the layout of the campus. As far as strength to carry off the body, she's thin but wiry and a little above average height for a woman. And I've seen some people on drugs do superhuman stuff."

"But wouldn't she have needed a car to get the body to Fort Point?"

"Her boyfriend had an old beat-up van that she used to drive sometimes. So that's a possibility."

"Is there anything else that points the finger at her?"

"In a sense, she may have the strongest motive of anybody we've talked to. The social worker said in her experience, mothers who lose their children can be obsessively malicious. She has fairly often heard of threatening behavior by mothers who lose their children, and she knew of one who even attacked a fellow social worker with a knife."

"That sounds ominous."

The clinking of dishes stopped for a moment, and from the kitchen, Jo Anne said, "Mother lions will fight to the death for their cubs. What are you doing to follow up, Roy?"

"We don't have the manpower to watch her all the time, but we're keeping an eye on her as much as we can. The most suspicious thing we've seen is her hanging around in front of the courthouse where the hearings took place. She hasn't tried to go in, though, and it's hard to say whether she might commit a crime. We might be able to catch her using or making a connection for drugs sometime, but I doubt whether arresting her right now would be a good idea. If anything, it might provoke her to do something drastic."

"Do you think she'd try to do anything about her child?" Clara asked.

"The address of the foster parents has been kept confidential. We plan to keep it that way. And you'll let us know if you see any signs of her around campus."

"Of course, and the same goes for Richard Piper. Have you had any luck locating him?"

"Unfortunately, no. I did dispatch a patrol car in the vicinity of the campus after he paid you a little visit, but we saw no traces of him."

"After I asked you not to, of course."

"Sometimes I get to make the calls, Clara. I'm the cop, remember?"

"I stand corrected. Anyway, do you think he'll be back?"

"There's no way to tell, but I wouldn't be surprised. The very fact he went to your office suggests he's a loose cannon, and he probably doesn't have much of a handle on reality. After checking the neighborhood, the officers in the patrol car paid a visit to the campus security guard and gave him a description."

"Did you connect it with his visit to my office?"

"No, I didn't think we should give the security guard any reason to think you might be doing anything with the police.

"Are you even suspicious of the security guard?"

Travis put on a rather bad French accent and said, "I suspect everyone, and I suspect no one."

Clara laughed. "That's the worst Clouseau imitation I've ever heard, Travis."

"What do you expect from an old Okie?"

"Okay, not bad for an Okie, if you'll forgive the pun."

"That's not even good enough to call it a pun."

"Cut it out, you two. You sound like a couple of kids," said Jo Anne. "I want to hear more about the case."

"Yes, ma'am," Travis said. "Back to work."

"So where are we on Piper?" Clara asked.

"More or less back to square one. We don't know where he is or when he might turn up, let alone what he might've been doing the night Vivian was killed. So what about the professors? You've told me what you learned from various sources, but how would you evaluate their possible motives for murder?"

"I can't say any of them have strong motives from what I know at this point. But you mentioned before you thought the killing was most likely a spur of the moment thing. A lot of people can lose it for an instant, do something violent, and then regret it in the next instant. It may be far-fetched, but that could apply to Lyle, Paula, or MacArthur."

"Take them one by one. How could it have happened with Lyle?"

"He's the one I think is the weakest suspect, because I believe he genuinely loved her. But they did have a few heated arguments, and we all know the potential downside of unfulfilled love. It's conceivable he could've become very angry, for example, if she might have said she'd never marry him, no matter what. So I guess it's possible he could've picked up a hammer that happened to be in front of him and hit her with it. It seems pretty improbable to me, though."

"What about Paula Kelley then?"

"I'd say about the same for her, or maybe even less of a motive than Lyle. First of all, we don't know for sure that she had a romantic interest in Vivian. Even if she did, she might not have much trouble accepting that a heterosexual like Vivian wouldn't return her love. That must happen to gay people now and then."

"Do you think she'd be capable of losing her temper enough to strike out, even a momentary impulse?"

"The only signs of anger I've seen in Paula are against men. I can't imagine her wanting to hurt a woman, especially Vivian, despite the old saying that we always hurt the ones we love."

"What do you think of her character overall?"

"She's one of the most principled people I've ever known. She's adamant in her opposition to the death penalty, she's against police profiling, and she's a supporter of almost all of the high ideals I hold dear. Maybe her solid values have made me a little biased, but I do think her compassion for others is sincere."

"That aside, do you think she'd be capable of getting the body to Fort Point."

"I have to admit that, yes I think she would. She's a large woman and a good athlete. She's a tough tennis player, which seems to have developed the upper body strength most women lack. There's one other thing that bothers me a little, but I don't want you to make too much of it."

"What's that?"

"In one of our conversations, she showed a substantial familiarity with Hitchcock films. I'm not sure she mentioned *Vertigo,* but she was definitely familiar with several of Hitch's films. You can hardly fault her for that, though, because I may know more about them than most people do."

"Don't worry. I know all those films, too, but not the way you do. I like them because they're well-made and just plain fun, but there isn't much positive police work in most of them. I think my favorite is *Dial M for Murder.* For once, the Chief Inspector solved the crime."

Jo Anne came into the living room wiping her hands on her apron and sat by Clara. "Would you two stop digressing? Which of the professors do you think is the most likely suspect, Clara?"

"If I had my druthers, it would certainly be MacArthur, if for no other reason than convicting him would be a nice way to eliminate him from the faculty."

"What do you think of his motive? Roy told me about his exploiting poor Vivian to do all the work on his book."

"Aside from my bias against him for his other negative qualities, I think he has the strongest motive of any of the faculty members, so far as I know anyway. It's not hard to picture him showing up in Vivian's office, confronting her about quitting her work on the book, and getting angry enough to pick up a hammer and deliver the fatal blow."

"I might be able to buy that, but the problem, of course, is proof," Travis said.

"Do we even know if he has an alibi?" Clara asked.

"I'm ahead of you there. I've done a lot more work on this than you know about. We've questioned every faculty member, as well as a lot of staff and other people connected with the law school. We always tell them it's a routine question to ask where they were at the relevant time of the crime, which of course it is."

"So how do they stack up?"

"Except for a couple of faculty members who were out of town and one who was at a late movie, all the rest claimed to be at home reading, watching television, or sleeping. Paula said she was reading the autobiography of Justice Sonia Sotomayor, Lyle was watching a rerun of *Guess Who's Coming to Dinner* on Turner Classic Movies, and MacArthur said he was sleeping, although not in the same bedroom as his wife."

"That's suspicious right there," Jo Anne said with a wicked wink. "What about Vivian's former boyfriend? You were focused on him for a while, Roy."

"You can't necessarily pin a murder on a guy because he's a jerk. So far as I can tell, that's Susskind's main contribution to this scenario."

"Does he have an alibi?" Clara asked.

"Sort of, though not conclusive. He claimed to have been out with a woman who's a secretary at another law firm, and, of course, we checked with her. She said she came back to his place, but they'd been drinking, and she was fuzzy on the time. He swears he took her home after one a.m., but she didn't absolutely confirm that. She said she thought it was at least after midnight, but from the way she described it, the time could've been early enough for him to get to BASL and kill Vivian."

"What do you think?"

"I think it might've been possible, but I also believe the woman who was his alibi was telling the truth, at least about being with him. I doubt that he would've gone straight to kill Vivian right after that."

"So are we left with nothing concrete?" said Clara. "What else have you been investigating, Travis?"

"We've been going back to everything since Vivian arrived in California. Even though we haven't turned up anything new on Peter Susskind, he'll stay on our list till we find some reason to exclude him. We've questioned some of her law school friends and professors, including Murdoch and a couple of others who seemed to have known her pretty well. One of the younger professors apparently asked her out after she was no longer his student, but she didn't accept the date, and he had moved on to the Yale faculty by the time of the murder."

"So that's it for now?" asked Clara.

"Seems to be. We'll keep probing, but the leads seem to be thinning out."

"Where do we go from here?"

"Maybe we need to think outside the box a little," said Travis. "One thing that's bothered me all along is why dump the body at Fort Point? I don't buy a Hitchcock connection. That seems too pat."

"Maybe we should revisit the spot. It might inspire us to think of something."

"Great idea," said Jo Anne. "We need to get some fresh air anyway."

Before they could say anything, she was getting jackets for herself and Travis and asking if Clara had one.

"I always keep a jacket in my car, even in August, which is handy since it's always windy at Fort Point."

Clara took the lead in her car, and Travis and Jo Anne followed in theirs. When they arrived at the Fort

Point parking lot, Clara joked, "Did you have any trouble following me, detective?"

The mood turned somber as they approached the spot where Vivian's body had been found. There were no signs of anything unusual, of course, just waves splashing up against the rocks. They milled around for a while, and along the shoulder of the road Jo Anne picked a couple of wildflowers that she tossed on the rocks.

To break the melancholy mood, they went into the fort and climbed to the top for a panoramic view of the bay. As always, it was windy but exhilarating. The Golden Gate Bridge rose majestically above, with the rolling coastal hills of the Marin Headlands beyond. To the right were Angel Island, Alcatraz, and the Bay Bridge, then the fabulous city and on around the bay and back to the Golden Gate Bridge again. After walking on the parapet, they roamed through some of the exhibit rooms and then sat on a bench and talked.

"Did either of you have any sudden revelations?" Clara asked.

Travis replied, "I guess I can't say the rocks spoke to me. But it was different being here this time without all the hoopla of the crime scene investigators and the coroner. I can't say exactly how, but it was different."

"For me, too," said Clara, "but for other reasons. I had been here several times before Vivian's murder, and it used to be one of my favorite places. I still think it's a special place, but I'll never again think of it as where Kim Novak went into the bay in *Vertigo*. I'm sure now I'll always think of it as where someone callously left Vivian Hall. I hope we find out who."

෴

All the way home, Clara could think of nothing but Vivian on the rocks with the surf pounding her fragile body. She could not imagine how anyone could do that to another human being. What could a gentle soul like Vivian ever have done to provoke such an act?

As soon as the thought struck her, she was repelled by it. She should know better than to blame the victim in any way. Whatever prompted the murder, Vivian was in no way to blame.

Clara was looking forward to a relaxing evening with a good book. Instead, when she got home, she discovered a frantic voicemail message. The voice sounded fearful. "Clara this is Amy, Kristen's foster mom. I'm really scared because I think we saw Gretchen near the park today. I've tried to call the social worker, but I couldn't reach her. I'm not sure if this falls in the category of your job of protecting Kristen's legal interests, but I thought you should know, too. Please call me."

She immediately called Amy, who picked up after the first ring but said nothing.

"Are you there, Amy? This is Clara Quillen."

"Thank you so much for calling back. I really don't know what to do. I tried calling Vanessa Delgado. You probably remember she's the social worker still assigned to Kristen, but on a Sunday I didn't get through to her on her cell phone. I got a message that her voicemail was all filled up."

Amy was speaking quickly but deliberately. She seemed anxious but in control.

"Tell me what happened, Amy."

"My husband and I were at the park with Kristen. It's the one about two blocks from here. You may have noticed it when you came for your visit. We saw a woman across the park, mostly behind a tree, and we both think it was Gretchen."

"What did she do?"

"I saw her first, and when I told my husband, he looked in her direction, and she pulled back behind the tree. We told Kristen it was time to go home, and at first, she resisted a little. She was having a good time in the sandbox, playing with another little girl. We promised her a treat, and my husband picked her up, and we headed straight for home."

"Did you see Gretchen anymore?"

"We think she followed us for almost a block as we went out of the park, but we didn't see her again when we got to a more open space and walked on home."

"How sure are you it was Gretchen?"

"I know I said I thought we saw her, but I really don't have any doubt it was her."

"Have you ever seen her before in your neighborhood?"

"No, the only time we've seen her was for her visits at Family & Children's Services and at the last hearing in court. Our address was never released to her, but I guess she could've followed us. A few times I saw her get into her boyfriend's old beat-up van after the visits. I never thought of looking to see if she might be following us."

"From what you tell me, it sounds as if we should get a restraining order against her. Even though her past threats have been a little vague, that along with the likelihood she now knows where you live will probably be enough to issue the order."

"Will it do any good?"

"I have to be honest with you. A restraining order would make it possible for her to know she cannot legally get too close to you, but it wouldn't necessarily keep her from trying. But at least it would give you some legal protection."

"I guess it's better than nothing. What should I do to get the order?"

"Let me check with your social worker. Since it's Sunday, we may not be able to do anything until tomorrow anyway. So, for now, just stay home where it's safe with Kristen."

"Sure, I planned to do that anyway. Please let me know as soon as you know anything."

"I will. Meanwhile, try to relax and enjoy your family."

As soon as she ended the call, Clara tried calling the social worker but got the same message about her voicemail being full. So she sent an email marked urgent with the essence of what Amy had told her and asked the social worker to call as soon as possible.

Two hours later, she called. "Hi, Clara, it's Vanessa Delgado. I'm sorry I didn't get back to you sooner, but I just now checked my email. I can't say I'm completely surprised Gretchen has popped up again. She's the kind who might easily pose a kidnap threat."

"I thought so, too. What do you think about getting a restraining order?"

"It's worth a try and about all we can do at this point. But you know as well as I do restraining orders aren't always effectual. If Gretchen is determined, she won't stop trying. Amy and her husband are really Kristen's best protection, of course. I have a lot of faith in them. They're level-headed people."

"So do you want me to help Amy with the restraining order?"

"No, I can handle it pretty easily. This isn't that unusual for our department, and we can usually help foster parents instigate an expedited temporary restraining order. Then I can help Amy follow through with the rest of the process for a permanent restraining order. I'll give her a call right now and do what I can to put her mind at ease."

"Thanks, and let me know if you need anything from me. I want to make sure Kristen stays safe."

Funny how a fundamental concept like being safe now had so many nuances.

Chapter 13

Suspicious Shifts

It seemed like a very long wait until her date with Greg the next Saturday. She was glad her class would be starting this week, meeting on Monday and Wednesday afternoons.

For her first class, she wore the true-blue skirt suit that she'd worn when she argued and won a case in the California Court of Appeal earlier in the year. She thought it would bode well to model proper courtroom attire for her students. She posted her office hours as one hour before and one after her classes and also by appointment as needed. She bought a bouquet of fresh flowers and put them in a Waterford crystal vase on the corner of her desk.

Naturally, she was more than prepared to teach her class. She had always been that way. It wasn't entirely her penchant for being conscientious, however, but more that she didn't want to be blindsided by the unexpected.

As it turned out, she wasn't blindsided during class but afterward.

Her class went very well, as she'd hoped. She felt

good about the rapport she'd established with the students as well as the content of the subject matter. Several students lingered to ask her good questions after class, and one said she'd like to talk further with Clara about the work she told them she was doing in her appellate case. She was glad for her interest and looked forward to discussing it with her, without giving the student any confidential information, of course.

For the drive home, Clara switched from her medium heel pumps to low heel shoes and changed from her suit jacket to a light blue cardigan. She was hungry after being on her feet for two hours teaching and thought about a place to eat on her way home.

She headed home via San Jose Avenue, Guerrero Street, and Gough Street. She decided against Mexican food in the Mission District because she'd recently had a Mexican lunch with Lyle. This would be a good opportunity to go back to the Zuni Café just off Gough at Market. She loved the innovative menu and tried something different every time she went there.

She parked on a side street a couple of blocks from the restaurant, but this time she was disappointed. She'd forgotten Zuni was closed on Mondays. So she walked a few blocks more to Hayes Street Grill and had a delicious dinner of Half Moon Bay Petrale Sole with King Trumpet Mushrooms. She had never felt uncomfortable when she had to eat alone in a restaurant, and she didn't bother to read a book but focused on savoring her food. For a long time now she'd been reminding herself to live in the moment, and this was one time she felt she was doing just that.

She was walking back to her car when she saw him. Richard Piper was wearing the same dark gray hoodie he'd been wearing when he came into her office the week before, and if anything, his eyes looked even more sunken, and his clothes were ragged.

At first, she couldn't be sure it was Piper. He was across the street in front of Davies Symphony Hall, leaning against a lamppost. She kept glancing over her shoulder, and he seemed to be following her. She quickened her pace, and he did the same. At one point, she looked back and didn't see him. She breathed a little sigh of relief, but the next time she looked, she saw him step out of a doorway.

She ducked into a Walgreens drug store and wandered around the aisles. She didn't see Piper anywhere, but when she came out she saw him again across the street. Should she call Travis? After all, Piper hadn't done anything threatening. But was his mere presence threatening?

As she walked another half block farther, she was worried about the side street where she'd parked. Travis had always told her to call if she ever felt uneasy, even if she didn't think she had a strong reason. He said he knew her well enough that if she felt anxious, it was worth checking out, and he'd far rather be safe than sorry. Besides, she knew Travis had tried to find Piper, and this might be his chance.

Having justified it in her own mind, she called him as she continued to walk. Luckily, Travis picked up right away. He asked her exact location and what she was wearing. He told her to keep walking down Gough on the east side of the street. By the end of the block, over her shoulder she saw a black-and-white coming down the street behind her.

The police car stopped by a fire hydrant on the corner, waited, and then started up again, continuing the same pattern and keeping a consistent distance from her till she reached her car. The female officer who was driving stayed in the police car, and her partner got out and spoke to Clara. "Good evening, ma'am," he said. "We don't know exactly what's up, but dispatch described you and told us we were supposed to find you and follow you to your car. After you're safely on your way, we're supposed to try to find a guy who was following you. Can you give us a description?"

"Yes, but I'm not sure you'll have any luck. As soon as you drove up, he disappeared. I haven't seen him for two blocks." She described Piper and asked, "Did you see him anywhere?"

"No, ma'am, but we didn't know who to look for till you gave us his description."

"Of course. I wasn't sure if I was supposed to approach you or what."

"No, ma'am, we were told you'd keep walking, so you did the right thing. Do you want us to follow you home?"

Clara was so glad for the police presence she didn't even mind being called ma'am, which she hadn't heard much since she left the South.

"You don't need to follow me. The most important thing you can do is try to find him. If you have any luck, call in and ask for Detective Travis. He's been trying to locate a person of interest."

"Will do, ma'am. We'll watch out for you till you drive away."

Neither of the police officers, unfortunately, had seen the disheveled young man in the gray hoodie get into his rusty VW parked on another side street and head in the opposite direction.

&⁊&⁊

When Clara got home, she realized she was still

shaking. It seemed odd, considering that she hadn't actually been aware she was shaking. On her mailbox, she
found a note from her neighbor that said, *We have two
packages for you, Clara. M & M.*

"Hi, Clara," Marge said, as she opened the door.
"We haven't seen hide nor hair of you for days. You must
be keeping busy. You're just like my daughter. She's always busy. I don't know how she keeps up with her boys
and everything else. She's a real dynamo."

Marge barely took a breath, and Clara hoped she
wasn't too obvious when she interrupted her. "You have
packages for me?"

"Yes, they were too big for your mailbox. They
should be right here somewhere." Marge rummaged
through a pile of things on her entryway table. She came
up with a book-size padded package from Amazon and
large manila envelope about a half of an inch thick that
looked the worse for wear.

"Honestly, you have to wonder what the post office
does with these packages. This one is so beat up you can
barely read the address. I'm surprised it even got deliv-
ered. And the return address is completely torn off. It's
no wonder the postal service can't make ends meet. Honestly, it's a crying shame."

Clara murmured agreement and thanked Marge.

"Won't you come in for a glass of wine? You do
look like you've had a hard day," Marge said.

"In fact, I have, and as appealing as a glass of wine
sounds, I think a warm bath sounds even better."

"Of course. Have a nice night."

As Clara entered her home, she looked at the packages. She opened the one from Amazon and found the
new mystery she'd ordered. The other one, except for being mangled, looked innocuous enough. It bothered her
that she couldn't see any return address. With the torn

corner, she couldn't tell whether there had been one or not.

She was afraid to open it.

How had she reached this point—afraid to open her own mail? Was she completely paranoid?

Did she dare call Travis again? She knew he didn't even have any way to know for sure that she'd seen Richard Piper following her. But she had seen him—she had no doubt. Even knowing he trusted her judgment, she didn't want to look like the boy who cried wolf.

She set the envelope down on the granite kitchen counter and poured herself a glass of wine. She carried the envelope and the wine to the coffee table in her living room. After she had drunk half of the wine, she began to open the envelope with deliberate caution. Right away she saw it was from the court. The cover letter had a brief note saying that several pages had erroneously been omitted from the record in the case of *In re K.M., A Person Coming under the Juvenile Court Law*. These pages were to be inserted into the appropriate place in the record as indicated.

She was relieved both because the envelope was harmless and because she hadn't called Travis. She worried that she was becoming too dependent on him. It was always so comforting to have him to rely on, to know he would always be there for her, but she didn't like the feeling of losing her sense of self-reliance. At the same time, what would she have done if Richard Piper had tried to harm her?

She didn't want to think about it. She'd think about it tomorrow.

తితి

She went to bed early and started reading her new

mystery novel, which was not one of the scary ones she sometimes liked. Instead, it was a modern British cozy where everyone was upper crust, and you knew everything would turn out all right in the end, but it wouldn't be the butler who did it. About nine o'clock, she jumped when her phone rang, and she waited to let her voicemail screen the call. She picked up as soon as she heard Greg's voice.

"It's reassuring when you're pretty sure somebody is screening her calls and then she picks up right away. How was your first class?"

"Fine, I think. You'd have to ask the students. But I felt good about it."

"I didn't doubt it for a second."

"Before I forget, I want to take you up on your offer for my class to visit your courtroom. Do you think it's too soon if we do it next week?"

"No, the sooner, the better. Your academic instruction will be much more meaningful for them after they've seen a couple of real cases."

"My class meets Mondays and Wednesdays from three to five. Which would be better for you?"

"Either is all right, but let's make it for Wednesday. That'll make it closer to the following weekend before I whisk you away for a surprise."

She was taken aback and wondered what sort of surprise he had in store.

"I like surprises, but only when I know what they are."

He laughed. "Why doesn't that surprise me? It's nothing devious, and I promise, you'll like it. Trust me."

"I'll think about it. Meanwhile, are we still on for the Turner exhibit at the de Young this Saturday?"

"Of course. You promised me a picnic in the park."

"By the way, I already have some tickets for the

Turner exhibition because I have a membership there and the Legion of Honor." She didn't tell him she had a substantial contributing membership that gave her a lot of privileges because her second husband had been a generous benefactor. His legacy foundation, in which she was still actively involved, was a significant supporter of San Francisco's fine arts museums.

"Maybe we can go to the Legion on Sunday if you like. They have a four o'clock concert there."

"Yes, I'd like that. How's the rest of your week shaping up?"

"It's the usual grind, but it's always challenging. How about your week?"

"Other than the Wednesday class, I'll probably be working at home most of the time, preparing for class and working on my appeal. I can even work in my jammies if I want to."

"Hey, I can wear my jammies under my robe if I want to—so there."

She laughed. "That's a little hard to picture, but I think you'd look cute in Dr. Denton's."

"It's kind of warm for Dr. Denton's, even in San Francisco. Guess I'll stick to my jeans and polo shirts."

"That's much more dignified, Your Honor."

"Nobody ever accused me of being dignified."

"Do you get the feeling this conversation is getting a bit silly? I suspect we're both a little tired."

"I noticed that, too, but I like talking to you, whether we're silly or serious. So if you want to be serious, what did you think of the dissent in the last Supreme Court opinion that was released in June?"

"Now that is silly. Maybe both of us should think about getting some sleep."

"Okay, but only if you promise we can do this every night before we go to sleep."

Clara was stymied by that one. Much as she was enjoying Greg, part of her was scared. She didn't want to hold back, but at the same time, she was reluctant to go forward too fast.

"Hmm, 'Promises, Promises.' Wasn't that a song back in the sixties?"

"Hmm, nice digression…"

"It's about time. Goodnight, Greg."

"Goodnight, Clara. Sweet dreams."

❦❦❦

Her dreams were sweet—for a short while. But they were confusing, too, and then disturbing. At first, she was dancing with a man in a tux, and then it became three different men in turn, all in tuxes, and all wearing masks. The masks were rigid, and they scraped her face. The dance had been pleasant at the beginning, but as her partners shifted her from one to the other, the music became discordant, and the tempo grew faster and faster. The dance stopped abruptly as the clock stuck midnight.

But it wasn't midnight. When she woke, she saw the red numbers two-forty on her digital clock. Other numbers rolled by as she tossed and turned. The last numbers she recalled noticing were four-thirty-seven before she began to have different dreams. Those were not sweet at all. They were frightening. She felt wet and slimy, and her head was pounding.

She awoke again a little before seven and tried to remember the substance of her last dream. It was dark and foreboding, with long shadows as she walked down a wet street. The street became a road to a rocky edge of the bay.

She decided the only sensible thing was to laugh at herself. She had simply seen too many noir films. Maybe she should pull out her DVD of *The Sound of Music* to watch that night. Great, that's all she needed, Nazis. Maybe she could try *West Side Story.* Oh, yeah, street gangs. How about *Singin' in the Rain?* Now there's a cheery movie for you. Just thinking about it helped her get out of bed, have her coffee, and start her day.

But she was not cheered by the story on the next to the last page of the Bay Area section of the *Chronicle.* In essence, it said there had been no significant progress on the investigation regarding the death of Vivian Hall. Other than referring to it as a homicide, there was little information that had not been in the very first article. There were vague references to the police following up leads, but no real news.

She thought again about the possible motives of Vivian's BASL colleagues, as well as those of Gretchen Miller, Richard Piper, and Peter Susskind. Maybe it was none of them.

She thought about when Travis had first called her about the case and asked if she would like to do some snooping around some people connected to her old law school. At that point, her only connection with Vivian had been UC Berkeley law school. Had she been spinning her wheels trying to find something suspicious at BASL? Should she have been more diligent in considering UC Berkeley possibilities before she maneuvered herself into teaching at BASL?

She tried to divert herself with work. She was absorbed in a law review article about child abuse and sipping hot jasmine tea, still in her pajamas, when her phone rang. She saw it was Travis, and his first words created instant apprehension.

"I don't want to alarm you, Clara, but I have uncovered some information I think you'll want to know." His tone was ominous.

"I'm braced. What should I know?"

"It may be no big deal, but it looks like your judge went out with Vivian at least once."

Clara took a sip of tea and nearly choked on it. "My judge? You mean Greg? Tell me about it, Travis."

"After our discussion on Sunday, I decided I had to go back and interview some of the people I'd talked to before. Yesterday, I talked to Peter Susskind again and didn't make any more headway than before. Then I went over to Berkeley to poke around the law school again, but I didn't really pick up anything new. This morning, I got back to Marilyn Aiello, the roommate. She added something she hadn't thought to tell me before."

Clara could sense the reluctance in his voice and asked, "What did she say about Greg?"

"I'd asked her before if Vivian had been seeing anyone since Susskind. She told me she knew Vivian had been seeing someone from BASL, but he never came to pick her up at the apartment, and Vivian hadn't confided in her about him other than to mention his name was Lyle.

"So where did Greg come in to the conversation?"

"She said Vivian mentioned having lunch with Judge Hart the weekend before she was killed. It was either a Saturday or a Sunday. She couldn't remember which. Aiello didn't meet him because Vivian met him somewhere else instead of having him pick her up."

"Did she say anything else?"

"Nothing of significance. That's what I mean about maybe it's no big deal. She said they apparently had a long lunch, and when Vivian got back, she said it was very beneficial. She had waited till after her case was finished in the judge's court, then asked him if they could get together to talk about how she had handled it."

"He never mentioned it to me. That's what bothers me about it. Are you doing anything to check into it further?"

"We figure it won't hurt to check where he was at the time of the murder, if for no other reason than to rule him out. Keep in mind, we know absolutely nothing to make us think he could be a suspect. We're not aware of any possible motive he might have had. So I repeat, we're just checking things out—don't go thinking he might be a suspect."

She was already thinking exactly that. "Are you going to interview him?" She didn't want to use the word interrogate.

"Not yet. On the remote chance he might be a suspect, I don't want to alert him. I'm going to try to find out from other sources where he was from eleven to one o'clock that night. I have a couple of people helping me check things, so we should know something fairly soon."

Clara felt as if somebody had punched her in the pit of her stomach. She winced from the physical pain in her midsection but otherwise felt numb. She didn't know what to say.

"Are you still there, Clara?"

"Barely, but let me know what you find out. Remember me, your old pal Pandora? I always want to know what's in that damn box."

"I know, kid. I'm working as fast as I can, and I'll get back to you as soon as I can."

She clicked off the phone. Funny, she had always mocked those phone calls in the movies where people end a phone call without saying good-bye.

She sat stunned for a while and then realized her next sip of tea was cold. Next, she realized she was having a migraine. She saw a bright aura in front of her eyes, and she could no longer read the words on the page.

She hadn't had a migraine for ages, not since a little while after Jon died. She'd first thought it was eyestrain and asked her optometrist about it the next time she had her eyes checked. He told her it was probably a migraine and she should check with her doctor. When she described the symptoms to her doctor, he agreed it was a migraine, but said she was lucky she didn't have the excruciating pain many people suffer, only the bright aura and a mild headache. He said it could be caused by stress and recommended trying to reduce the stress instead of using medication.

Sure enough, she found that calming herself through yoga meditation relieved the symptoms, and gradually the migraines went away. She tried that now, sitting in lotus position and breathing deeply and rhythmically. In less than half an hour, the symptoms were gone, and she tried to go back to reading the article.

ᑖᑑᑖᑑᑖ

She had finally managed to engross herself in reading when the melodious ring of her phone interrupted. She had programmed the beginning of Bach's *Second Brandenburg Concerto* as her ringtone, with the naïve notion that it could not lead to a phone call that would bring bad news. She knew it was a silly notion anyway, yet as she thought of what news Travis might bring her, she was reluctant to pick up. But of course, like Pandora, she did.

It wasn't Travis.

"Hi, Clara, it's Vanessa Delgado. You remember, Kristen Miller's social worker?"

"Of course. I talked with Amy yesterday, and she said she hasn't seen any signs of Gretchen since the court issued the restraining order. I hope you're not calling to give me any bad news."

"I'm not sure what to call it, maybe good news or maybe bad news, depending on your point of view."

"What is it?"

"Gretchen Miller is dead—drug overdose."

"Now I understand why it was hard to say whether it was good news or bad news. Do you know what happened?"

"Only in a general way. I had a call about it late this morning. She was discovered in a homeless shelter in the Tenderloin. Apparently, the staff does a bed check every morning, and she seemed to be sleeping. When they couldn't wake her, they discovered she was dead."

"That's awful. How did they know to call you?"

"They ran a background check on her, and the juvenile dependency case came up. They weren't sure who to contact, but I was listed as the social worker, so they thought I'd know who her relatives might be. I gave them the information on her mother and sister in Oakland. They've been notified."

"I don't know what to say. It seems everything related to Gretchen's life is so sad. Have you told Amy about it?"

"Yes, I just got off the phone with her. I think she's still in shock. I told her you'd be calling to tell her the legal ramifications of the situation."

"Sure, I'll do that right away. Thanks for all you've done to help me in this case, Vanessa."

"I've enjoyed working with you. I guess my last duty will be to call county counsel so they can file a request for dismissal of Gretchen's appeal."

"Yes, do you think they'll file it promptly?"

"I'm sure of it. This is one case they'll be glad to see go away."

"I don't suppose we'll have much reason to be in touch any more now."

"We might wind up on another case together sometime. You never know."

After the call ended, the phrase "You never know" echoed in Clara's head. Now would she ever know whether Gretchen was the perpetrator in Vivian's death? Did Gretchen die with a guilty secret that no one would ever know?

As she tried to quell her thoughts, Clara called Amy.

"Hello," she said in a hollow voice.

"Amy, it's Clara Quillen. Vanessa told me she gave you the unsettling news about Gretchen."

"Yes, I'm still having trouble processing it. I'm completely shaken."

"I can imagine. You must be feeling very mixed emotions right now."

"Yes, and that's a huge understatement. Part of me feels guilty because I know I sometimes wished Gretchen would disappear, but I'd never have wished this on her. Sometimes I even fantasized that she might finally get her act together and we could establish a positive relationship when Kristen was older."

"At least now you don't have to worry about Kristen's safety."

"I'm grateful for that. I was beginning to look over my shoulder every time I went out."

"It may be a while before it sinks in, but I think you'll have a lot more peace of mind now."

"That's already beginning to happen. I guess this means the appeal is over, right?"

"Yes, all but the legal formalities. Now that the appellant is deceased, the appeal is moot, which means there's no way for it to continue. County counsel will file a request for dismissal and remand of the case back to the juvenile dependency court. As soon as that happens, the court will reinstate the final order regarding termination of parental rights and the order for the adoption to proceed. That can happen pretty quickly now."

"What a relief that'll be. It's wonderful to know Kristen is going to be our child now for sure. It's hard to base our happiness on Gretchen's misfortune, but I don't think I could be happier."

"Enjoy your happiness. Gretchen's misfortune was her own doing, and now you can go ahead with all the great plans you have for Kristen. I wish you all the best."

"Thanks, Clara. Is it okay if I keep in touch with you about how Kristen is doing?"

"I'd love that. It'll be a pleasure to see how she develops."

✎✎✎

After that phone call, Clara realized she had momentarily forgotten about Travis's further investigation of Greg. She tried not to think about it, but still she found herself reading the same paragraphs over and over again. Finally, Travis called again.

"You can relax now. We found out the judge was at a conference in Los Angeles the weekend Vivian was killed. After the conference, he had dinner with his cousin in Santa Monica and took an eleven o'clock flight back that night. The flight arrived at SFO at twelve twenty-nine a.m. and reached the gate at twelve forty-six."

"Could he have gotten to BASL by one o'clock?" Clara asked anxiously.

"We're pretty sure he took BART because that's also how he got to the airport. After the flight arrived, it would've taken several minutes to get to BART, and the first train he could possibly have taken had a scheduled departure at twelve fifty-three. Assuming it was on time, he'd have arrived at the Glen Park station about twenty-two minutes later, and then he would've had to walk a couple of blocks to BASL. By that time, Vivian was already dead."

"Besides, if he took BART, he wouldn't have had any way to transport her body to Fort Point," Clara said, amazed at how coolly analytical she could be under the circumstance.

"Right. So we don't have any serious doubt the judge took BART home. To cover all the bases, we even considered the possibility he could've rented a car at the airport, but that would've taken at least another fifteen or twenty minutes after his flight arrived, maybe more. Then he'd have needed another twenty minutes or so to drive to BASL. Anyway, there was no record of a rental at that time with any of the airport rental car agencies. Bottom line, we're as sure as we can be he couldn't have done it."

"Thanks, Travis. I do feel better, on one score at least."

"I understand. You may have a few questions of your own for the judge about why he didn't tell you about his lunch with Vivian, but it's good to know he's off the hook for murder."

"Important consolation, I guess. Thanks again. I'll talk to you soon."

She had the afternoon ahead of her, and she tried to think what to do with it. She was having trouble focusing. She felt she had to do something proactive.

೮೨೮೨

She showered and dressed in a camel-colored pantsuit with a pastel print blouse in varying shades of yellow, apricot, and ecru. She used to wear scarves with her suits, but she had gotten rid of all of them after she was nearly strangled with one the last time she investigated a murder with Travis.

She'd had only half a bagel that morning and was ravenous. She made an omelet with mushrooms and artichoke hearts and finished off the rest of the bagel. All the while she'd been mulling over where she should start next, and instinctively she was drawn back to Berkeley.

As she drove across the Bay Bridge, she wondered why she was going there. What could she hope to learn about Vivian that she hadn't learned already?

When she got to Boalt Hall, she first wandered around the classrooms. Most were in use, and as she peered through the small window in the door, she could see students who reminded her of herself not so long ago. Unlike her, however, they seemed to be assiduously tapping on their laptops as if trying to take down every word the professor was saying like a bunch of diligent court reporters. She had always been more selective in her note taking, listening intently, jotting a pertinent word or phrase, and writing up more complete notes after class.

She strolled through the faculty offices. She made a point of going by the offices of professors who had taught her as well as Vivian, but none of them were in their offices.

The only professor with her office door open was Professor Karen Smithers, who had been her Criminal Law professor, but her office had changed. She now was in the office that had been Professor Murdoch's.

Professor Smithers was a diminutive African-American woman with bright eyes that looked up over narrow rimless glasses.

"Hello, professor. I'm not sure if you remember me," Clara said.

"I definitely remember the face, but please remind

me of the name. I've given up trying to recall the names of my students."

"I'm Clara Quillen, and you were my professor in Criminal Law a couple of years ago."

"Of course, I should've remembered you, Ms. Quillen. I still recall the closing argument you presented in our simulated case, one of the best I ever had from a student."

"Thank you, and now that you're no longer in a position to give me a grade, I can tell you that you were unquestionably the best law professor I ever had. I loved the combination of your practical experience and academic knowledge. You had a way of inspiring us without making us feel we were neophytes, which, of course, we were."

"I'll take the flattery. It usually comes only from students who think they have something to gain by buttering me up. What brings you back to campus?"

"A little nostalgia, I guess. But it's different to see you in this office, where I spent so many hours as Professor Murdoch's research assistant."

"He retired at the end of the last academic year and only recently vacated this office. I was the next in seniority to inherit this lovely corner space. Isn't it a beauty?"

"It certainly is with you in it. I like the touches of African art you've added. And that print with portraits of all the female Supreme Court justices is terrific."

"It's from the National Portrait Gallery, and I couldn't resist. I'm still waiting for a female justice who's closer to my complexion, though."

"Maybe the next one. We can always hope. I gather Professor Murdoch took all of his decorative items with him."

"That was fine with me. His taste was a bit more conventional than mine."

"Yes, I know. He even had a portrait of Justice John Marshall."

"He offered to leave it for me, but I politely declined. I told him if it was Thurgood Marshall instead of John Marshall I'd gladly have taken it. He seemed to have no hesitation about shedding his worldly goods, though. He gave nearly all of his books to the library."

"Do you know how he's doing since he retired?"

"He didn't look well the last time I saw him, but maybe he's rested a bit since then."

"Isn't he planning a trip with his wife fairly soon?"

"I wouldn't think so. I guess you haven't heard. She filed for divorce. Rumor has it their long marriage was one of convenience only, but you know how rumors are."

"I know he rarely talked about his wife, except he mentioned he was planning a trip with her. That was only a few weeks ago."

"That's odd. I understand it was months ago that she moved out and filed for divorce."

"As you say, you know how rumors are. I met her once at their house, a big Victorian in the Berkeley hills. It was an annual gathering of a few of his chosen students. His wife was gracious, the perfect hostess."

"That was my impression, too, although I saw her only at occasional faculty social events. Now tell me, what are you doing these days?"

Clara gave Professor Smithers a brief account of her former work at a law firm and her current appellate work and teaching at BASL.

"Good for you. I'm glad to know you're teaching as well as doing public interest work. BASL is a good small school, very different from here. Isn't that the school where Vivian Hall was teaching?"

"Yes, you heard what happened to her?"

"Awful tragedy, wasn't it? I haven't heard any recent news, though. Coincidentally, her name came up the last time I was talking to David Murdoch. He became uncharacteristically quiet about it. He said she had been one of his best students."

"That's what I understand. She graduated second in her class the year before I did."

"Now that you mention it, I remember."

"She wasn't one of your students, was she?"

"No, I'm not sure who was her professor for Criminal Law. I don't recall that I had any direct contact with her, but naturally, it's always sad when a promising young person dies."

"From all accounts I've heard, she had a lot to offer the legal profession."

Professor Smithers looked up at the clock on her wall and said, "I don't want to cut you short, but I'm due in class in ten minutes. Maybe we can have coffee sometime."

"I'd like that. Let's keep in touch." The two petite women shook hands firmly.

As Clara walked back toward the parking lot, her thoughts turned to Professor Murdoch, and she began to feel uneasy about him. She wondered why he seemed to have purposely misled her about his plans to travel with his wife.

He hadn't mentioned the divorce, which might be understandable, but he'd certainly led her to believe they were still together.

She also wondered about Professor Smithers's comment that Murdoch did not look well. He had seemed to make an effort to look lively when they talked only a few weeks ago. Her curiosity was rising to the surface, and she could hear Travis saying that was half of what made her a good detective.

So what would a good detective do now?

Chapter 14

Final Piece of the Puzzle

S he gave it only a moment's thought and lost no time going straight to her car. She vaguely recalled the general area where Murdoch lived, but she had no idea what the exact address might be.

So before she started off, she Googled Victorian houses in Berkeley on her smart phone and came up with an enclave in the area of Fulton and Blake streets. She set her GPS and followed Malcolm's British voice to the area. When she got there, she drove around a few blocks before spotting the house she remembered. She recalled having admired the periwinkle blue color, the graceful white arches above the veranda, and the lacy latticework.

It was a quiet street, shaded by towering old trees, and she saw no one as she parked in front of the house and climbed the steps to the front door. She rang the bell and waited, but no one answered. She knocked, but no one answered. She knocked again, rang the bell again, and waited again, but there was no sound from inside. All she could hear was the twitter of a few birds in the lofty, leafy trees that shadowed the windows.

She started to turn away, but on an impulse, she tried the doorknob. To her great surprise, it turned in her hand. She gave the door a gentle push and heard a creaking sound as she said, "Hello."

She waited again and said hello again, this time adding, "Hello, is anybody here?"

She stepped into a gloomy entryway that looked as if it hadn't been dusted since Queen Victoria was on the throne. She tentatively entered a wide-open space and was assaulted by a musty odor that permeated everything. Just to the left was a curving staircase that led upward.

To her right was a formal parlor. One end of it was a sort of music room, dominated by a baby grand piano draped with an elaborately embroidered Spanish shawl, once brightly colored but now dull with dust. There was even dust on the dustcovers that shrouded every surface.

She crossed the open space and looked to her left at what had been an imposing room. It was the room she remembered from a little over a year before, where she and a select group of other students had gathered to sit at the feet of their esteemed professor. It had been an impressive library at that time, but now it was dusty and in disarray. For some reason, it made her think of the disheveled appearance of Richard Piper, whom she could imagine as having once been a good-looking young man, now reduced to a shabby shell. An analogous deranged deterioration seemed to have afflicted this house.

Beyond the stairs on the ground floor was an elegant dining room with a huge mahogany table, although like everything else, now laden with dust. It led to an unexpected modern kitchen, which at some point had apparently been gutted and replaced with modern equipment. Even it looked forlorn, however, as if abandoned by someone who knew how to use it but no longer wanted to.

She heard occasional faint creaking sounds, but as far as she could tell, there was no one in the house, although she hadn't yet ventured up the curving staircase. She felt compelled to go up, but, as she did, she gradually began to catch the scent of an odor she had never smelled before. It was decidedly unpleasant.

When she reached the top landing, the odor became stronger, and she discovered it was more pungent when she turned to the right than when she turned to the left. When she looked to the left, she could see through an open door into the first bedroom, decorated in what had been fluffy pink and white, now more of a dingy gray.

The first bedroom to the right was in stark contrast, all leather and wood with a rumpled dark blue spread on the four-poster bed, but it had the same forsaken look as the rest of the house. Next was a large bath with a claw-footed bathtub and relatively new fixtures designed to look old. As she passed another bedroom, the odor expanded into a stench, and she began to feel lightheaded.

At the end of the corridor was a final door, closed and foreboding. She stood in front of it and listened—again, not a sound. She heard a rustling behind her, but when she turned, all she saw was the dusty silk of the draperies swaying in a gentle breeze.

She faced the closed door again, fearful of what might be on the other side. But it seemed no more to her than another version of Pandora's Box—she had to open it. When she did, the stench almost knocked her down.

She was horrified, though not entirely surprised, at the source of the overwhelming smell. She saw Professor's Murdoch's decaying body lying stretched on a dark blue brocade chaise lounge in what once had been a charming sitting room. He was wearing a long black velvet robe and black velvet slippers that had an embroidered crest on each toe. Arranged nattily at his neck was a scarf that had once been white silk. The scarf was now mostly a shade of drab brown that could only be dried blood.

Most gruesome of all was his face—or lack of it. What had been his face was now a hideously grotesque, dark-colored mush. Before she turned away, Clara caught only a glimpse of a gun lying on his chest. His left hand was just below the gun, and his right arm dangled off to the side of the chaise lounge.

When Clara dared to look again, on a small table beside him, she saw several sheets of bond paper with bold writing in black ink. She recognized Murdoch's elegant scrawl from the days she had received handwritten memos from him. His prized Montblanc pen was capped and lay lined up beside the papers, alongside a gold chain with a V.

Overwhelming nausea had swept over her before she was even consciously aware of it.

Clara then realized she had been holding her breath, and she staggered back into the corridor. She went into the adjacent room and stood by the open window, gulping deep breaths of air from outside. She felt as if she had been drowning and was just beginning to breathe again.

She was dizzy and sat down for a few minutes. After regaining her composure, she opened her handbag and took out a handkerchief. She covered her nose and walked back into the sitting room. She held her breath and then used her handkerchief to take hold of the sheets of paper.

She knew she wasn't supposed to disturb the scene, but she could not possibly read anything in that room, nor was it possible to wait to read what was on those papers. Taking care to handle them with her handkerchief was the best concession she was able to make to those she knew would be investigating every detail of the grisly scene.

She took quick steps down the stairs, went into the library, stood by an open window, and savored the cool gentle breeze from outside. She sat on the dustcover of a leather chair and began to read the document titled Murdoch Manifesto. The first line began with a question.

Where does one begin to demarcate the end of one's life? The adage is, begin at the beginning. Yet that is the difficulty—to delineate the beginning.

In a sense, it began when I married. Much like the story of Ivan Ilyich, a girl fell in love with me, and just as Ivan said to himself, "After all, why not marry?" I had no more reason than that.

Elizabeth was a mere twenty-one, and I was twenty-nine. By the time she was twenty-nine, I was well into my first affair with an adoring young student, and Elizabeth was the disappointed wife of a disappointing husband.

I did not know it at that point, but I had begun a pattern of affairs that would serve me well until I was in my sixties, which began five years ago. Every three years, I would identify a piece of fair fresh fruit, ripe for the picking.

At the beginning, it did not take long to groom each one and prepare her to serve me until her graduation from our illustrious law school. I was dashing to those starry-eyed young women, who typically said they admired my mental acumen even more than my physical prowess, which was considerable. As I grew older, it became somewhat more challenging, but my charms continued to succeed as I entered my final decade.

Perhaps because I subconsciously knew she would be my last conquest, Vivian was different from all the rest. While it may have begun as the usual dalliance, it

evolved from the mere selection of my prey to incremen-
tally stronger emotions. I cannot explain, even to myself,
how merely being intrigued by an attractive young wom-
an at the beginning could progress to total obsession at
the end.

I do not know with any degree of certainty the pre-
cise time when Elizabeth became aware of my dalliances,
but no doubt, long before Vivian became my goal. It may
have been when she insisted on separate bedrooms. It
mattered little, as we had barely shared a bed even from
the beginning. In any event, she never told me she knew,
even when she moved out of our house on the first day of
spring this year. How apt that there would be none of her
compulsive spring-cleaning this year.

Her lawyer did not state anything explicitly in the di-
vorce papers. After all, this is a no-fault state. Nor did
Elizabeth say anything except, "I'm leaving for Paris as
soon as the divorce is final," and I found out later it was
to be with a man five years younger than she. There was
almost a sense of relief when she left, allowing me to live
as I wanted, free of her fanatically fastidious tidiness.

So, I cannot say I was pained by her leaving. Eliza-
beth had no power to give me pain after I was rejected by
Vivian. Only Vivian could not be won over. I prefer to
think it was because she was so virtuous rather than be-
cause of my own failure to maintain my manifest mag-
netism. Vivian was to be my last and finest conquest. I
knew my virility would not endure forever, and I wanted
my final affair to be my best.

The shame came in the stalking. After Vivian rejected
me, I became obsessed with her. I learned every detail of
her life, and I cringed with every detail of her moments
with that inferior swine Susskind. I followed her when I
could and kept records of her every movement. In the at-
tic, I created my shrine to her. I spent my day yesterday

destroying it, but it is already preserved in my cosmic memory, just as she is.

Along with her photographs, many that were taken long-range and some close-up when I dared, was a list of every aspect of her life: what she wore, what she ate, where she went, whenever and wherever she would come and go. My last notation of her was on the last night of her life, although I did not know at the time it would be her last night.

I DID NOT MEAN TO KILL HER. Of all the things the reader of this document must understand, that single declaration is of paramount importance. While my astute colleagues may debate many of the legal nuances of my culpability, I adamantly insist that they consider the reliability of this one fact because it is based on this, my final testament, which may be equated with a dying declaration. Thus, any analysis must include this essential irrefutable fact: I DID NOT MEAN TO KILL HER.

I had been waiting outside her flat, as I had done so many times. I watched her as she walked toward the Civic Center Station, as I had done so many times. She walked with such assurance. She had the air of one who believed intuitively that if she strode with confidence, no harm could come to her, even in an area of the city known for its threat of harm.

I knew where she was going, for I had stood near her open window and heard her tell her roommate (the woman I so envied for her daily proximity to Vivian). I could have followed her on the train, but she had never seen me follow her, and I was not going to take the chance of her discovering me.

So, I drove the familiar route I had driven many times before and arrived shortly before she did. I parked just outside the campus of that inferior little school where she taught, and I had my usual perfect spot with its per-

fect view. I watched her walk into the building and saw the light go on in her office, through the branches of the olive tree.

I crouched beneath the tree just out of sight of her window. I was only a few feet from her, watching her lithe body as she arranged the books on her bookshelf. She looked so lovely with her hair flowing freely, not bound up in the chignon she wore when she taught her classes. I saw the security guard come to her door and speak to her, and I despised him for being so close when I was unable to approach her myself.

I watched her measure and decide where she wanted to hang her artwork and especially her diploma with the words Summa Cum Laude. I was proud of my contribution to that lofty accolade. When she was finished, I knew she would be leaving soon, and I couldn't bear the thought of once again having to follow her from afar. I had to get close to her.

I went through the passageway between the buildings to the interior door on the quad. I had been there many times before, and thus I knew it would be unlocked. After I entered, I waited a while in the hallway, knowing there was no way I could explain my presence. I could hold back no longer and tapped softly on her door so as not to frighten her.

She must have assumed it was the security guard because she opened the door without hesitation. To say she was surprised to see me is a vast understatement. She expressed her surprise, but her face was clouded with more than that. Although it had been a long time since I had last made a direct effort to get close to her, I could see she remembered and still resented my intrusion.

Even so, she allowed me to enter. For a while, I tried to talk with her about ordinary things, but I could not resist asking her if she was finally free of the young men who courted her. I had seen her go from Susskind to the Shelton fellow, and I knew they were mere boys who could never appreciate her—worship her—as I did.

At first, she tried to assuage my ego. She told me I was an attractive man and age had nothing to do with her rejection of me. She, of course, did not use the word rejection, but that was undeniably what it was. At last, she said she was sorry, but there simply was no way, ever, that she could return my devotion to her.

All the while I had been inching closer to her, smelling her sweet fragrance, wanting to touch her soft skin. She said she did not want to make me uncomfortable, but she was going to turn away and then she wanted me to be gone—forever—when she heard the door close.

I had not even realized my hand was on the hammer until my fingers started to close around the wooden handle. I raised my hand and struck her, only once, but very hard, and she slumped to the floor. I did not, and do not, know what possessed me. I DID NOT MEAN TO KILL HER.

I cradled her in my arms and kissed her face, but she remained limp and lifeless. It took a while for me to realize the latter because I could not imagine that I had rendered her lifeless. A gold necklace with a V encircled her lovely throat, and I gently removed it and put it in my pocket.

It was then I began to realize the gravity of what I had done. I knew it could not be undone. I felt that reason had left me, but at the same time reason was telling me I must do something.

I cannot say why, but suddenly I thought I could not leave her there. Did I wonder if that would somehow make it possible for someone to figure out what had happened and how it happened? The thought was irrational, but I asked myself what I should do with her and believed I should take her away somewhere.

I knew if I took her away, I would have to carry her to my car, a block away. I was not so worried about my ability to carry her small body as I was fearful that someone would see me. Yet something, I know not what, compelled me to take her away. She deserved a better resting place than that insignificant little office.

Before I did, however, I remembered the importance of removing any signs of my crime. I wiped the hammer carefully, so there were no fingerprints, and I wiped every other surface I had touched. I also wiped the small trace of blood and hair that was on the hammer. I looked carefully for other signs of blood. There were a few small spots on the carpet and a couple of them on the wall. I poured water from the bottle sitting on Vivian's desk and thoroughly doused and blotted every spot with my handkerchief until no blood was visible.

Her cellular phone was on the desk, and I put it in my pocket. I knew I had called her repeatedly from a disposable phone that was not likely to be traceable. I had hung up without saying anything, but I was not certain calls could not be traced. All of these thoughts and actions occurred very quickly, and I was eager to depart.

Despite her small size, I was surprised by how heavy her dead weight seemed. I stumbled several times in the dark, and there were moments when I was tempted to drop her and run. Yet I simply could not leave her in such an undignified place.

Once I reached my car and put her in beside me, I drove for a long time. At first, there was some pleasure in having her with me, but as I became more lucid, I became more aware of the enormity of what I had done. My mind was racing as I continued to drive, trying to think where I should take her.

Eventually, I saw a wooded area ahead and then the sign for the Presidio. I had been there numerous times before, but not for a long time and never in the dark. I thought I might be able to find the military cemetery, but even if I did, I did not want to leave her among the dead. She was so full of life. I do not know how I could have thought such a thing with her lifeless body beside me.

I thought primarily of finding a secluded place, and then it occurred to me I might find a place that would help to disguise how she died. I remembered the rocks by Fort Point and thought leaving her there might give rise to the presumption that she slipped and fell on the rocks, or perhaps she jumped in an attempt to end her own life. People often do not know why their loved ones kill themselves. Sometimes there are no warning signs.

I must have driven in circles for a long time and thought I would never find the turn off to the fort. Then I saw the small sign, pointing down the little road. There was not another car in sight, and I did not fear being seen.

I could hear the surf pounding, just as my heart was pounding. I irrationally believed if I put her there, it would be assumed she died on the rocks.

I thrust her body quickly, with one forceful motion, before I could lose my nerve. I felt a great sense of release because I could go home and begin to forget. I naïvely believed my long torment because of Vivian would finally be over. I did not know she would continue to haunt me, in every waking moment and in my dreaded dreams.

As I drove up toward the main road, I began to breathe easily again. Then I remembered I still had her cellular phone in my pocket. I stopped and heaved it as far as I could into the bay.

I hardly know how I reached my home, which had ceased to be a home, except for my shrine in the attic. My dreams that night were nightmares, and the next day was agony. Exhausted, I roamed from room to room. Finally, I watched the evening newscast, knowing I would hear the dreaded news, and I was appalled by the dispassionate reporting of the body found on the rocks at Fort Point. How could I go on with my life after such a life-changing event?

I went in to my office the next day to continue the process of clearing it out for my retirement. In the afternoon, I had a visit from another former student who had been one of my research assistants, and, in the course of conversation, I was taken aback when she mentioned Vivian. I could barely control myself as remorse came flooding over me. Yet I managed to maintain my composure, after years of practice in the classroom of showing only a façade, regardless of my inner feelings.

It was unnerving the next day when a police detective came and questioned me, but I had already heard he had been questioning other professors who had taught Vivian. So it was relatively easy to show the proper degree of sympathy without giving any indication of a personal relationship with her.

I am not sure exactly when, but at some point, I had already begun to disintegrate even before that fateful night. Perhaps it was weeks before when my colleagues gave me an extravagant retirement dinner and a gold watch—how cliché if it had not been for the fact that it was a ridiculously extravagant Apple watch. I could hardly think of anything I would want less.

No, that was more likely the culmination. I knew my mind had been slipping. Even though I expected my body to give way when I could no longer run marathons, I could not face losing the power of my mind, which had been the mainstay of my life. In lucid moments, I could see the irrationality of stalking Vivian.

I could even see how foolish it was to think putting her on the rocks would cover a crime. There was no way she could have been there without someone placing her there. It made no sense that she would have found her way there and slipped or jumped.

So finally, everything converged: the end of my marriage, the end of my career, the end of my days of loving an exquisite young woman. I no longer maintained any doubt about whether I had a single reason to continue living.

I considered confessing and letting justice take its course. Justice! After all my years in the law, I know how fickle that can be.

I had no desire for a circus of a trial, and that is surely what it would have been. I decided there could be only one way to achieve true justice, and that is to take my life as I took Vivian's. I would even do it the same way if that were possible. In the end, I cannot bear the thought of great physical pain, but I assume this method will be no more painful than the instantaneous pain Vivian must have suffered.

The most magnanimous thing I believe I can do for Vivian is to leave this explanation of how and why I took her life. I saw her parents at the memorial service, and I can understand it must have been agonizing for them not to know how their daughter died. One often sees a victim's loved ones make reference to closure, and sometimes they say there can be no closure. Yet this meager gesture may provide some degree of closure, if not genuine solace.

So now the only comfort I can give them is to provide answers. It may help them to know she did not take her own life. I hope it also gives some comfort for them to *know she suffered no prolonged, agonizing pain. It was quick, and I am sure she did not suffer unduly.*

Of course, I do not expect forgiveness from them or anyone else. I cannot forgive myself. So how could I expect anyone else to forgive me?

I cannot bring Vivian back. All I can do now is to remove myself from the face of the earth. While I deplore the triteness of the Dickensian words, I can express the sentiment no better than he: "It is a far, far better thing that I do, than I have ever done; it is a far, far better rest that I go to than I have ever known."

So now I have come to the end of my life. I have no more to say.

David Murdoch

As Clara read Murdoch's words, her reading became slower and slower because she was weeping. The handkerchief she had used to hold the confession was saturated. She had felt sad before, just knowing Vivian had been killed. Now she felt utter desolation as she realized even more what a waste it had been for Vivian to lose her life in such a meaningless manner.

She read it again, this time with the more detached analytical mind of a trained lawyer. She could see Murdoch weaving erratically from reason to ego to dementia, intertwining them as he made a futile attempt to justify himself.

She included herself in a long list of people who would never forgive David Murdoch.

∽∾∽

Clara sat for a while until at last her tears dried up. She would not go back into the room where he lay, even to take the papers back to where she had found them. She didn't think it would really matter if she simply left them for Travis when he got there. She was sure it wouldn't take him long, and then she would begin to be all right again.

She wiped her own fingerprints from the front door-knob, the only surface she had touched with her bare hand. It was time to go.

Epilogue

Travis, of course, had no difficulty clearing the case after Clara gave him the essential information. He received credit for discovering Murdoch as Vivian's killer, although he would much have preferred giving Clara credit for solving the crime. She reminded him she hadn't actually solved Vivian's murder but had merely discovered her murderer, which was not the same thing. She convinced Travis it was better for everyone concerned not to release any information about her role in the investigation.

So the official story was that Travis received an anonymous phone call to go to Murdoch's house to find the solution to Vivian's murder. In essence, it was even the truth, because when Clara called him, she said, "Hi, Travis. This is an anonymous telephone tip. You need to go immediately to the address in Berkeley I'll give you." She gave him not only the address but also a brief summary of what he would find there. She told him to be sure he was the first to find the manifesto in the library so he could decide what was best to do with it.

He took with him everything he needed to process the scene and alerted the Berkeley police to meet him, timing it so they would get there soon after he did. It didn't take long for Travis and his crew to arrive at Murdoch's house, but by the time he got there, Clara had already paid the toll and was heading back to San Francisco on the Bay Bridge.

Her thoughts were flooded with the account Murdoch had written, so cogent in its own twisted way, and yet so different from her weeks of speculation and investigation. It appeared the choice of Fort Point was merely fortuitous, not connected in any way with Hitchcock or *Vertigo*. Only one thing seemed similar, the progression of Stewart's emotional state compared with Murdoch's: he was at first intrigued, soon entranced, eventually smitten, and finally obsessed with Vivian. The final stage ended in tragedy for them both.

Clara couldn't help wondering, though, if even Hitchcock himself would have dubbed her pursuit of the *Vertigo* connection as a MacGuffin. It had propelled her forward in investigating Vivian's murder, although ultimately it had no direct relevance to the solution of the crime.

The news was released that night and appeared in the *Chronicle* the next morning. The full version of Murdoch's manifesto was not released, by agreement of the police chiefs of both San Francisco and Berkeley, with a court order sealing the papers. A substantially sanitized account was released to the public after Travis first told it to Vivian's parents. Omitting any lurid detail, it indicated that Murdoch, who had been suffering a severe bout of depression, had gone to BASL to see his former student for reasons that were not entirely clear.

The account stated that, at some point, they had presumably disagreed about something, and he had picked up a hammer she had been using to put up pictures in her office. He hit her once with the hammer, and the single blow took her life. The sanitized account emphasized she had suffered little if any pain and the homicide was the result of impulse rather than intention.

The account further said Murdoch then apparently panicked and decided to transport her body to Fort Point, hoping her death might be considered an accident or suicide. Upon reflection, Murdoch experienced extreme remorse and decided to take his own life. The facts became known because he left behind a handwritten confession indicating how he had killed Vivian and disposed of her remains.

Greg had called Clara as soon as he saw the news on the Web. He seemed surprised she didn't seem eager to talk about it, as she had not seemed squeamish about the murder before when the subject came up. She said she had a headache, which was true, and she would talk to him later.

The next day, Clara didn't go to BASL until early afternoon, but the campus was abuzz with news of how Vivian had died. In class, Clara allowed her students time to talk about it and express their emotions, and she then talked to them about Vivian's work in dependency law. She also told the class the coincidence of her own appointment to the same case at the appellate level and said she would keep them abreast of the case as much as she could, while at the same time protecting the confidentiality of her child client.

One of the students asked if she had made arrangements to visit the court as she had mentioned in the first class. She told the class it was tentatively scheduled for Wednesday of the next week, but inwardly she was unsure how things would stand between her and Greg when the time came.

When he called her on subsequent nights, she kept the conversations short and said she was working on some things that were time consuming. She said she'd explain when she saw him on Saturday.

She knew he sensed her pulling away from him, but decided to confront him in person about going out with Vivian rather than on the telephone. She wanted to see his face when she asked him about it. She was doubtful about resolving her concerns on their Saturday date, leaving her apprehensive about seeing him at all. But she knew she had to see him.

❡❦❡

Two days had never seemed longer, but finally Saturday came. She prepared a delectable picnic, partly because her heart wasn't in it and she figured she'd feel guilty if she made only a halfhearted effort. She didn't want her lack of enthusiasm to taint the preparations she had originally planned to make.

He brought a bottle of good champagne, chilled to perfection in a cooler, along with brie and a baguette to start things off. After they parked and found a good spot beneath a shady tree, he spread a blanket and said, "Okay, let me have it. I thought everything was going well with us, and suddenly you became colder than this champagne."

"I don't want to prolong this, so I'm going to come right out with it. Why did you give me the impression you knew Vivian only in your court, when you had actually dated her?"

"Dated her? I never dated her."

"You also acted as if you barely knew her. You didn't even let on you knew she was teaching at BASL."

"That's true. I knew she said she was teaching somewhere, but when we met for lunch, we got so busy talking about her case, we didn't talk about much else."

"So you admit you took her to lunch."

"I'm not sure I would even call it taking her to lunch. There was nothing to it. After her case was concluded, she called me and asked if she could talk with me so I could give her some feedback on how she had handled the case. I said I'd be glad to. I do that sort of thing all the time. I love to help people new to the field get better at what they do."

"Are you saying you went to lunch, but nothing more?"

"I'm certain it couldn't have been anything more innocuous. We met on a Saturday at the hot dog stand across from city hall, which she said wasn't far from where she lived. I had some work to do in my chambers, and it was an easy place to meet. We sat on a bench and talked about her case for maybe an hour or more, I'm not sure. That's all there was to it."

"Nothing personal?"

"Of course not. Well, not quite. I admit—I did pay for the hot dogs."

Clara finally smiled. But she still wanted reassurance and asked again, "You're sure there was nothing personal?"

"Now that you mention it, there was one thing, but it wasn't personally related to me."

"What was that?"

"Toward the end of our conversation, I told her how important it was in this kind of work to keep balance in your life. She said she'd been thinking about that, and she told me she'd been seeing someone she really cared about. She said she had some misgivings, but she didn't tell me what they were. I didn't think I wanted to come across like a Dutch uncle, but I said if she really cared about the guy, maybe she should go for it. All she said was she'd think about it."

"And that was it? That's all there was to the date?"

"It wasn't even a date. Didn't you and I have a conversation like this on our first date?"

"I guess we did," she said sheepishly. "But I wasn't even sure it was a date at the time, and I wasn't clear about you and Vivian."

"So my meeting with Vivian is the reason you've been giving me the cold shoulder?"

"It wasn't thinking it was a date that concerned me. It was thinking you'd deliberately deceived me, or at least misled me. I guess I have some trust issues. But that's another story."

"Are we okay now? Do you have any lingering doubts?"

She laughed. "I guess not unless I think of some more."

"Do you think we'll be able to have a good afternoon then?"

"I don't see why not."

He had been inching closer to her as they talked, and then their lips touched.

They enjoyed the picnic followed by the Turner exhibit at the de Young Museum. Afterward, Greg asked if she'd like to stop by his house for coffee and dessert. He had gone to a bakery that morning and made no secret of hoping she would come home with him. She wasn't sure how long she would stay, but she was curious to go to his house. He'd mentioned living on McAllister Street, within jogging distance of his court.

He drove out of Golden Gate Park, then east on Oak Street, and turned toward the picture postcard Victorian houses by Alamo Square. He began telling her about how fond he was of his own house, which had been a fixer upper when he and his wife bought it years before. She had taken it in hand and supervised the complete renovation of the house, while keeping true to the historic architecture.

He took Steiner Street over to McAllister and pulled up in front of an exquisite Victorian house. It was painted periwinkle blue and had graceful arches above a small porch, topped with fine latticework. Clara instantly became queasy.

There was no way she could explain to Greg what had triggered her sudden attack of nausea. She thought fast and conjured up a story about feeling uneasy to be with him in the home his wife had restored with such care. She needed some time to get used to the idea. He said he understood and asked what she wanted to do instead.

She could see Greg's disappointment, which she assuaged by making plans to see him the next day. She promised she would be in a better frame of mind. He reminded her he had a surprise planned for the following weekend, and this time she agreed without hesitation. Reluctantly, he took her home, but she was true to her promise and the next day they had another fine Sunday together.

ଏ୪ଏ୪

The following weekend, all Greg would tell her about the surprise he had planned was to dress comfortably, and he would pick her up at eleven in the morning. Not knowing what that really meant, she wore tan slacks, an attractive teal-colored blouse, and walking shoes. Prompt as always, he came for her on time and drove to the Sunset District of San Francisco.

As they arrived and parked in front of a pleasant house painted a cream color trimmed with peach molding, Greg said, "Welcome to Peaches 'n' Cream, as my mother dubbed it. This is where I grew up, and you're about to meet the two people who made that possible."

Soon she was introduced to two of the nicest seventy-something-year-olds she had ever met. After a pleasant lunch, they strolled over to the ocean and back, completing as agreeable an afternoon as Clara had ever spent. On the way home, she said, "I had a great time, Greg, but why did you make it a surprise? I would've looked forward to meeting them."

"I remembered how terrified I was the first time I met my wife's parents. Her father had been a symphony conductor, and her mother played the cello. I was awed by their knowledge of music, but it was a great relief to find out they were really nice people. I didn't want you to be apprehensive about meeting my parents."

Clara laughed as she told Greg something he didn't know. "I'm insecure in a lot of ways, but that doesn't happen to be one of them. I was the kind of girl guys always wanted to introduce to their parents. I don't think I ever met a fellow's parents who didn't like me."

Her relationship with Greg, already off to a good start, seemed to blossom progressively after that.

❧❧❧

The fall semester continued to go well, and Clara thought Paula and Lyle gradually began to make their peace with Vivian's demise. One day Lyle told Clara that he believed it had made it easier for him to know how Vivian died, although he had a long way to go in dealing with his anger at the senselessness of Murdoch's crime. He said he was particularly glad Murdoch was dead because otherwise, he had no doubt that he would have wanted to kill him. Paula never revealed any special feelings for Vivian other than a deep friendship.

There was joy in Mudville when John Knox MacArthur announced he would be retiring at the end of the school year. It was whispered he announced early to give everyone plenty of time to prepare tributes to him. Maybe there would even be some, so great was the pleasure at his leaving the law school. There would be no tributes for the publication of his electronic book, however, as the deal fell through when he failed to produce anything substantial by the second deadline.

Travis finally tracked down Richard Piper, even though he no longer had an official reason to because of any connection he had with Vivian's murder. Travis still had some lingering concerns about the possibility that in his twisted mental state he might transfer his antipathy for Vivian to Clara. He was glad to learn Piper's brother had become his conservator and placed him in a Pennsylvania mental health facility where he was making slow but gradual progress.

cɔcɔ

The legal procedures related to Kristen's adoption took place in record time. Following the dismissal of the appeal, Clara personally undertook the required paperwork for the adoption, and Greg expedited the matter in his court. One further fact came to light when an autopsy was performed on Gretchen. She had been approximately two months pregnant when she died. Only necessary authorities were privy to the information, which was not released to Gretchen's family or Amy's family.

Clara and Greg attended the joyous occasion of Kristen's adoption ceremony, officiated over by one of his colleagues. Clara took lots of pictures and made an album for the newly formed family. Kristen's adoptive father received a promotion and a raise, and he and Amy began looking for a three-bedroom house closer to his work in a highly rated school district. Amy called one day to tell Clara they were fostering an Asian baby who had been neglected by a young unwed mother, and if all went well, they hoped Kristen might eventually have a sibling.

∽∾∽∾

One more detail fell into place in an unexpected way when Clara received a phone call from Marvin Morrison.

"Hi, Clara, I hope you're doing well."

"I am. And you?"

"I'm always well, but right now I'm rather enjoying a bit of news about the young associate you asked me about, Peter Susskind. I imagine you'll be interested to know we've dismissed him from the firm."

"Really, how did that come about?"

"I was thinking of him recently when I saw the news about Vivian Hall's murder having been solved. For some reason, it aroused my curiosity about Peter, and it occurred to me to take a look at some of the cases he'd been working on. As a result, I discovered something that astounded me."

"What was that?"

"I have to admit I didn't discover it all on my own. I had to get our best tech expert to help me. I saw some suspicious things in one of his cases. Frankly, it was a complicated process tracking things down, and I don't know exactly how our tech expert did it."

"Sounds intriguing. What did you discover?"

"I won't bother you with the details, some of which fall within attorney-client privileged information anyway, but the bottom line is he found Peter had hacked into some private accounts for access to information to benefit one of his clients to make himself look good. Once we traced everything and we were sure, we called Peter in and dismissed him on the spot. He didn't even protest. He knew he was caught."

"That's amazing, Marvin. I had no idea he was capable of doing anything like that."

"Nor did we, of course. We'd thought his technological ability might be an asset to the firm, but we never expected him to use it unethically. So obviously we're glad to be rid of him. We don't want anyone with such questionable ethics to be associated with our firm."

"You don't know it, but you've made my day. This turn of events makes me think there's a very good chance Peter may have been the one who hacked into my email and read some attachments that were private documents from Vivian Hall's laptop."

"How despicable. So perhaps he used his computer skills to hack into information in any number of ways that were ethically improper."

"I wouldn't be surprised. In fact, I wouldn't even be surprised if he somehow hacked into the grading system at Boalt and manipulated the numbers so he'd graduate first in his class. Wouldn't it be wonderful if it turned out we could determine whether he did that?"

"Do you think there's any way to find out?"

"There might be. The police have some remarkable experts in the tech field. I'll check with Travis."

As soon as she finished her conversation with Marvin, she called Travis and filled him in. His first reaction was it made sense that hacking into Clara's email and getting access to Vivian's laptop would be consistent with Susskind's penchant for tracking down information that could reflect unfavorably on him.

He also thought it was consistent with Susskind's personality to try to cover his tracks by sending the email that was written in substandard English. Ironically, if it hadn't been for the email, Clara wouldn't have known her account had been compromised. "But how would he even have known I might be working with you, Travis?"

"I'd be willing to bet he saw me go into your office the day of the memorial service. He probably put one and one together and got two."

"So if he did that, do you think it's possible he might have hacked into the UC Berkeley system and manipulated the law school grades? And if he did, do you think there's a way to find out?"

"Maybe. I could call in a favor off the record and have one of our tech people look into it. Let me see what I can do."

To Clara's amazement, the very next day he had an answer for her. It had turned out to be a relatively easy problem to solve.

The biggest hurdle was the red tape of getting into the system when it wasn't actually a police matter. But as soon as it was made clear to the law school administration that grades might have been changed, they were glad to cooperate.

All the tech expert had to do was track down the original grades that had been submitted by the professors in all of Vivian's and Peter's courses and then compare them with the ones fed into the final program that determined class rank.

It soon became obvious that there was a discrepancy in the grades, and once the correct grades were entered and reprogrammed, the accurate class rank became clear. And the only person who could possibly have anything to gain from the changed grades was Susskind.

Best of all, there was no doubt—it was not Vivian who had been second in her class. It was Susskind. Vivian had been first.

c/ɔc/ɔ

Clara continued to see Greg and was beginning to consider the possibility they might have a future together. Still, she was cautious, even though Travis and Jo Anne had given their wholehearted stamp of approval. Every now and then they ventured to ask about her love life. With Clara's natural inclination to protect her privacy, she typically said something like, "I don't want to get my hopes up. After two marriages that ended sadly, I'm reluctant to expect too much."

Prophetically, Travis had a standard reply: "Don't forget, the third time's the charm."

But his "third time" comment wasn't the only "third" reference that shaped Clara's life with the events that followed. Instead, as she perused the *San Francisco Chronicle* one morning, she read about an apparent homicide that had happened in a local art house movie theater. The article started off with, *The strains of the "Third Man Theme" could still be heard as a bloodied man staggered out of the Roxie Theater in the Mission District and collapsed. He was pronounced dead from three gunshot wounds to the chest shortly afterward at a nearby hospital.*

This time she was almost expecting Travis's call. She wasn't surprised when he said, "Hi, Clara. Want to go to a movie?"

About the Author

J. E. Gentry was a lawyer and law professor until she decided to devote herself full time to writing. She earned a bachelor's and a master's degree in English before going to law school, and then earned a Juris Doctor degree. She has traveled extensively and now lives with her husband in the San Francisco Bay Area. She enjoys classical music and classic movies, and also show tunes and cool jazz. She is somewhat like her central character, Clara Quillen, but in the books Clara is better looking, nicer, younger, and much wealthier.

The author's Facebook page is
https://www.facebook.com/J.E.Gentry/

39164562R00152

Made in the USA
Columbia, SC
08 December 2018